W9-BIJ-510

"Is that your phone in your pocket," Kate drawled in a damn fine version of Mae West's comment to Cary Grant, as Nick's phone vibrated, "or are you just happy to see me?"

"A little of the first, a whole lot of the second." Her nearness had his gut tangling in a knot of sexual awareness as he pulled his cell phone off his belt.

Her breath was sweet from the sugary beignets she'd eaten. And warm. The thought of those sweet, silky lips on his body, moving down his chest, over his stomach, which was knotting even tighter at the fantasy, then lower still, taking him deep, nearly undid him.

He might be a SEAL. But he was also a man. A flesh-and-blood horny man who couldn't resist plucking at those amazing lips.

"The talent for storytelling is obviously embedded deep in Ms. Ross's bones."
—*Romantic Times*

No Safe Place is also available as an eBook.

Out of the Mist

"The story's robust momentum and lively characters make this a fun, energetic read."

—*Publishers Weekly*

"Ross weaves the search for the missing family treasure and the growing attraction between two creative spirits with aplomb in this charming romance."

—*BookPage*

Magnolia Moon

"Perennial favorite JoAnn Ross wraps up the hugely engaging Callahan trilogy in great style. Filled with emotion, passion, and a touch of suspense, this is just plain fun reading."

—*Romantic Times*

River Road

"Skillful and satisfying. . . . With its emotional depth, Ross's tale will appeal to Nora Roberts fans."

—*Booklist*

"The romance . . . crackles, and their verbal sparring keeps the narrative moving along at an energetic clip. Readers . . . will be heartily entertained . . . delightful."

—*Publishers Weekly*

Blue Bayou

"Ross is in fine form . . . plenty of sex and secrets to keep readers captivated."

—*Publishers Weekly*

JOANN ROSS

NO SAFE PLACE

POCKET BOOKS

New York   London   Toronto   Sydney

An *Original* Publication of POCKET BOOKS

 POCKET BOOKS, a division of Simon & Schuster, Inc.
1230 Avenue of the Americas, New York, NY 10020

This book is a work of fiction. Names, characters, places and incidents are products of the author's imagination or are used fictitiously. Any resemblance to actual events or locales or persons, living or dead, is entirely coincidental.

Copyright © 2007 by The Ross Family Trust

ISBN-13: 978-1-4165-0166-4
ISBN-10:   1-4165-0166-5

This Pocket Books paperback edition March 2007

10 9 8 7 6 5 4 3 2 1

POCKET and colophon are registered trademarks of Simon & Schuster, Inc.

Cover design by Lisa Litwack
Cover illustration by Craig White;
photo of woman © Tony Garcia/Workbook

Manufactured in the United States of America

For information regarding special discounts for bulk purchases, please contact Simon & Schuster Special Sales at 1-800-456-6798 or business@simonandschuster.com.

To the people of New Orleans, as well as all the others in Louisiana and along the Gulf Coast who suffered—and are still struggling—from the devastation of Hurricane Katrina.

ACKNOWLEDGMENTS

With heartfelt thanks to Fredericka Meiners, Chris Foutris, Blythe Gifford, Debbie Pfeiffer, Margaret Watson, and Diane Whitton-Brown, for answering questions about Kate's scenes in Chicago.

Also, I could not have completed this book without *The Times-Picayune*, which won a much-deserved Pulitzer Prize for its spectacular coverage of Hurricane Katrina. The paper's continuing stories about life after the storm proved hugely helpful, as did contributions from New Orleans bloggers, particularly freelance writer Troy Gilbert, who came to my aid when I was searching for marinas, which allowed Nick Broussard to stay on *The Hoo-yah*.

1

New Orleans

THEY CAME FOR NICK BROUSSARD IN THE DARK, guns drawn, harsh shouts shattering the night.

It was 0430 hours, a time in the morning that the navy referred to as "oh-dark thirty," when all but the most determined party animals or chronic drunks were asleep—or at least passed out—in bed.

As he'd been. Until they'd stormed onto his ketch, dressed all in black like ninjas, pistols drawn.

"On your knees!" one of them screamed, his voice cracking with the same nervous adrenaline that slammed into Nick's bloodstream like a Stinger missile. "Hands on top of your head."

"Hey, stay cool, *cher*. I know the drill."

Hadn't he been on the other end of it enough times? Both as a Navy SEAL and, more recently, before he'd been thrown off the force, an NOPD cop.

Nick's head nearly exploded as he crawled out of bed, laced his fingers together on top of his pounding skull, and refused to flinch when the metal barrel pressed against his temple.

The kid on the other end of the pistol had a shiny, beardless face that made him look as if he hadn't made it out of adolescence.

Had he ever been that freaking young?

Nah. When your father was Antoine Broussard, an angry, brawling man with an explosive, white-hot temper, you grew up real fast.

A storm had boiled in from the Gulf; the torrential rain hammering on the deck of *The Hoo-yah* created a thick, slanting curtain of white noise that must've been why he hadn't heard them coming.

It had to have been the rain. Or all the damn Jack Daniel's he'd drunk last night. Because the only other possibility was that he was losing his edge. Which would suggest he might be getting old.

And wasn't that a fun thought?

Nah. Couldn't be. Six months ago he'd been running black op missions in Afghanistan and Iraq. Sure, he'd been wounded, but a little shrapnel in the thigh and chest couldn't make a guy go downhill that fast.

Could it?

Hell, no. Still, getting older was definitely preferable to an up close and personal meeting with the Grim Reaper. Which could well be in his future if these thugs decided to take a little drive out into the swamp.

There were four of them, and one of him. Which might present a problem for some Delta Force dog-face, but if you were a SEAL, well, hey, that just meant the odds were in your favor.

His problem was, he had to keep his eye on the mission. Which meant if he took the bad guys out, he might fail to infiltrate Leon LeBlanc's organization. Which wasn't an option.

"Y'all cops?" The easy conversational tone wasn't easy given that his mouth was dry as Death Valley and tasted like he'd sucked up every last bit of mud in the Mississippi delta. "Or maybe LeBlanc sent you?"

Getting the attention of the guy who ran the South Louisiana rackets was what had put him in that Algiers bar last night. And that, in turn, was responsible for what he suspected was going to end up being the mother of all hangovers. The trouble with going undercover was that you had to act like the bad guys. Who last night had appeared to be trying to drink the state of Louisiana dry.

"Shut the hell up!" A big ugly thug, built like a refrigerator, slammed a steel-toed boot into his back.

A shock of fiery pain tore up Nick's back. Hell, he'd be pissing blood for a week.

If he stayed alive that long.

Nick wasn't afraid of death. Back when he'd been providing rapid response in hot spots all over the world, he'd faced it down more than once. Besides, any guy afraid to die was a guy who was afraid to live. And the one thing Nick had always had in common with his brawling, alcoholic old man was that he believed in living life to the fullest.

"Let's go, Broussard." The refrigerator jerked Nick to his feet.

"Y'all gonna let me get dressed first? Even down here during Mardi Gras, dragging a guy off to jail naked might make some bystander a tad suspicious."

Nick figured he'd be lucky to be going to jail.

Proving that he wasn't exactly dealing with NASA scientists, the men seemed stumped by his request. He watched as they exchanged dumbfounded, what-the-fuck-do-we-do-now looks. Finally, fridge guy lifted his knuckles off the floor long enough to scoop up the underwear lying on top of the discarded pile of clothes Nick couldn't remember stripping out of, and he tossed them at him.

"Thanks."

Nick snagged them out of the air and yanked them on. The gray knit boxer briefs were a long way from a suit of armor, but if a guy had to go into battle, and it looked as if he was going to be doing exactly that, it was a helluva lot more preferable to tuck your balls away beforehand. He'd never gotten why so many of his old SEAL team found going commando a cool thing to do.

The thug yanked his arms behind his back so hard, he was surprised his shoulders didn't pop out of their joints. A pair of handcuffs locked around his wrists, digging tightly into his skin. Nick had always enjoyed that click of metal, which was so much more satisfying than the rasp of plastic the military was using these days. He did not enjoy it now.

Everyone on the boat, including Nick, froze as a siren from a cop car screamed nearby on Lake Marina Avenue. Then faded into the distance.

"Let's go." His captor pushed Nick toward the splintered door that was hanging by its hinges.

"Since you asked so nicely, how can I refuse?"

"You keep mouthin' off, numbnuts, and you gonna be gator bait."

It was not, Nick suspected, an idle threat.

2

Chicago

THE SKY OUTSIDE THE APARTMENT WAS STILL A deep, dark purple as Kate Delaney set her treadmill to a grade more likely found in the Rockies than the flat Midwest, then cranked her iPod up to blast out her eardrums. As Pearl Jam spun the black circle, she began to run, her snazzy new Nike Shox Turbos pounding on the endless rubber track that wasn't nearly as satisfying as running outdoors.

Southern born and bred, Kate hated the cold, but given the choice between the treadmill and having her cheeks chapped red by the icy Chicago wind, she'd choose the wind any day.

"I hope they end up in the lowest hub of hell," she muttered, damning the cretins who'd so screwed up her life. "Forced to spend eternity in polyester white leisure suits, listening to canned disco music 24/7."

Outside the floor-to-ceiling windows, the city lights sparkled over the landscape like jewels spilled from a pirate's chest. The view was one of the reasons she'd rented a loft in a building that was still undergoing renovation. Even with the raise she'd gotten with her last promotion, lake views were beyond a cop's salary. Then one day, while she'd been trying on shoes at Marshall Field's, a fellow shopper had her bag snatched.

Barefoot, Kate had chased him through the store and down State Street. After half a block, she nailed him with a flying leap that knocked the breath out of him and gave her concrete burns on both knees.

After the perp had been hauled away in a black-and-white cruiser, the woman, hugely grateful to have her pricey Prada bag back, gave Kate her card and told her to call if she ever happened to be in the market for a house. Or even, she'd amended, taking in Kate's decidedly midpriced dark suit, an apartment.

Coincidentally, Kate just happened to be.

The real estate agent had not only found Kate this loft, she'd gotten the building's owner to pay the power bills, which made it not cheap, but at least affordable. So long as she was willing to eat Rice Krispies for dinner twice a week.

Her first night in the loft, Kate had watched, enthralled, as the city kept changing before her eyes between dusk and dawn. Her grateful real estate agent had left a bottle of champagne in the refrigerator. It'd been domestic, not imported, but the difference would have been lost on its recipient, anyway, and in between hot, steamy lovemaking sessions with the man who'd taken advantage of her uncharacteristically romantic mood to propose yet again (only to be refused, yet again), Kate had toasted her good fortune, blissfully unaware that her luck—and her life—were both about to take a drastic turn for the worse.

The same windows that offered Kate a bird's-eye view of Chicago also allowed people to look in. Was someone in that building across the street watching her now? Through one of the many telescopes she knew residents had set up in their apartment windows?

Or worse yet, was she being watched through a sniper's scope? Was she, even now, in the crosshairs?

Hating the feeling of being so exposed, Kate cranked up both the volume and the speed and began running faster. Harder.

An hour later, her aggravation somewhat eased by exertion, she showered, blow-dried her unruly curly hair, twisting it into a braid so tight her temples hurt, then dressed in one of the black pantsuits she'd bought when she made detective.

She'd chosen the suits because they were practical and didn't show dirt or blood. Not because they proved an appealing foil for her light auburn hair and ivory complexion. Today she was counting on the unrelieved black to provide her with gravitas and keep attention on her words and not her looks.

Standing at the kitchen counter, looking out over the sweeping spread of city lights, feigning a composure she was a long way from feeling, just in case anyone might be observing her, Kate gulped down her third mug of coffee, then poured one more for the road.

Sufficiently wired with the caffeine that overrode her sleepless night, she strapped on her leather shoulder holster, grabbed her coat from the rack by the door, squared her shoulders, and then, feeling a lot like Russell Crowe's gladiator entering the Colosseum, marched out the door.

The ancient elevator, formerly used for freight, took its time clanking its way up to the top floor. When it finally arrived, she swept a quick look around the interior, then, assured it was empty, stepped inside.

She'd been offered protection. In fact, the federal prosecutor had called again just last night, trying to get her to accept an armed bodyguard. Which was, in Kate's mind, ridiculous. Cops were the ones who protected and served. They didn't need protection. Especially from other cops.

She'd turned the offer down. As she had dozens of times over the past months.

Knowing that the yellow-livered bastards she was testifying against wanted her to believe that every breath might be her last, Kate refused to give in to the dark and creeping feeling of doom as, with an ominous grinding of gears and a jolt that rattled her bones, the elevator began its descent. Their goal was to make her sweat the everyday stuff, to make her live her life on that gut-gnawing, razor-sharp balance between fight and flight.

But the thing was, if she allowed the bad guys to get under her skin, they'd win.

And for them to win, she'd have to lose.

"Which is so not an option," she muttered darkly as the elevator suddenly rattled to a jerky stop on the fifth floor.

A jolt of adrenaline hit her already coffee-jazzed

bloodstream. Prepared to draw her Glock, she let out a quick, relieved breath as the door opened to reveal a man clad in a black cashmere coat.

"Good morning," he greeted her.

"Morning." Kate's tone was brusque. She didn't return his smile. But, recognizing him as a tenant, she did take her hand from beneath her coat.

"They say it's going to snow all day," he said.

She shrugged as the elevator began clanking back down again. "It's Chicago. That's what it does. Snow."

And snow. And snow. When it wasn't sleeting, which was even worse.

"Doesn't sound as if you're much of a fan of our winters."

"Snow's okay, I guess, when you're a kid." Not that she'd ever experienced a white winter as a child, growing up in the hot and steamy South. "Once you're an adult and have to deal with driving in the stuff and salt eating through your car and mountains of brown slush until spring, it sort of loses its appeal."

"Ever go skiing?"

"No."

"You might change your mind about snow if you did."

Kate figured there was a better chance of her being appointed police commissioner. The odds of which, after today, would be . . . oh, say, a bazillion to one.

He filled in the silence surrounding them when she didn't respond. "I've got this place in Colorado."

"Hmmm," she said noncommittally, in no mood for conversation.

"In Purgatory."

Which was exactly what this ride was beginning to feel like.

"Skiing's great this time of year. White powder like you wouldn't believe."

The only kind of white powder she'd ever been interested in came in bags. More bags than people outside the cop business—including those politicians who were constantly passing drug laws—could ever believe.

"I'm going back there next week."

"Lucky you."

Personally, she couldn't figure out why anyone would escape Midwest winter weather only to go to a place with even more snow, but she'd witnessed a lot weirder stuff in her years on the force.

As he continued to extol the wonders of racing hell-bent down an icy 14,000-foot mountain strapped onto two narrow pieces of wood or whatever skis were made of these days, Kate zoned out, focusing her mind on her upcoming testimony.

She'd always been good in court. No, better than good. She was effin' great. Attorneys in the DA's office loved her because she kept her answers brief, never wandered from the question, never offered a personal opinion, stuck to the facts, and, most important, was never, ever rattled by the opposition.

Of course, she'd never been personally involved in a case, either. Until now.

"Thought you might like to go with me."

That got her attention.

"With you?" She must've heard wrong. "To Colorado?"

They'd met a month ago, when he'd been moving in. He'd been carrying a six-foot ficus up to his new apartment, and Kate—whose black thumb had never met a plant it didn't immediately murder—had admired the leafy-green tree. They'd exchanged brief greetings in the garage a few times since then, but this was the longest conversation they'd had.

"Your case should be pretty much wrapped up about then, right?"

Every atom in Kate's body went on red alert. Although his mouth was curved in a benign smile, she'd known stone-cold killers who enjoyed snuffing out a life.

Especially a cop's life.

As if on cue, the already dim overhead light flickered.

Once.

Twice.

A third time.

Just as his gloved hand reached inside his black overcoat, the light went out, pitching the elevator into darkness.

3

New Orleans

THE SMELL OF THE EARLIER RAIN LINGERED ON air scented with camellias, salt, and diesel oil from the nearby river. As she made her tentative way across the uneven, shell-strewn ground, Desiree Doucett tightly clutched the dark hand of the man who'd brought her to this spooky City of the Dead.

Even pre-Katrina, no cautious woman would have ever entered St. Louis Cemetery No. 1 during the day, let alone at night. Not that anyone would ever call her cautious.

But still, some risks seemed acceptable. This one did not.

The fact that her companion, Toussaint Jannise, had paid a drug dealer from the neighboring redbrick housing project to accompany them into the cemetery did little to calm Desiree's nerves. Bald, glowering, huge enough to play linebacker for the Saints, and, she suspected, heavily armed beneath that black trench coat he was wearing—what was to prevent the oversize homeboy from deciding he could make more by robbing them in the deserted cemetery?

Or killing them, just for kicks?

Or robbing them, then killing Toussaint, finally ending his Mardi Gras crime spree by raping and killing her?

Nothing. They were literally at his mercy.

Nerves jangled, her pulse hammered in her throat. Desiree swallowed and tasted the metallic flavor of fear.

A thin slice of moonlight had managed to slip through a gap in the heavy rain-black clouds, causing the crumbling tombs, barely visible through the swirling thick fog, to gleam like mute, white ghosts.

They stopped at a tomb covered with brick dust X's. Coins, shells, and shiny Mardi Gras beads littered the ground around it. The tomb belonged to Marie Laveau, the famed nineteenth-century Voodoo queen. The X's signified bequests, the offerings gifts of appreciation for wishes granted. Or, just in case.

She watched as Toussaint, who was her teacher as well as her lover, knelt in front of the tomb and, after singing a few African-sounding words she wasn't going to begin to try to understand, began sprinkling yellow cornmeal onto the ground. Although she hadn't been studying Voodoo very long, Desiree understood that he was creating a *vever*, a tribute to Damballah-Wedo, the most popular father-god, who, when in his serpent guise, had formed the hills and valleys on earth and brought forth all the stars and planets in the heavens. When he'd shed his skin in the sunlight, releasing water all over the land, the sun he'd created shone in the water, creating the rainbow.

His wife and life partner, Aida-Wedo, a short-coiled, iridescent serpent, shared Damballah-Wedo's function as cosmic protector and giver of blessings. It was Aida-Wedo's image Desiree had tattooed on her breast.

While Toussaint worked to create the *vever*, Desiree carefully laid out their offerings: a bottle of specially blended perfume, a rosary with multicolored beads to signify the sacred rainbow, a ripe banana, because that's what the rainbow-hued snake preferred to eat, and seven shiny silver dollars, which she suspected their "protector" would return for as soon as they'd left.

Most people left silver dimes.

Then again, most people weren't in as much trouble as she was.

He stood up. Brushed his palms together. *"C'est tout."*

He put his arm around her and together they looked down at the yellow cornmeal drawing of the two standing snakes with a line of five pointed stars between them.

"That's beautiful," she said.

"There are those who could do much better," he responded with the humility that had attracted her to him in the first place. In her line of work, she didn't meet many men confident enough in their masculinity to be humble. "But hopefully the god and goddess will find my small effort pleasing."

He reached into the pocket of his slacks, pulled out a charcoal crayon, and handed it to her. The church, which oversaw the upkeep of the cemetery, had been complaining about people damaging other tombs in order to obtain brick to write with. That was another thing Desiree loved about this man. The fact that he was so thoughtful of others. Another rare commodity in her world.

"Now," he said. "Make three *X*'s on the tomb while silently telling Marie Laveau of your desire."

That was an easy one. She wanted to stay alive. Then, if she was allowed a bonus request, she wanted to live happily-ever-after with Toussaint Jannise.

"*C'est tout,*" she said, echoing his French, when she was finished with her silent request.

"*Bien.*" He took her hand in his, the contrast between his dark skin and her fair reminding her yet again of all the ways they were so different.

But she was changing. Thanks to him.

He folded her fingers into her palm so her hand was now a fist. "Knock three times on the tomb where you've made your marks," he instructed.

As she followed his instructions, he began to sway, his chants ringing with the musical tones of the Caribbean.

His remarkable turquoise eyes were closed, his handsome face illuminated, as if a thousand candles had been lit beneath his skin. He lifted his arms, palms up, toward the sky. A wind, seemingly seasoned with incense and mysterious spices, gusted in from the river, lifting his beaded hair until it flared out, an ebony halo around his head.

"Shit, man," said the bodyguard whom she'd forgotten was standing nearby. "This is some fucking weird stuff."

"You even think about leaving and this man will have Marie Laveau turn you into a goat," she warned, not taking her eyes from Toussaint as the ground began to roll beneath their feet. "And then he'll sacrifice you to the darkest, most evil of all the Voodoo gods. Horned fuckers so bad you can't even imagine them in your worst nightmare.

"And then, after he's sliced you open with his machete, and eaten your still-beating heart, we'll roast you on a spit and cut you up into little pieces and serve you to all your drug-dealing enemies."

"You are some tough bitch," he complained.

"You know it, homie." Not that she'd ever had much choice.

A storm raged around them: deafening thunder boomed like cannon fire, forks of white lightning flashed like fiery comets across the sky. Stars began to tumble; the full white moon floating over the City of the Dead began to pulse. Slowly at first, then faster and faster, until it rivaled the wild beat of her heart.

The wind roared; the earth trembled. Hot rain poured down in a deluge, the water sizzling on her skin. Having absolute faith in the man and his mojo, excitement and power and, yes, even hope burning through her blood, Desiree watched, enthralled, as the ghost galleon moon broke free of its moorings and came crashing toward earth.

The tomb glowed blinding bright. A brilliant blue light shot up from the top and speared the moon, tossing it back up through the roiling black clouds.

And then all was quiet.

The rain stopped as if turned off at a tap. Toussaint's beads settled back around his shoulders. As his arms lowered to his side, the earth steadied.

The spinning stars became fixed once again, sparkling like diamonds on velvet, while the moon continued its peaceful journey across the midnight-blue sky.

"J'ai fait tous ce que je pouvais," he murmured. "I did all that I could."

Although he was six feet tall and built like a sprinter, he appeared drained. And no wonder.

"You have"—she put her arms around him, not to seduce but to comfort—"done more for me than anyone else ever in my life."

"Damn," the dealer croaked. "Can we go now?"

Toussaint smiled benignly, not looking anything like a man who'd turn anyone into a sacrificial goat. "Of course."

They left the cemetery hand in hand.

"That was," Desiree said, "amazing."

"Was it?" he asked.

"You didn't know?"

"No." He shook his head. "I suppose I was caught up in the moment."

"Well, let me tell you, darlin', it was one freaking cool moment. If that didn't get Marie Laveau's attention, nothing will."

Desiree knew that some people—like her charlatan mother, who'd certainly done more than a few woo-woo gigs herself—would say Toussaint had merely pulled off a grand charade. She'd explain how he'd obviously set up the speakers and multimedia show earlier, before they'd arrived.

That he'd played to his audience's weaknesses, laying the groundwork and letting their imaginations fill in the rest.

He's a showman, just lying to you, baby. It's only your imagination.

It was what her mama always told her whenever the demons came. But then Antoinette Carroll Pickett St. Croix had never been known for her veracity. Although supposedly wellborn into a fine Savannah family whose antecedents had fought in the American Revolution, Antoinette—actually a product of a cabaret singer and a disbarred alcoholic southern lawyer—had always lived by her razor-sharp wits and the honeyed lies that came so trippingly off her tongue.

Her mother's daughter in looks, attitude, and ambition, Desiree knew a lot about lies. She also knew something her mama didn't.

Sometimes the demons were real.

4

THE STORM BLEW TOWARD THE NORTHEAST, taking its drenching rains into Mississippi, leaving behind moist air pregnant with the dank, cloying odor of decaying vegetation. The chirr of crickets provided a sharp counterpoint to the deep bass croak of bullfrogs, and the drone of the outboard motor felt like a dentist's drill behind Nick's eyes. Still handcuffed, sliding from drunk to hungover, and soaking wet from being dragged out into the rain, he'd been driven across the Mississippi into St. Bernard Parish. Now he was lying on his back on the flat bottom of a pirogue cutting its way through the bayou's twists and turns.

Overhead, Orion—the hunter—armed and in search of prey, strode across a sky as black as the oil floating on top of the water the boat was cutting through. Being in the swamp, especially at night, was like taking a trip back in time to prehistoric days. Nick wouldn't have been surprised to see a pterodactyl suddenly flying through the silvery Spanish moss hanging from the knobby cypress and tupelo trees, or a towering brontosaurus emerging from the lush, moonlit tangle of ferns.

The dark didn't bother him. Hell, before returning home to Louisiana, he'd spent fifteen years working under the cloak of night. "The enemy fears the dark," Chief Jake O'Halloran always said. "For we SEALs are in it."

They'd been more than *in* the night. They'd fucking *owned* it.

When they reached a spot that was more mud than water, the larger of his two captors turned off the engine and began poling. After about twenty minutes, they came around a bend and the muddy waterway opened up onto what appeared to be a small lake. Located on the bank of the lake, beneath the gnarled, spreading limbs of a centuries-old oak, stood an old-style planters' cabin, set on stilts.

Nick had heard rumors about this camp since joining the force, but he hadn't run across anyone who'd actually found it. Which made sense since, if you believed the stories, the last person to give away the location had been fed to the gators, limb by limb, while still alive.

The camp's location was isolated even by bayou standards. Nick wondered if the fact that he'd been brought here meant he was about to suffer a similar fate.

And wouldn't that be ironic . . . to survive a damn mortar attack in the mountains of Afghanistan only to end up killed by some asshole Louisiana wiseguy.

The interior of the cabin would have made a Trappist monk's cell look luxurious by comparison. The four straight-backed chairs and large table that took up most of the single room had been built from local cypress; there were no cushions on the seats for comfort.

A few army-green cots lined the walls. A Confederate flag hung on the wall along with some Hometown Hotties torn from the pages of *Maxim* magazine.

The kerosene lantern on the table revealed a dark amoeba-shaped bloodstain spread over the rough plank floor.

Of course, this could be a hunting cabin, the blood from some unlucky wild animal.

Sure it was. And he was Vin freakin' Diesel.

For a guy who'd grown up on the mean streets of Algiers—Louisiana, not Africa—Leon LeBlanc cleaned up real good. His three-thousand-dollar Italian suit looked custom-made, the thick silver hair sweeping back from his forehead had been expensively scissor-cut, and his nails had been buffed to a mother-of-pearl sheen. Stick him in the stands at a Tulane game and he might look like a banker or stockbroker alumnus from one of those tall glass business towers in the CBD. Until you noticed the .38 handgun pointed at Nick's chest.

"Welcome, Mr. Broussard." His tone was casual, but if a gator could smile, it'd look a helluva lot like LeBlanc. "How nice of you to drop by."

"Nice of you to invite me," Nick drawled. And about freaking time. Nick had begun to think it'd be easier to get a meeting with the president. "Though if I'd known this party was formal, I'd have taken time to have my old dress-blue uniform pressed."

LeBlanc's smile didn't fade. But Nick sensed animosity seething from the hulk looming behind him.

Apparently picking up on the same vibes, LeBlanc lifted a hand. "Why don't you boys go outside after you take the cuffs off Mr. Broussard?"

It was more order than suggestion and everyone in the cabin knew it. Nick was reluctantly impressed when the goons shuffled out.

"Good trick." He resisted rubbing his chafed wrists. "They've already proven they know how to fetch. Do they bring you your paper and slippers in the morning, too?"

"I don't wear slippers." As if deciding Nick didn't offer a threat, he put down the pistol and reached into a cooler sitting on the floor beside the table. "I leave those for the girly men." He skimmed a gaze over Nick. "Seems you don't favor them, either. Which isn't surprising, you having been in the military and all. And, who your daddy was."

Deciding it wasn't a question, Nick didn't respond.

LeBlanc pulled two bottles of beer from the cooler. Dixie, which, since Katrina had taken out the hundred-year-old brewery, had become as rare around these parts as a FEMA official with a checkbook. He held one of the bottles out to Nick.

"Why don't you have yourself a seat, Broussard? And we'll have ourselves a little chat."

"How about I go home and leave you to chat with your oversize lapdogs?"

"They're good boys. Maybe not as sophisticated as

some, but they're loyal, which is a rare commodity these days." Gold eyes, rimmed with a darker brown, skimmed over Nick. Took in the bruises. "They were rough on you."

"You could say that."

Having grown up sitting in for his father during the weekly poker games, Nick knew when to hold 'em. And when to fold.

Given that LeBlanc had dealt himself a hand of aces, Nick sprawled in the wooden chair and took a long pull from the bottle, enjoying the faint tang of the barrels the beer was aged in. There were beer snobs who probably wouldn't consider Dixie the best beer in the world, but Nick had been drinking it since he was fifteen, and as far as he was concerned, there wasn't anything on the planet better with crawfish.

"Good man, your daddy," LeBlanc said. "I was sorry to hear he'd passed on."

"Well, that makes one of us."

Nick knew damn well that although he probably hadn't been the one to pull the trigger—LeBlanc hadn't survived all these years by risking capture while doing his own dirty work—the mobster's fingerprints were all over Big Antoine's so-called suicide.

He put the bottle down on the table and went for the bluff. "Look, LeBlanc. You may have half the cops in the parish on your tab, but I'm not my old man."

"So I've heard. Antoine used to say you might be wild, but you were as clean as a fuckin' altar boy."

"Excuse me if I have trouble buying that."

A patrician silver brow arched. "Which? That your father thought you possessed integrity? Or that he talked about you at all?"

Nick shrugged and took another long drink of the beer. Talking about his old man made him thirsty.

"He was real proud of you," LeBlanc continued smoothly. Despite the outward convivial tone, this was not, Nick knew, a casual conversation. Wiseguys like LeBlanc didn't send their goons to haul a guy out into the bayou in the middle of the night because they were looking for someone to chew the fat with. "Didn't understand you worth shit. But he was proud."

"You got cell-phone signal out here?"

The older man's brow furrowed at the seeming non sequitur. "It's spotty. Why?"

"Because you might want to use that friggin' phone to call someone who cares."

Nick suspected not many people would have the nerve to mouth off to Leon LeBlanc. At least that's what he was counting on.

Bingo. LeBlanc threw back his head and roared. "Damned if you ain't your old man's kid after all."

He rubbed his palms—which looked as if they'd never done a lick of physical work—together with apparent glee, enjoying some private joke he wasn't prepared to let Nick in on.

"Hear you got yourself into a little trouble with the cops."

Nick shrugged. "I was set up."

"That's your story and you're sticking to it." LeBlanc

winked, beaming like a vinyl-siding salesman at his own humor. "But you know, it got me thinking."

Always a dangerous thing.

"Taking payoffs from some low-rent hot-sheet places, like you were busted for, isn't usually enough to make even a ripple in the department."

Not in this city, anyway. "I suppose gettin' my picture on TV didn't win me any political friends."

"Sure enough, that's a possibility. Cops never like seein' one of their own on the nightly news. Unless, of course, one of them can be spun as a dead hero. Still, that type of pissant stuff tends to blow over."

"So did Katrina."

LeBlanc's lips curved into a satisfied smile. "That hurricane may just turn out to be the best damn thing that ever happened to this city."

"I suppose that depends on what side of the government contracts you're sitting on."

Leon LeBlanc's Crescent City Construction Company had been tearing condemned buildings down for months. While his waste management trucks hauled mountains of debris away. When they started handing out government contracts, LeBlanc had been first in line at the public trough. Any subcontractors wanting a piece of the rebuilding of New Orleans parish had to pay LeBlanc to play.

"Maybe so. The thing is, Broussard, I've been givin' a lot of thought to your situation."

Again Nick didn't respond.

"And I've decided that either you're the unluckiest

sumbitch who ever lived, or just maybe you've pissed off some people in the department. Given your previous reputation as a Boy Scout, I'd say it's the latter."

"If people get pissed off, hey, that's not my problem."

"Unless those pissed-off people just happen to decide to get you out of the way. By framin' you. But here's the kicker." LeBlanc folded his hands and leaned forward over the table. A glacier-size diamond pinky ring glittered like ice in the lantern light. "I did me some diggin' and I can't find a single solitary soul who'll cop to settin' you up for that bribe that got you busted."

Unsure where this conversation was headed, Nick had the niggling little suspicion that he may have miscalculated the situation.

"Lots of stories in the Big Easy," LeBlanc said amiably. The smile in his eyes was about as trustworthy as a government promise. "Some truer than others. I figure you got railroaded out of the department because you're the one thing everybody hates. A hypocrite."

"That's your opinion." Nick polished off the Dixie. "You're welcome to it. And, for the record, that little trouble turned out to be the best thing that ever happened to me. Now I got my own business. Nobody tells me what to do. Or how to do it. There's no Big Brother looking over my shoulder."

"There's the state licensing board."

Nick laughed derisively. "Yeah. Right."

"You got a point." LeBlanc's eyes crinkled at the corners. "Been a while since Katrina, but everyone's still a bit distracted."

Distracted. That was one word for it.

"Guess that's how you managed to get yourself a license without taking the required forty-hour PI course."

"You *have* been keeping an eye on me."

"Big Antoine and I went to Redemptorist High together. We were friends. I'll always feel guilty that he didn't come to me with his problems before—"

"Blowin' his damn head off with a shotgun?"

LeBlanc shook his head. "I heard it wasn't pretty."

"Brains splattered all over a bedroom wall seldom are."

Actually, when he'd seen the police photos, Nick had been surprised the son of a bitch had any brains left, considering his father had spent most of his life—at least the part of it after he'd returned home from Chu Lai with two Purple Hearts and a serious jones for booze—trying his best to pickle every damn cell in his body.

"As for my skipping that PI course, with the police department shorthanded these days, certain, shall we say *friendly* members of the licensing board believe it's more efficient to get cops back on the streets. Even private ones."

"What did that cost you?"

"Not a red cent."

LeBlanc chuckled. "You're a fair-to-middlin' liar, Broussard. But I'm not buying it. You're runnin' on fumes, boy."

"Yeah, but I got me some snazzy new business cards. I figure I'll snag myself a hot case soon enough."

So far he had three clients. The first was a former high school girlfriend who wanted him to run a check on a guy she was considering getting serious about, the second a friend whose dickhead of a husband was too quick with his fists.

Nick had refused to take money in either case. The first he figured he'd owed, having pretty much dumped her to join the navy after high school. In the second case the woman was a victim, and no way would his conscience allow him to make money off that.

The third was a trickier situation. And, he was beginning to suspect, the real reason he'd been dragged out here tonight.

"Ask and ye shall receive. Because, as it happens, I've got a job for you, boy."

Nick leaned back in the chair, balancing on the hind legs. *Bien.* This was better. Now things were getting back on track. "What kind of job?"

"Let's call it a missing-persons case."

"Lots of people still missing since Katrina scattered folks to the four winds."

A shitload of cops had taken off that weekend, too. Some in cars they'd "borrowed" from local dealerships.

"Ain't that the truth. But this particular person shouldn't be so hard to find. Given that you and she are . . . well, shall we say, close?"

Hell. Damn if she hadn't gone and done it.

It took a Herculean effort, but Nick managed to keep his expression and his voice bland. "I'm close to a lot of people. Especially those of the female persuasion." He flashed the kind of grin two guys might share when a well-endowed female sashayed by.

"Another way you're like your old man. Antoine liked the ladies, too, back in the day. But the word on the street is that you and Desiree Doucett have been doin' the nasty together."

"The street doesn't know shit about what I do behind closed doors."

LeBlanc exhaled a long, patient sigh. "You're not bad at bluffin', boy. But you know what they say. About a picture bein' worth a thousand words."

He reached into the jacket pocket, pulled out an envelope. Then fanned the photos out on the table like a poker player showing off a royal flush.

Fuck, fuck, fuck! Nick pretended scant interest in the photos even as his mind spun like a damn Tilt-A-Whirl.

There they were together, Desiree all smooth, perfumed, and powdered magnolia skin, him still fully clothed, which didn't really let him off the hook. Especially when he took in the others: photographs of Desiree in his arms, Desiree's lush ripe mouth on his, Desiree wrapped around him like a damn python in her pretty iron-frame bed.

"I don't suppose you'd believe I was visiting a sick friend?"

"I'd believe you and that little chippie were playing doctor, sure enough," LeBlanc said. "You being so close to her, you'd probably know where to find her."

Ice skimmed up Nick's spine. "And you're looking for her why?" His voice was steady. His palms moist.

Trust the crazy, willful redhead to screw things up.

Well, he'd wanted to infiltrate LeBlanc's cadre of killers, thugs, and thieves.

But, dammit, not this way.

He'd suspected the criminal boss might give him a hit right off the bat, to test how far he'd fallen. How desperate he might be.

As a SEAL sniper, Nick had taken lives before. In the line of duty. For flag and country. But no way would he commit cold-blooded murder. Unfortunately, when he'd come up with what had seemed, at the time, a crackerjack plan to uncover who was really responsible for his father's death, he'd decided to set fire to that bridge when he got to it.

Problem was, he'd never foreseen the proposed target being a woman. And, damn it all to hell, not just any woman. A confidential informant.

He couldn't tell LeBlanc he'd been at Desiree Doucett's apartment so she could feed him information about the South Louisiana rackets. Not if he wanted to walk out of here alive.

And not if he wanted to keep Desiree alive. Which it sounded like involved finding her first.

Jesus, Mary, and Thibodoux. Nick had gotten himself into some tight situations over the years. But this was the first time he really understood the old cliché about being between a freaking rock and a hard place.

"The girl stole somethin' of mine. Somethin' she has no right to," the mobster growled. "I want it back."

Roger that. No problem. Desiree might not like it, but even as reckless as she was, the woman wasn't stupid. When he explained the alternatives, she'd see the light.

"So, you gonna tell me what it is I'm supposed to get back?"

"Desiree knows what it is. What I want is for you to bring her to me. So she and I can have a come-to-Jesus meeting about how stealing's not only a crime, but a sin."

Like LeBlanc wasn't personally acquainted with all seven deadly sins?

"So why haven't you sent your goons after her?"

"Let's just say this job needs a bit more finesse. Plus, I can always use a PI on my team. This seems a good way for you and me to see how well we work together."

"Okay. So I bring Desiree Doucett in for that little chat. Then what?"

"*Then* ain't none of your business."

The man's expression hardened. His eyes turned flat as a gator's. Gone was the jovial wiseguy known for the best Jazz Fest parties and Mardi Gras fireworks on the Gulf Coast. In his place was the stone-cold killer Nick knew him to be. Unfortunately, knowing a guy was rotten to the core didn't necessarily mean you could get a conviction when said guy was as connected as Leon LeBlanc was.

"You want the job or not, Broussard?"

He took a hammered gold case from the same pocket from which he'd pulled the photos, stuck a cigarette in his mouth, and lit it with a black Zippo adorned with a retro sixties *Playboy* cover girl. Adding this piece of evidence to the pinups on the wall, Nick concluded LeBlanc liked women.

When he wasn't trying to kill them, that is.

"And just in case you decide you need time to think about it, let me explain how things work," LeBlanc said on a stream of smoke that hung on the humid bayou air. He then proceeded to offer a sum equal to what it would've taken Nick five years in the military to earn. "The deal is, boy, it goes down ten thousand dollars a minute for the next ten minutes. Then, it's off the table."

He stood up, shot his snowy cuffs. "I'll let you think about it while I go talk to the boys."

Not wanting to let LeBlanc and his thugs have themselves a little powwow about what to do with him, Nick decided he could think later. "I'll take it."

"I rather thought you would." A satisfied chuckle rumbled up from the older man's chest. "Did I mention the job comes with an end date?"

"I don't believe you did."

"You've got forty-eight hours to bring that little gal to me."

"And if I don't?"

"Well, the obvious thing is you won't get paid. But you never know what kinda accidents a fella might have." He shook his head, took one last hit on the cigarette, and dropped it into the beer bottle, where it sizzled and went out. "Sure would hate to think about that boat of yours goin' up in flames some night. Even worse if you happened to be there when it happened."

It was a threat, pure and simple. And both men knew it.

Now all Nick had to do was figure out how the hell to keep reckless, headstrong Desiree Doucett from becoming a New Orleans homicide statistic, solve a murder—no way would his old man kill himself—and, oh yeah, manage to keep from being clipped himself.

Piece of cake.

5

Chicago

AS STANDOFFS WENT, IT DEFINITELY WASN'T the most life-threatening she'd ever encountered.

The adrenaline still pumping trip-hammer fast through her veins, Kate double-handed her Glock as she faced off against a . . . flashlight?

Oh, hell.

Strangely, the man she was pointing the pistol at didn't seem all that nervous. Instead, he merely smiled and sort of waved the flashlight, a yellow beam shooting over the walls and ceiling.

"After getting stuck in here for twenty minutes last week, I've started bringing my own light with me," he said mildly.

"That's a good idea." One of the good things about having been a patrol cop was the Mag-Lite Kate had carried on her utility belt.

"It doesn't keep the elevator from getting stuck. But at least I won't be in the dark next time." Somehow his attention shifted to the gun, though he kept his eyes on hers. "I'm one of the good guys. So you can put that away."

"Sorry." There were cops in the department with itchy trigger fingers. Kate had never been one of them. Until now.

Welcome to Paranoiaville.

"You've been under a lot of stress lately."

She was holstering the gun when his words sent another little jolt through her. "You know who I am?"

"Of course. Even if you weren't the best-looking police officer I've ever seen, it would've been hard to miss all the media coverage."

"Damn vultures." Like most cops, Kate had never been that fond of reporters. The past few weeks had not altered her opinion that most were carrion who fed on human tragedy.

"It's a compelling story. There's a tall blue wall inside every police department dividing the good guys from the bad guys. The rules behind that wall are the cop counterpart to omertà, the mobster code of silence."

She tilted her head and studied him as the elevator reached the ground. "And you know this how?"

His smile was quick and friendly and made him appear absolutely harmless. "I'm a psychiatrist."

Could her day get any better? Shrinks rated below reporters on Kate's personal hierarchy. They were all the time wanting you to talk about private stuff. About your mother. Yeah, like that was going to happen anytime in this millennium.

"Good for you." Her tone said otherwise.

"I've consulted with the department before."

Her heart jumped as adrenaline, laced with a cop's instinctive caution, spiked through her. "You're not—"

"Stalking you? Watching you for police brass who undoubtedly aren't all that pleased to have one of their own turn Serpico on them?"

"I was going to say keeping me under surveillance."

"No." He shook his head. "My moving into the building was just a coincidence. But perhaps"—the steel door opened—"a fortunate one."

He reached into his coat pocket, took out a leather folder, and handed her a business card. It was ivory, the lettering in bark-brown raised type. Classy.

"If you want someone to talk to," he said, "I'm told I have an empathetic ear."

"I'll keep that in mind."

She gave a smile as false as her words as she slipped the card into her coat pocket. Mephistopheles would be ice fishing in hell before she spilled her guts to anyone. Let alone a shrink with ties to a department that believed she'd betrayed it.

"And I don't want to boast, but I also make a mean lasagna, if you're ever in the mood for a homemade Italian dinner."

How did he know she didn't cook? Had he seen one of her microwaveable meal cartons while searching through her garbage?

And can you get any more paranoid? He's only asking you to dinner. Like a casual date. You do remember dating, don't you?

Sure she did. Just barely.

"How about I give you a rain check?" Kate forced a bit more warmth into her tone.

It wasn't this shrink's fault her life was screwed up. Or that she'd decided—after her unsurprising breakup with one of the cops she'd be testifying against in the Justice Department's police corruption case—to embrace her celibate side.

"I'll hold you to that," he said as they left the elevator together. "Good luck in court."

"Thanks."

Kate watched as he walked in the opposite direction, stopping when he got to a black BMW sedan that was both conservative and expensive. He was six feet, a hundred eighty, maybe a hundred ninety pounds, hair brown, eyes hazel. And, although he was not the kind of guy who usually hit on her, he seemed nice enough. If she'd been in the market for a man, she probably could have done worse.

Hell, you've done a whole lot worse. Which brought her back to the celibacy issue. And the fact that nice guy or not, he was still a man. Which meant he'd undoubtedly expect payoff for pasta.

The sedan even sounded expensive as it drove out of the garage. Leaving Kate all too aware of being alone. If this were one of those chicks-in-jeopardy movies that seemed to run 24/7 on cable, right about now the bad guy would come leaping out of the shadows and grab the defenseless airhead heroine.

Fortunately, this was real life and Kate was neither an airhead nor defenseless.

But that didn't mean she didn't have bad guys gunning for her.

A fact she was all too well aware of every morning. Over the past weeks she'd developed a routine, which began with opening the hood of the humiliatingly ugly-as-sin Crown Vic currently hunkered down on balding tires in the building's garage.

Okay. No signs of an ignition-fired bomb. So far, so good.

Next she took the red creeper she'd bought at the Auto Zone and wheeled herself beneath the car's rear end. Although she hated this part of the morning routine, even worse than risking grease on her coat would be to end up like that Gangster Disciple, the one who'd been blown up by a heat-fired incendiary device some Latin Warlord enforcer had attached to the muffler of his pimped-out Escalade during last year's turf wars.

Again, nothing.

Sliding back out, she checked beneath the handle and along the edge of the door, then climbed into the driver's seat. When her heart started to threaten to glitch out on her again, she looped her hands over the steering wheel and tried not to think about the fact that if any of those cops who'd been calling with anonymous death threats were serious, this could well be her last peaceful moment on earth.

She counted backward from ten, watching the numbers float in front of her, all soft and shimmering, like moonlight on misty fog banks. It was a mental trick she'd developed as a kid. Usually it helped her relax. Not today.

"Hell. May as well get it over with."

She didn't exactly close her eyes. That would be like waving a white flag to the bad guys. But she did slit them just a bit.

Drew in a breath.

Held it.

Then twisted the key.

The Crown Vic's engine roared to life. Okay, so technically it was more a whimper than a roar, but in this case, that was a good thing.

"Yes!"

She blew out the tension on a rush of relieved breath. Shook her wrists to release the nerves that had coiled in her gut like a tangle of rattlesnakes. Then finally fastened her seat belt and backed out of the garage.

Night slid into morning as she pulled onto Lakeshore Drive. Blustery winds stirred up whitecaps and blew ice, like tumbled stones, across the steely gray surface. Although the Crown Vic's windows were tightly shut and the ancient heater was blowing hot air out of the dashboard and floor vents, Kate imagined she could hear strange hissing sounds the ice made as the almost otherworldly shapes rubbed against one another.

Never peaceful this time of year, Lake Michigan echoed her own tumultuous mood.

Though Kate hated the winter with a passion usually reserved for child molesters and Internet predators, some of her most memorable moments had been spent sailing on the lake in the summer, savoring the fresh air, the warmth of the sun on her face, the brisk wind tangling her long red hair into an unruly cloud, and, most of all, the exhilarating feeling of freedom.

But after all that had happened, the memory of the last time she'd been on the water was a faint, misty memory, like a dream upon waking. Had it only been six months ago?

"Stop feeling sorry for yourself, dammit!" She flexed her fingers, which had tightened into a death grip on the wheel, as a stuttering sun colored the sky a pale lemon yellow. "It's a new day. Filled with possibilities. And you're not going to die."

At least not this morning.

She hoped.

6

New Orleans

IT'S ONLY YOUR IMAGINATION.

You're not being followed, Desiree assured herself as she forged through the raucous, jostling carnival crowds jamming the French Quarter.

It was two days of libertine frivolity before the relatively austere season of Lent. A cacophonous jangle of jazz, zydeco, and blues poured out of open doorways and the night air was rich with scents of spicy boiled crawfish, spilled beer, and sweet, sticky cocktails.

Many of the shops and bars remained shuttered, and although the city was still in the midst of rebuilding after Katrina, its long-term future unknown, tourists had returned. Drunken frat boys crowded onto balconies, dangling strands of beads over lacy black iron railings, urging women passing on the street below: "Show us your tits, baby!"

The women, caught up in the frivolity, happily lifted their tops, flashing for beads. The larger the breasts, the gaudier the beads—an unfair barter system, perhaps, but the Big Easy had never been a bastion of political correctness.

Which was what Desiree loved about the hedonistic city.

A waddle of nuns, looking like shiny penguins in black-and-white fetish latex habits and sporting prominent Adam's apples, drunkenly cheered encouragement to a horned devil chugging a pink frothy Hurricane from a plastic to-go cup.

After polishing off the lethal blend of rum and passion-fruit punch, the demon's midnight-black eyes, framed by a scarlet half-mask, clashed with hers.

Desiree froze. A knot, sharp as barbed wire, tightened painfully in her stomach.

Is he the one?

He swiped the back of his large, black leather-gloved hand across his wet mouth. Grinned evilly. Then tossed her a saucy wink before disappearing with his cohorts into the crowd.

Desiree's breath left her lungs in a long, relieved whoosh.

Normally, it would only take thirty minutes to walk to her destination, then back to Toussaint's shotgun house. But tonight, because of the crush of people, it had already taken nearly an hour. Not helping were the ice-pick heels Jimmy Choo definitely hadn't designed for walking on uneven cobblestone streets.

A shiny dime hung from a thin platinum chain between her breasts. As her fingers curled around the gris-

gris Toussaint had given her for protection, she could have sworn the metal warmed.

She had no business being out here again tonight. Not alone. She knew Toussaint would be furious at her for taking such a risk. Although he'd done everything he could to protect her, he'd always told her that such things were ultimately out of his—and her, and every other human's—control.

But after he'd taken her back to his home, where she'd promised she'd remain until he returned from his night job as a waiter, she'd decided that keeping the videotape under his roof was too dangerous. Which was when she'd gotten the idea of exactly where she needed to hide it.

The *click click click* of her heels on the cobblestones echoed in the swirling mist, an accompaniment to the off-key peal of bells calling saints and sinners to St. Louis Cathedral.

The church, with its tapering, slate-covered triple towers bathed in spotlights, stood sentinel over Jackson Square. Desiree had often found it ironic that local Catholics could arrive at the church by carriage, confess their sins, then walk two blocks to one of the most sin-drenched streets in America. At the moment, she wasn't thinking all that much about her own sins, but of sanctuary.

A handful of people were scattered around the Romanesque building, raising funds for a local homeless shelter. A young, fresh-faced nun handed her a flyer, which Desiree stuck in her bag without bothering to read it.

Instead of turning onto Royal, she cut through Pirates Alley. The alley was supposedly haunted by the ghost of Father Pere Antoine, the cathedral's first priest, who'd not only baptized Marie Laveau but had performed her wedding, as well.

Rumors said that he'd loved New Orleans and its people so much, he couldn't bear to leave them behind when he died. According to local legends, on certain rainy nights in the hours before dawn, a male voice could be heard singing the *Kyrie*.

Desiree didn't believe in ghosts any more than she believed in God. But she did admire the priest for his efforts to free women of color and his work for the city's poor and oppressed, including the city's prostitutes.

A sound behind her—like the rattle of dry leaves or, worse yet, the scurrying of a wharf rat—caused her to shoot a quick, nervous glance back over her shoulder. A frisson of fear brushed over her, like fingers of fog against her suddenly icy skin.

Not watching where she was going, she stumbled on a broken stone and tripped straight into the arms of a black-robed stranger.

She opened her mouth to scream, but there was something about the stern warning in the man's eyes, which gleamed in the stuttering white glow of moonlight, that caused the half-born sound in her throat to die.

Dark brows dove down to a sharp nose, but Desiree, an expert at reading male intent, noted a softening of his expression. He leaned toward her, close enough for his breath to fan her icy skin as his lips touched her ear.

"Faites attention, ma jeune femme."

His whispered words were little more than a zephyr of night breeze drifting in from the river. Having picked up some French from her lover, Desiree understood that he was warning her to be careful.

A cloud drifted across the moon, throwing the alley into shadow. When the cloud moved on, he was gone.

It couldn't be. All those stories about the priest haunting the alley couldn't actually be true. Could they?

"I ain't afraid of no ghosts."

Saying the line from *Ghostbusters* was like whistling in a graveyard. Desiree brushed her clammy hands down her skirt, took a deep breath.

She'd only taken another two steps when a tender touch, like silken fingertips, skimmed against her cheek.

"Priz pour votre âme," the ghostly voice whispered in her ear as a different, all-too-human man, dressed in black jeans and a black leather jacket, stepped out of the shadows. *"Go with God."*

"I'm afraid it's too late for that, Padre," Desiree murmured with a sinking heart, as the flesh-and-blood male flashed a deadly smile she knew all too well.

The last time Stephen LeBlanc had looked at her like that, she'd ended up with four cracked ribs, a broken wrist, and a concussion that had her seeing double for a week.

It had been, he'd coolly informed her as his father's goon slammed a steel-booted foot into her ribs, her punishment for breaking the rule by doing a few tricks on the side.

It was time she learned who made the rules. Who she belonged to.

That had been three months ago. And she'd recovered. At least physically.

But it was the next morning, as she'd stood beneath the shower that was pounding hot water onto her bruised and battered body, when Desiree began to plan her revenge. A revenge that began with hottie Cajun cop Nick Broussard, who'd warned her that she'd be better off taking up nude alligator wrestling than trying to pull anything over on the Gulf's most ruthless—and most politically connected—wiseguy.

Now, as she took in her adversary's deadly cobra smile, Desiree figured she had two choices.

She could stay here and be killed.

Or she could take her chances and try to escape. And probably end up being caught, anyway. Then forced to die a very slow, very painful death.

As Stephen LeBlanc's black-gloved hand reached for her throat, Desiree made her decision.

Spinning on a stiletto heel, she took off running. For her life.

7

DAMN. HE WAS TOO LATE. DESIREE DOUCETT was found dead, her neck—and a great many other bones, including those in her surgically enhanced face—broken. She'd decided to take a dive out the window of her apartment.

"Any sign of forced entry?" Nick asked his partner.

Make that his *former* partner. Given the way Nick left the force in public disgrace, he knew Remy Landreaux could get reamed just for talking to him. Let alone sharing details of a crime scene. Nick appreciated the loyalty, especially since he'd been treated like a leper ever since he'd been shown doing the perp walk on WWL's *Eyewitness News*.

It was one thing for a cop to bend the rules.

Another thing entirely for him to be caught doing it.

And, especially after Katrina, being caught on camera pretty much made you a pariah.

Nick's meeting with LeBlanc had reminded him that there were more important things than his own ego. Or even his reputation. The death of any informant would've driven that idea home, though that was, more often than not, the breaks. Informants, after all, tended to live on the edge.

In fact, there was an old cop Q&A joke about what to do when all your informants were shot dead.

Answer: *Open another can of informants.*

Now regret warred with an icy fury that this particular informant had been a woman he'd honestly cared about.

"Non." Remy shook his head. Took a long drag on a cigarette. That was one thing Nick didn't miss: driving around inside a car that smelled like a week-old ashtray.

Nick watched as uniformed EMTs lifted the red-haired corpse into the waiting ambulance.

"Apartment was locked from inside when Homicide got there. Only way out was the window," Remy divulged. "Manner of death is the medical examiner's call, but unofficially we're ruling it a suicide."

Hunching his shoulders against a rain that had turned ice-cold, Nick lifted his gaze to the open window, where white lace curtains billowed in the breeze.

"Just like that?" Nick wished he could be surprised that the brass was so willing to jump to the easy judgment.

"The door was locked," Remy reminded Nick. The tip of the cigarette glowed red as he inhaled. "From the inside. Looks like she'd barricaded herself inside by pushing a bunch of furniture against the door."

"And no one found that a little strange?"

"Hell, Nick. You know as well as I do that this fuckin' city is strange on a good day. During Mardi Gras . . ."

He shrugged his Burberry raincoat—clad shoulders. Remy Landreaux had always liked the good life. Fortunately, thanks to trust funds bequeathed him from a doting *grand-mere* and various elderly aunties who'd passed on, he could afford it.

"Besides, the girl was a junkie," he said.

"She'd been clean for six months."

His former partner's look asked what crawfish truck he'd just fallen off of.

"Addicts fall off the wagon, *cher*," Remy said gently. " 'Specially during this time of year when people go buck wild."

And didn't Nick know that all too well? Back when he was a kid, he'd learned to stay out of the old man's way from Thanksgiving until Lent.

"I gotta go."

Remy tossed the cigarette into the gutter, where it hissed, then winked out. He gave Nick a long, searching stare. The kind a cop gives a "person of interest" when he's trying to decide whether or not to read him his rights.

Then he shook his dark head, turned on the heel of his Bruno Magli tasseled loafer, and began to walk away.

"What?" Nick demanded toward his back.

Remy stopped at the openly belligerent tone. He glanced back over his shoulder. Pursed his lips, exhaled with obvious frustration.

"How long have we known each other?"

"I don't know." Nick shrugged. "Twenty-five years. Going on twenty-six, maybe."

They'd met back in grammar school, when Remy's mother moved back to her hometown after her husband died in an explosion on an oil rig out in the Gulf. The new kid had been in Nick's class all of two days when they'd gotten into a playground fistfight over the favors of Evangeline Rochefort, a flirtatious, dark-eyed, seven-year-old beauty who would go on to represent the state of Louisiana in the Miss Universe pageant.

"And all that time, we've been straight with each other, right?" Remy demanded.

"Right."

Nick may have told a helluva lot of lies in the past six months, but this was one thing he wanted on the record.

"So, what the hell happened?"

"If you don't know, you haven't been watching *Eyewitness News*."

"I know the media's saying you're just another crooked NOPD cop. I know the friggin' brass is saying pretty much the same thing while doing their damndest to wash their hands of you. Ditto the cops on the street, who figure you've gone over to the dark side. Some even say you're aimin' to outdo your old man by becoming LeBlanc's top enforcer." He dragged a hand through his fifty-dollar haircut. "But you've never said a single damn thing. Not even to me.

"Your *partner*," he stressed. "The guy who stood up beside you at your wedding. And got tanked with you the night you came home on leave and found your wife shaggin' her hairdresser."

"That was a long time ago. But, hey, thanks for reminding me."

His former partner's heavily lidded dark eyes—which Nick had heard more than one female call "bedroom eyes"—turned sad. "What the hell happened?"

Nick shrugged. "You know what they say, *cher*. Shit happens."

Remy's gaze drifted toward the ambulance that was taking off, the rooftop bar lights dark, the siren silent. There was, after all, no need to hurry.

"Isn't that the truth." He scrubbed a hand down his face. "I don't suppose it'd do me any good to suggest you try to stay out of trouble?"

"Hey, I've got me a new business, a new lease on life. No way am I goin' to screw all that up."

"Desiree Doucett was a train wreck waitin' to happen, Nick. It's best just to let sleeping dogs lie."

"You got any more clichés you want to throw at the situation?"

Being a hotshot detective, he could tell from Remy's dark scowl that his former partner was less than amused. Well, didn't that just make two of them?

"She was also a fellow human being," Nick said. "Was she flawed? *Mais*, yeah." That was, in Desiree's case, a vast understatement. "But aren't we all?"

"Word on the street is that she got greedy and tried to run a blackmail con on Leon LeBlanc. Which, if true, given how that guy controls his empire, means she'd committed suicide before she took a flying leap out that window."

Remy shot a killer glare up at the rain that was making dark spots on his tobacco-colored coat. Then he looked back at Nick.

"You stay out of trouble, y'hear?"

Nick flashed a grin that was as phony as everything else about his life these days. "Roger that."

They both knew it was a lie.

Again, Remy was not amused.

Nick watched his former partner walk back to the courtyard. Watched him talk with the detective who'd caught the case.

Martin Dubois made *The Pink Panther*'s bumbling Inspector Clouseau look like Sherlock Holmes. It wasn't so much that he was carrying an extra eighty pounds on his five-foot-eight frame (which he was), or that he apparently believed a comb-over would hide the fact that he was going bald (it didn't), or that he sweat like a bureaucrat facing a congressional committee hearing (which he did, even in the middle of winter).

It was that he was, hands down, the most crooked police officer Nick had ever known. And considering he'd grown up in New Orleans, with a cop father who routinely returned home with pockets filled with cash, that was saying something.

Desiree Doucett, admittedly, had been screwed up. She had also been, at times, greedy. Impatient. And headstrong.

Some of the dangerous choices she'd made—like

ripping off the LeBlancs, for chrissakes—might lead someone to believe she was suicidal. Someone, that is, who didn't know her as well as Nick had.

There was no way the woman would jump out a window. A dramatically slit wrist in a bathtub, maybe. Pills, sure. And though it would be a tragic sight, he could easily picture her clad in a body-clinging white nightgown artfully posed on the bed so as to leave behind a beautiful corpse.

But kill herself in a way that would not only break bones, but shatter the already pretty face that a Gulf Coast plastic surgeon had enhanced to a movie-star ideal?

No way.

It was obvious she'd been murdered.

Just as it was obvious that Dubois—who couldn't find his oversize ass with both hands if someone drew him a picture—wouldn't be able to find Desiree's killer.

If he even wanted to. Which Nick didn't believe for a minute he did. How coincidental was it that the cop known to everyone in the city to be Leon LeBlanc's own personal bagman just happened to be on duty when the 911 call about a hooker's suicide came in?

Slim to none.

Zero.

Zip.

But dammit, someone had to stand for the murdered. Especially when no one had stood for this particular victim in life.

"Looks like you're fucking elected." Which was precisely what Nick did not need.

8

DARK WAS FALLING AS KATE LEFT THE DIRKSEN Federal Building through the underground parking garage after her second and—thank you, God!—final long day of testimony. Although the prosecutor had arranged for a phalanx of federal marshals from Judicial Protective Services to keep reporters from rushing her car as she left the twenty-eight-story black glass tower, that had not stopped a contingent of uniform cops from lining the sidewalks. Seeing their folded arms and stony expressions, Kate doubted she was going to win the Fraternal Order of Police congeniality award anytime soon.

Another clue that she'd fallen out of favor was the used condom left on the driver's seat of the Crown Vic while she'd been inside the courthouse. There was, of course, no point in asking any of the JPS court-security officers if they'd seen anyone approach the car.

The CSOs may have been assigned to protect her, but she suspected that deep down, where it really mattered, more than a few of them shared that one-for-all, all-for-one cop mentality. By crossing that blue line of police silence to testify against some of her own, she'd earned a jacket she'd never overcome. After today, she was pretty much out of the cop business.

She was about to cross the river when, despite the crush of afternoon traffic, a patrol car suddenly pulled in front of her.

Another closed in behind.

A third on her driver's side.

Kate's fingers tightened on the steering wheel, and she knew that if there'd only been enough room, they would've put her into the center of a diamond formation, a classic cop intimidation technique.

They continued that way for several blocks. When they all stopped for a red light at Ohio, the cop to her left continued to look straight ahead, not giving any sign at all that he knew or even cared who was beside him.

Which was a crock. If there was one thing all patrol cops paid attention to, it was cars anywhere in their vicinity. She knew because she'd once been one of them. And, like them, she would run the plate whenever she was behind a vehicle at a stoplight. Because you just never knew when you might stumble across a stolen car. Or better yet, a wanted felon.

The damn light seemed to be lasting forever. Although she'd managed to get through hours of testimony, including being badgered by the attorneys for the police defendants, without breaking a sweat, moisture began to gather beneath her bangs. Under her arms. Even on the palms of her hands, which had a death grip on the wheel.

Never let them see you sweat.

It was the first thing she'd learned in the police academy and was even more important for a woman cop here in this macho, sports-crazy land of Bulls and Bears, ribs and beer.

It had begun snowing again, thick, fat flakes driven by wind off the lake that splatted against the windshield.

The cop to her left still hadn't looked at her. But Kate knew he was every bit as aware of her as she was of him.

The light—finally!—turned green. The cars peeled away, like a Navy Blue Angels flying team. Her heart pounding jackhammer-fast, jackhammer-hard, just as they intended, Kate had just turned right, toward the lake, when her cell phone rang.

The display read "private number." Given that it was next to impossible to keep those threatening cops from getting her unlisted phone number, she'd been changing cell phones every few days. So far, the only people who knew this number were on the federal prosecutor's staff.

"Hello?"

"Ms. Delaney?" an unfamiliar male voice asked.

"Who's calling?" A cop still down to her toes, Kate wasn't about to give out any information to a stranger.

"This is Lieutenant Remy Landreaux. From the New Orleans Police Department. I'm calling for Ms. Kathleen Delaney."

"How did you get this number?"

"From information. Your other one has been disconnected," he told her, nothing she didn't already know.

"Information should have told you I'm unlisted."

"That's exactly what the operator said. Until I explained to her supervisor that I'm a detective, calling on police business." Meaning doors would open magically for him as soon as he pulled his shiny NOPD badge.

"What precinct house are you calling from?"

"I work the cold-case squad out of the Eighth District. That's the French Quarter," he revealed.

She took a pen from the center console. "Give me your number. I'll call you back in five."

As much as she disliked Chicago winters, Kate was grateful for the frigid temperature, which kept the press from camping out in front of her building.

She waited until she was upstairs, inside the loft, with the three double bolt locks fastened and the drapes pulled, before returning the call. But only after double-checking with information to make certain the number he'd given her actually belonged to the NOPD.

"So," she said when he answered, "you're calling about a cold case?"

"Cold case is my squad. Other districts have their own homicide departments, but we don't get many death by murder in the Quarter, so we sort of pitch in when needed. Technically we're the Major Cold Case Homicide Squad."

"I see," she said, not seeing anything at all.

"Do you have a sister named Desiree Doucett, Ms. Delaney?"

"It's Detective Delaney. I'm a Chicago PD lieutenant."

"Sorry," he said, switching gears, "the notation in her address book doesn't mention that."

"Also, no, that name's not familiar."

Though she wouldn't be surprised to discover Tara was living under an alias.

"But you *do* have a sister?"

"Yes." Kate blew out a frustrated breath. No wonder so many civilians disliked cops. "But her name is Tara Carroll."

"Okay," he said, shuffling some papers. "That works, too."

This couldn't be good. What trouble had Tara gotten herself into? "And you're calling because . . ."

"I'm sorry."

Kate knew that tone. Hadn't she used it herself when breaking bad news to a civilian? She braced herself for the words she knew were coming.

"I'm afraid your sister's dead, Detective."

"Dead?" And wasn't that the same thing civilians inevitably said in response?

She began to pace the chestnut plank floor, her mind scrambling to make sense of this call. "You said homicide."

"That's right, ma'am. Uh, Detective. Actually, your sister's death appears to be a suicide, but legally we're required to treat it like a homicide until we get the official cause-of-death report from the coroner's office."

That was how it worked. But one thing wasn't ringing true. Despite all their problems, despite having been estranged ever since Kate had taken the opportunity to escape to Chicago, they were still twins. Their DNA was identical; despite the difference in lifestyle, they could've been the same person. If Tara was dead, she'd know it. Wouldn't she?

"You've made a mistake."

"You *are* Kathleen Delaney?"

"Yes, but—"

"And your sister's Tara Carroll, who also went by the name of Desiree Doucett?"

"I don't know anything about her using the name Desiree."

Whatever name she was using, her sister would never commit suicide. No more likely to than Kate herself.

"She must be running some kind of scam," Kate decided.

"A scam."

It was not a question, but she understood that she was expected to answer it. This was not a story she enjoyed sharing. Especially with another cop.

"Look, Detective Landreaux. My sister and my mother are grifters. They lie for a living. They're also big on staging phony scenarios."

Kate's first job had been at age five, when her mother—wearing a pillow beneath her dress to simulate a late-term pregnancy—fainted during a champagne brunch at a historic hotel in Biloxi. As the well-heeled crowd rushed to help, her sister, displaying natural acting skills, wailed to high heaven while Kate moved like a shadow around the dining room, slipping billfolds from purses.

By the time she was eight, her mother had graduated to insurance falls. Store managers might suspect a lone woman of pulling a con, but it was hard to believe two such sweet and visibly shaken little girls would lie through their pretty white teeth.

When she was in high school, her mother—who'd always insisted her daughters call her by her first name, Antoinette—had moved them to Memphis, where she began pulling off sweetheart schemes, using her considerable sexual appeal to scam money from emotionally vulnerable males, more often than not men ancient enough to have forgotten what *dementia* meant.

"This is undoubtedly just another game they've cooked up. Probably to cheat some insurance company." Kate could far more easily picture them getting the idea to pull off a phony death scheme than imagine Tara dead.

There was a pause on the other end of the line. Not one of those cop pauses designed to get the other person talking. But one that told her Detective Landreaux was processing this information.

"And your mother would be?"

"Antoinette Carroll Pickett. But I heard she'd recently married again."

The invitation had come from out of the blue to the cop shop six weeks ago, with the notation that her mother was registered at the Canal Place Saks. Like sure, Kate was going to rush out and buy a pricey set of Waterford champagne glasses for the newlyweds.

How about not in this lifetime?

"To a Martin Le Cru. No, that's not right." It was like the island, she remembered. "St. Croix."

"You're sure of that?" His tone sharpened. "That the name is Martin St. Croix?"

"Absolutely." Now that she'd recalled the name, Kate could picture the groom's name calligraphied in raised gold type on that gilt-edged invitation.

There was another pause. This one longer than the first.

Then, "I think you'd better consider a trip to New Orleans, Detective."

"Why?"

"Because your sister listed you as her next of kin to be notified in the event of her death. And she definitely *is* dead, Detective. Her body's in the morgue as we speak. And, coincidentally, your mother's new husband is in the hospital. In critical condition."

Oh, God. Kate's mouth went dry. "Why do I suspect he's not there because he keeled over from a heart attack?"

Or any normal occurrence. Heaven forbid her family should ever be involved in anything *normal*.

"It was hit and run," the detective said.

Of course it was.

Kate rubbed her temple. The headache that had been threatening since those cops had boxed her in as she'd left the courthouse was now exploding full-blown.

"How old is he?" she asked over the sound of evil maniacs pounding sledgehammers against slate behind her eyes.

"Early seventies."

Which put him around twenty, twenty-five years older than his new bride. "Is he rich?"

"Let me put it this way. He owns a car dealership. A *Mercedes* dealership," he tacked on significantly.

Of course he did.

"Are you saying you believe his accident and my sister's death might be related?"

"A link hadn't occurred to me when I called you," he allowed. "Because I didn't know the connection between Desiree Doucett and Mrs. St. Croix. But now that I do, I'm going to have to consider the possibility. Unfortunately, your mother's left town and we haven't found anyone who knows where she might have gone."

Kate blew out a long breath. Well, at least she no longer wondered about what she'd be doing tomorrow. "I'm on my way."

9

NICK'S FIRST THOUGHT WHEN SHE APPEARED at the dock was that he was seeing a ghost. Or hallucinating. Those goons had roughed him up pretty good before throwing him into that boat. Maybe they'd shaken a few brain cells loose.

She was tall, lean, and reminded him a lot of Nicole Kidman in her *Days of Thunder* days, before she'd gotten all sleek and polished and become a high-class clothes hanger for dress designers to the rich and famous.

Thanks to a warm front that had moved in from the Gulf, she'd left her black suit jacket open; a white silk blouse clung to pert breasts, which, while not as voluptuous as Desiree Doucett's silicone-enhanced ones, were still damn fine.

Her copper-penny hair had been pulled back into some sort of twist at the nape of her neck, but heat and humidity had it springing out into a bright cloud around a face that belonged on one of those cameos in the antique-shop windows on Magazine Street. Her eyes were cat-green and tilted upward, just a bit at the corners. Her nose canted slightly to the left, which kept her from being classically perfect.

But her mouth! Good God almighty, Angelina Jolie, eat your heart out! Although she'd chewed off most of her lipstick, that didn't keep his obviously injured mind from conjuring up potent sexual fantasies of those top-heavy, cotton candy-pink lips pressing against the swollen flesh around his black eye.

Then against his chest, soothing the pain in his rib left by a well-placed punch. And that was just for starters.

In the fantasy that sparked through his mind like one of Louisiana Power and Light's infamous power surges, those amazing lips began traveling lower. And lower. Until . . .

He jerked his unruly, horny mind back from where it had been about to get him into real trouble. As it was, if she happened to look down, she'd take him for a pervert and probably get back in that cab idling at the pier and leave.

The funny thing was that although Desiree, who'd been an expert at using sex to get what she wanted, had pulled out all the stops trying to get him into bed the past few months, Nick had never been interested. It wasn't so much that he doubted she could count the number of men she slept with in any given year.

Call him crazy—and he knew a lot of men undoubtedly would—but the top-dollar call girl had never gotten his dick to stand at attention like it was doing right now.

Her lips were moving, but her words sounded as if they were coming from the bottom of the lake. Maybe the concussion the thugs had given him had affected his hearing.

"Are you Nick Broussard?"

It was her voice, edged with an impatience you only heard around these parts from northern tourists, that finally tipped him off.

The woman whose bright brows had beetled over those remarkable catlike eyes wasn't Desiree. But the sister. Cathy? Karen? What the hell had Desiree told him her name was?

"That's me," he said. "And you'd be Kate." That was it! "Kate Delaney. Desiree Doucett's sister."

Her uptight law-and-order *cop* sister, Nick remembered.

Surprise came and went so quickly that had he not been watching her face carefully, Nick would've missed it. They might be identical twins, but Kate Delaney had definitely learned how to conceal her thoughts a helluva lot better than her sister.

Her lips drew into a tight line. In a nanosecond she'd gone from fantasy female to a clone of Sister Mary Francis, a habit-wearing harridan who'd struck terror in the hearts of her entire third-grade class.

"My sister's actual name was Tara Carroll. And how did you know her?"

Could she actually think he might be one of Desiree's—Tara's—johns?

And jeez, wasn't that an ego boost?

He resisted the urge to assure her that he'd never had to stoop to paying for a woman.

"New Orleans may look like a city, but it's pretty much a small town." A lot smaller now than it'd been eighteen months ago. "Everyone pretty much knows everyone else. And if you go back enough generations, you'd probably discover that most of us are related one way or another . . . I'm sorry for your loss."

"Thank you." A sheen that might have been tears brightened her eyes. Then she resolutely blinked it away. From a boombox down the pier, Jimmy Buffett and Alan Jackson were claiming it was five o'clock somewhere. "I went to the police station straight from the airport. Unfortunately, I didn't receive a lot of cooperation, but Detective Landreaux gave me your card and said you might be able to help . . . I tried to call before coming over, but I kept getting dumped into voice mail."

"That's because I turned the phone off."

There were a lot of things about this case that weren't adding up. Things Nick had needed to think about. Like how come LeBlanc would hire him to find Desiree if he already had a contract out on her. Something LeBlanc had sworn, when Nick had confronted him after watching her body get taken away, he hadn't done.

Not that LeBlanc was ever going to win any medals for truthfulness.

Since mindless labor always helped him sort things out, Nick had decided to spend some time working on the boat.

He also wondered if, considering how understaffed NOPD was, even after the recent reorganization, Remy had sent her here hoping that his former partner might be able to do an end run around Dubois and solve whatever crime might've occurred.

"Doesn't turning off your phone make it a bit difficult for prospective clients to reach you?"

"Gotta point there," he said agreeably.

Not that he wanted any clients, since this entire PI scheme was just for show. Something to do after getting tossed off the force.

But, of course, Remy didn't know that. Maybe his old friend didn't have any ulterior motive. Maybe he was just trying to help Nick drum up business.

"Well, when you didn't answer, I decided to take a chance on catching you at your office." She looked past him. "I didn't realize your office was on a boat."

"It's my office and my home. Makes commuting convenient." He glanced past her to the black-and-white cab idling on the street, meter ticking. "Why don't I pay your taxi, *chère*, then I'll pipe you aboard and you tell me why you're here."

And afterward we'll get naked and have sex. Get married. Sail off to Tahiti where we'll lie naked on the beach and feed each other juicy ripe passion fruit, and you can have my babies.

The crazy ideas had struck like a jagged jolt of lightning from a clear blue summer sky. The really weird thing was, they sounded pretty good to him.

Maybe the goons *had* given him brain damage.

"It's Detective," she corrected, not making a move. "I came here to discuss hiring you to find my sister's murderer."

Damn. That was what he'd been afraid she was going to say. Wasn't that just what he needed? A hotshot Yankee detective mucking around in Desiree's death?

She tilted her bright head, seeming to rethink her decision to come here. Apparently, she wasn't finding the bruises that had bloomed overnight as appealingly rakish as he'd hoped.

If he'd had the brain God gave a gator, he'd just let her go back to wherever the hell she'd come from. Unfortunately, from the stubborn set of her chin, and the way she'd squared her shoulders, Nick suspected the lady wouldn't go. And having Desiree's cop sister running around the city half-cocked would stir up a hornet's nest of problems that could make the other night's visit out to the bayou look like a Sunday-school picnic.

"Don't be put off by appearances," he said, imagining how he must look to her, with his banged-up face, ratty old torn T-shirt, and grease-stained jeans. "And, though I can understand it might be hard to accept, the police are calling your sister's death a suicide."

"They can call me the pope," she shot back in an intriguing flare of heat. "But that wouldn't make it true . . . Look, if you don't want to help me—"

"Did you hear me say I didn't want to help?"

Let her go, the little voice of reason in the back of his head advised. *Like your daddy always said, never get in the middle of someone else's quicksand.*

Trouble was, Nick had never been real good about listening to his old man.

"No point in running up taxi fees while we stand here talking. I'll pay the driver off. Then we'll discuss it."

She glanced past him at the boat again. From her frown, he suspected she was viewing a flashing red sign reading "Den of Iniquity."

"Or, though it wouldn't be nearly as comfortable, if you're nervous about being alone with a stranger, we can stand out here all night."

"This isn't going to take all night. Besides, I'm a cop. There's no way you could make me nervous."

"That's a start." His grin pulled painfully at his puffy lip. "And don't forget I come highly recommended by New Orleans's finest."

She snorted. "From what I could tell, that's an oxymoron." He watched the wheels turn in her head as she made her decision. "I'll get my bag and be right back."

"Now what kind of gentleman would I be if I didn't carry a lady's suitcase and pay her taxi fare after she's come all the way from Yankeeland to visit?"

She tossed up a chin that somehow managed to be delicate and strong at the same time. "This isn't a visit. It's business. And if I do hire you, I expect you to put that fare on my bill."

Desiree hadn't been kidding. Kate Delaney was definitely Ms. Law and Order. But she also smelled a helluva lot better than any cop he'd ever met.

He skimmed a long, slow look from the top of her

bright head down to narrow feet clad in a pair of sensible black flats.

To please himself, he mentally exchanged the white, buttoned-up blouse she was wearing beneath a trim black suit jacket for a lacy, scarlet-as-sin camisole.

Her gaze sharpened, letting him know she'd caught him looking at her breasts. But hell, he was a man. And, although she might be wearing more camouflage than a SEAL recon team out on maneuvers, he wasn't going to apologize for looking. Or for his imagination.

"We can work out the details later," he said as he pulled some bills from the front pocket of his painfully-too-tight jeans.

He managed to make it to the curb on a swollen knee without limping too badly, paid the driver, and as he watched her watching the cab pull away, Nick caught another fleeting moment of indecision, which he suspected was not Kate Delaney's usual state of mind. Then again, it couldn't be easy to learn that your twin sister—essentially your other half—was dead.

"Like I said, this place is a bit of both home and office," he said as he picked up her suitcase and, taking her hand, helped her onto the ketch.

God, she really did smell delicious. Unlike her sister, who'd always favored pricey, heavy French perfumes, Kate Delaney used a shampoo, or soap, or whatever it was clinging to her neat, trim body, that smelled fresh and clean. Like spring rain or freshly laundered sheets drying in the breeze.

"She's a beautiful boat," she said. A little grudgingly,

Nick thought, as if she disliked approving of anything about him.

"I like her well enough."

He kept his tone deliberately casual, but she would've had to have been deaf not to hear the pride in his voice. *The Hoo-yah*, which he'd bought at hurricane sale prices from a doctor at Charity Hospital who'd decided to move his family to arid Arizona, was the one good thing that had come out of his trip back home.

"You enjoy sailing?"

"I did." She tugged her hand free and ran it over the gleaming brass railing he'd just finished polishing. "I haven't been out on the water for a while, though. And speaking of water, aren't you concerned about living on the same lake that flooded the city? What if another hurricane hits?"

"Oh, one will, sure enough. But if you spend your life waiting for somethin' bad to happen, you'll never have any fun."

"And New Orleans is all about fun."

"Laissez les bon temps rouler," he agreed. "Let the good times roll. Things may have gotten more serious since Katrina came blowin' through town. But you can't keep a good town down. Meanwhile, most people are just taking things one day at a time."

From the stiff set of her shoulders beneath that trim and tidy black suit, he suspected it'd been a long time since the pretty cop had allowed any good times to roll. He also expected that she had never taken things one day at a time. In fact, he bet she was one of those who made lists. Lots and lots of lists. Then color-coded and alphabetized them.

Not that there was anything wrong with lists, he amended, mentally making his own list of all the things he'd like to do with Kate Delaney. Beginning with his tongue in her wide, fuck-me-big-boy mouth and working his way down her naked body, sucking her polished toes.

"You want somethin' to drink, *chère?* Maybe a beer?"

She didn't look like a suds type of girl, but sometimes appearances were deceiving. He'd seen Desiree toss back more than a few Dixies.

"I think I've maybe got some Hurricane mix in the pantry."

Not that he was trying to get her drunk so he could have his perverted way with her or anything. *Right.*

"No, thank you. I'm fine."

No, she wasn't. She was wound as tight as a seven-day clock on the eighth day.

"My office is right down here." He took her elbow, leading her down the steps to the belowdecks salon. "It might not be as fancy as some overlooking the city from those glass towers of the CBD, but my hourly rate is cheaper."

"Money isn't an issue."

"I don't remember your sister telling me you were rich."

"What gave you the idea I was rich?"

"I don't know how it works up North," he said. "But down here in the swamp, the pay of your average law-enforcement officer fits somewhere between the guys who sweep up the streets after a Mardi Gras parade and a bouncer outside a Bourbon Street strip joint."

A redhead's temper—something she definitely shared with her twin—sparked in those emerald cat eyes.

Jesus, he *had* to get this woman into bed.

"Are you insinuating I'm a crooked cop?"

He lifted his hands, palms out, in a gesture of innocence, and tried to concentrate on the conversation while his rampant imagination conjured up a scenario involving a can of whipped cream, melted Hershey's bars, and Pop Rocks.

"*Non, chère*. It's just that most people want to dicker about price before we get down to the details of the case."

She sat on the leather chair he'd gestured toward and decisively crossed her legs. "I'm willing to pay whatever it takes. Within reason," she tacked on, as if to let him know right off the bat that she wasn't a pushover. Just in case he hadn't figured it out for himself. "I have some savings put away."

It was good she had a rainy-day fund, Nick thought. Since trouble would start pouring down like a delta storm if she actually started digging into her sister's cockamamie extortion scheme.

"One thing I've always been is reasonable. My usual rate's a hundred dollars an hour. Plus a flat thousand-dollar retainer and expenses."

Not that he'd made a dime yet. But the lady didn't have to know that.

"That seems high."

Hopefully high enough to make her go back home to Chicago.

"It also includes video, for surveillance cases. And you know what they say, *chère*. You get what you pay for."

Risking splitting his lip again, he flashed what more than one lover had assured him was a lady-killing smile. "And believe me, I'm worth it."

10

HIS TONE DROPPED TO A LOW, SEXY BARITONE.
From the moment she'd caught sight of him as she'd
walked down the long dock, all black tousled hair, face
that even all those bruises couldn't keep from being
movie-star handsome, ripped T-shirt, and raggedy jeans
that cupped his sex in a way that had every female nerve
ending leaping to alert, he'd reminded Kate of Marlon
Brando steaming up the French Quarter in *Streetcar*.

What was she doing? Thinking about sex when her
sister was dead?

Shaking off the unsettling sensation, Kate reminded
herself that Lieutenant Landreaux had recommended
this man. But that didn't necessarily mean he was any
good. The good-old-boy network was definitely alive and
well in Chicago; wouldn't it be the same, perhaps even
worse, here in a city infamous for its corruption? She
wouldn't be all that surprised to discover that Broussard
was paying his former partner kickbacks for referrals.

"Did you get that black eye on a case?"

"I don't suppose you'd believe I walked into a door?"

She folded her arms. "Sorry."

"Okay. There was a bit of a misunderstanding. But hell, if you think I look bad, you should see the other guy."

He flashed her a slow, sexy smile she suspected had charmed its share of bayou belles out of their lacy thongs.

"I'd want you to keep your investigation confidential."

"That goes without saying," he assured her.

"Well, I, for one, would like to hear you say it."

This time his puffy lips barely quirked, just a little, at the corners, but his lake-blue eyes—fringed with long, dark, beautiful lashes that were wasted on a man—brightened as if lit by summer sunshine. Dammit, he was laughing at her.

"Do you find murder humorous, Mr. Broussard?" she asked in her stiffest just-the-facts-ma'am, Joe Friday tone.

"No, ma'am." He immediately sobered. "And I apologize if I gave you that idea. But I was just thinking . . . damn, you're beautiful."

The last thing Kate needed in her life right now was some hot Cajun player. Especially one who so easily scrambled her mind and had her thinking of tangling hot sheets with him beneath that slow-moving, paddle-bladed fan.

"Do you always come on to prospective clients?"

He shook his head. "Not that I recall. In fact, I know for certain that this is a first. But then again, it's not every day someone as classy as you shows up at the office. It kind of reminds me of when Ruth Wonderly sashays into Sam Spade's office and gets him involved in that hunt for the jewel-encrusted black bird."

She just looked at him.

"You know." He smiled encouragingly. "From *The Maltese Falcon.*"

"I've never seen the movie. And don't hit on me again."

"I'll try my best to refrain from giving in to my baser instincts. How about this . . . next time I hit on you, feel free to shoot me."

"I may just take you up on that. Now, about your credentials—"

"I served fifteen years in the navy, then six months working NOPD before going private last month."

"I can't see you in the military." If he'd radiated this much rebel bad boy when he'd been in the navy, she didn't know how he'd made it through basic training.

"Neither did I in the beginning. But SEAL teams allow for more, well"—he rubbed his jaw, which was sporting, along with the multicolored bruises, a sexy five-o'clock shadow—"let's just call it creativity."

This man with the shaggy poet's hair and lake-blue bedroom eyes had been a Navy SEAL? Well. That was a surprise.

Intelligent, physically fit, motivated, resourceful, and *good with weapons* went down on the plus side of the mental ledger she'd begun keeping the moment she'd first seen Nick Broussard.

Reckless was listed as a potential negative.

"If I hire you, you'd have to understand that you wouldn't just be working for me. We'd be full partners.

I'd want to know everything you learn and I won't have you running off on your own, like some bayou Rambo."

That unshaven jaw stiffened. His eyes hardened. Brando had just left the building and in his place was this . . . well, *warrior* was the only word Kate could think of.

"Rambo was fiction. SEALs don't go charging machine-gun nests hell-bent for leather like some Hollywood director's idea of war. That's what the marines are for.

"SEALs work the margins, doing jobs other people don't want to do in places no sane person would ever want to go—the dark, jungles, swamps, deserts, you name it. If it's ugly and deadly, we'll claim it," he said in a brusque, take-no-prisoners tone that suggested she might just be an idiot.

"Individually, they're the goddamn best the military has to offer. But the thing is, if team members don't work together, they can end up pink mist, which, if you've ever been unlucky to see it, you'd know isn't all that pretty."

He folded his very well muscled arms across his chest and looked down at her. "There's no *I* in SEAL team, Detective Delaney, and I can play damn well with others when my life—and the lives of others—and the success of the mission depend on it."

Okay. Kate didn't need any detective skills to realize she'd hit a hot button. If his glower hadn't tipped her off, the clipped, harsh tone definitely would've.

"Well." She cleared her throat. "Thank you for clarifying that."

His nod was quick and sharp. She'd always been good at reading people; cops needed to be, because often their lives depended on it. But it seemed she'd misjudged Nick Broussard; he definitely wasn't merely the laid-back, sexy southern charmer she'd first taken him to be.

He sat down behind a desk that was encouragingly neat, suggesting an orderly mind.

Then again, it could also mean he didn't get all that much business.

"So." The chair squeaked as he leaned back in it. He braced his elbows on the wooden arms and tented his fingers. "Did you talk to Detective Landreaux on the phone? Or have you already been to the cop shop?"

"Both. He called me last evening to tell me Tara was dead. Obviously I booked the first flight I could get out of Chicago to here, and the station was the first place I went after I arrived."

"How did Remy—Detective Landreaux—know to call you?"

"I wondered about that as well. He said Tara had listed me in her address book as her next of kin. I was surprised by that, especially since my sister and I haven't spoken for the past twelve years. Ever since I left home. Which was in Memphis at the time."

When she'd received the wedding invitation, Kate figured her mother must've run out of marks in Memphis and had decided to take her game back down to the Gulf.

"I would've thought she'd have listed our mother, but perhaps they weren't getting along."

"I hear that's often the case with mothers and daughters."

"True." It definitely was in Kate's case. "I was surprised that Detective Landreaux didn't know about the connection, though."

"What connection?"

"I thought you said this is a small town. That everyone knows everyone."

"That's true for the most part. In most circles, anyway."

"So, are you saying you weren't aware our mother is married to Martin St. Croix?"

"No. Well." He whistled softly. "That's interesting."

"You really didn't know?"

"Desiree—Tara—never mentioned it."

Unless he was a really good actor—which, given what she'd heard about SEALs going undercover, was possible—he really hadn't known that part of the equation. If her mother and sister had been involved in some scam that had gotten Tara killed, it could certainly explain why Antoinette was nowhere to be found.

Which meant, Kate decided, she was going to have to help him track down her mother. And wasn't that going to be fun?

"So, what did you learn at the station that made you think you needed to hire a private detective?" he asked.

"It was more what I couldn't learn. It was obvious I was getting stonewalled. For example, when I asked to identify Tara's body, that obnoxious overweight detective in charge of the case—"

"Dubois."

"That's him. Well, he told me it'd already been identified. But no one could—or would—tell me by whom."

"I saw her." He could not have surprised Kate more if he'd told her that he was running an al-Qaeda terrorist cell out of his boat.

"You saw my sister's body? When?"

"Yesterday morning. Shortly after the police had already arrived on the scene."

While she'd been in federal court, testifying against a former love to that federal jury. "So it was you who identified her?" And wasn't that a handy coincidence?

"No. But Desiree was the friendly type, well known in the Quarter. Any number of people could've told the cops who she was before I'd arrived on the scene."

"And you just happened to be driving by?" Kate wasn't buying it.

"That's pretty much it. And in the interest of full disclosure, I was across the street, and she was being put in the coroner's ambulance when I arrived, but it sure as hell looked like her. And the body was lying in her courtyard."

"When I said I wanted to see her, Dubois gave me the runaround. He told me she was scheduled for an autopsy."

"That's routine."

"I know. But something's fishy. Neither he nor your pal Detective Landreaux could tell me when the autopsy's scheduled."

"This is New Orleans. Post-Katrina," he reminded her yet again. "The crime rate's going off the chart again, gangbangers are shooting each other every night over turf, and a lot of neighborhoods are like Dodge City back in the cowboy and outlaw days.

"Every public agency, including the medical examiner, *especially* the medical examiner, is backed up. The morgue's understaffed and working under less than ideal conditions. They're not set up for visitors."

It was, damn it, the same thing that obnoxious Dubois had told her. And she couldn't deny that it made sense.

Still . . .

"I'm not a visitor," she said, repeating what she'd stated back at the station. "I'm a cop."

"A *Chicago* cop. Which, down here, makes you a civilian. This isn't your jurisdiction."

"God, you could be channeling Dubois," she muttered, folding her arms.

"Ouch. Now that's a really low blow."

He didn't exactly appear wounded. But she could tell he wasn't very flattered by the comparison, either.

"I could get a court order."

"You could try, sure enough."

As an outsider her chances would be what? How about slim to zero? What she needed was to ally herself with someone who knew the territory. And the players. Someone with a total disregard for rules. Someone like Nick Broussard.

"Look," he said on a long-suffering sigh. "That sound you hear is doors slamming all over the city. *If* your sister was murdered, and I'm not saying I necessarily believe she was, then the best thing you can do, Detective, is keep a low profile. Because New Orleans doesn't work anything like Chicago.

"We're our own little enclave here. We're not anything like the rest of the United States. Hell, we're not like the rest of Louisiana. Most folks who live here consider it an oasis, even now, after Katrina.

"People have been coming to the Crescent City for years because we're a party city, then they stay. And they try to change us. But New Orleans has always been impervious to outside influences.

"So, the thing is, if you start nosin' around in intimate southern closets, all you'll succeed in doing is make things more difficult."

"Which is why I should hire you?"

He shrugged. "At least I know all the players," he said, unwittingly echoing her earlier thought. "And where most of the bodies are buried." He cringed at that. "Sorry. Bad metaphor. But you could do a helluva lot worse. Of course, there's another alternative."

"And that would be?"

"You could go back home and leave this for the cops."

Right. Go back to Chicago? Where the best she could probably hope for would be meter-maid duty? Obviously, she'd burned all her Chicago bridges. But, dammit, Nick Broussard made her nervous.

No. Not nervous. Edgy. Stirred up. Enough that under normal conditions, this would be the last man she'd want to work with. Unfortunately, this situation was far from normal; it was obvious the cops had already made up their minds about her sister's death, and it was also becoming more and more apparent that this Navy SEAL-turned-cop-turned-PI might well be her only chance to discover the truth.

"I believe I'll hang around here a while. So, since this is your town, what do you suggest we do first?"

"It probably wouldn't be a bad idea to check out her apartment."

"Dubois told me it's still sealed off as a crime scene."

"That's standard procedure. Probably even in Chicago."

"In a suicide? When, as you pointed out, the police force is overworked and understaffed?"

He tilted his dark head. "Good point."

"I'm a cop," she reminded him. "It doesn't make any sense that they'd declare it a suicide, then keep it locked up."

"Maybe they're still looking for something."

"Maybe they are." And maybe, whatever it was, she'd find it first. "How good are you at breaking and entering?"

His deep chuckle had something inside her turning over. "Sweetheart, you are now playing my favorite tune."

"HEY, NICE MINIVAN," KATE SAID DRYLY AS Nick led her to a black Humvee parked in the lot.

"Gotta keep up the tough-guy image." He could've been wearing Kevlar, the way the barb just bounced right off him.

"Yeah. Hummer . . . the ultimate penis extender." She climbed up into the behemoth vehicle and decided the ALPHA stamped onto the back of the black leather seats in big block letters was definitely overkill. "If your ego's in such a need of a boost, why didn't you just buy a gun?"

"I already have a gun."

Obviously he was going to refuse to bite, which took all the fun out of the other penis jokes she had waiting in the wings.

It wasn't that far of a drive back to the Quarter, where she'd suffered through that frustrating meeting with Landreaux and Dubois, but the neighborhoods they passed through would not have looked out of place in a war zone.

Despite the optimistic photos she'd seen on the news of Jazz Fest and Mardi Gras, designed to show New Orleanians getting on with their lives, there were blocks and blocks of houses without roofs, many without walls. Several homes had washed off their foundations and stood open to the elements; broken furniture and plumbing fixtures littered vacant lots, rusting cars were overturned, sometimes piled up on top of one another, as if discarded by a giant toddler during a tantrum. Chest-high brown weeds grew up through the vehicles' windows.

There were mountains of moldy Sheetrock and twisted metal littering the medians, which he told her were called neutral ground here in New Orleans, for miles on end. They passed two pickup trucks, one with Arkansas license plates, parked on the dead grass.

"Damn scavengers," Nick said with acid derision as he watched the Arkansan pile some of the discarded metal into the bed of his truck. "It's not so bad when they just take the refuse, so they can make money off taking it to the scrap center—because they are, in their own twisted way, helping with cleanup. But a lot of them don't stop with that. I've seen them ripping copper plumbing pipes out of houses that are still boarded up and waiting for cleanup."

"What did you do?"

He shrugged. "Shot 'em with my big penis-extending gun."

"You're not serious."

"No. But it's a damn nice fantasy. Remember that old Mel Gibson movie, *Road Warrior?*"

"Of course." It was one of her all-time favorites, and not just because young Mel had defined hunk.

"Well, sometimes around here, that story doesn't exactly seem like fiction."

Refugee camps of unadorned house trailers had sprouted like mushrooms on parking lots of deserted strip malls; uniformed and armed national guard troops dressed in camouflage and patrolling the near-empty streets in military Humvees added to the war-zone feeling.

While several buildings remained boarded up, the French Quarter was in much better shape. Which, Kate assumed, contributed to many Americans' mistaken belief that the City That Care Forgot had nearly recovered.

Kate suspected that up on Bourbon Street, with only two more nights remaining until Fat Tuesday gave way to Ash Wednesday, the carnival atmosphere would be in full swing. But in the part of the Quarter nearer the river, the streets were surprisingly quiet and hushed.

Fog was drifting in from the river, the air so thick with humidity that Kate could feel her curly hair taking on a life of its own.

Tara's apartment took up the top floor of an Italianate three-story town house. Outside, the iron was rusted and the stucco was falling off the brick in large chunks; inside, the air was musty with age and dampness.

"Well, one thing's for certain," Kate said as they turned the corner at the narrow second-floor landing. "Dubois didn't do the apartment investigation."

"And you know this why?"

"Because he'd be lucky to make it halfway up the first flight of stairs before he had a heart attack."

"Good point. The man does enjoy a good meal. And it shows."

"What shows is that when he's not enjoying that good meal, he spends the rest of his time sitting around on his ass," Kate said as they passed the second-floor landing.

Yellow and black crime-scene tape barricaded the door to the top-floor apartment.

"Damn. I was afraid they'd have used tape," Kate muttered. Like everywhere else in the building, the paint was peeling off the door, and she was afraid that once they removed it, they wouldn't be able to stick it back on again.

"No problem." Nick snapped on a pair of latex gloves, then dug into the small duffel bag he'd brought along and pulled out a roll of identical tape. "Didn't I mention I was a former Eagle Scout when I was giving you my credentials?"

"I don't believe so."

She found it difficult to believe. Although she'd learned the flaws in profiling in the police academy, she would have pegged Nick Broussard as the quintessential bad boy.

"You also don't believe it." He dug into the bag and brought out a small black leather case.

"Let's just say I have a hard time imagining an Eagle Scout owning a lock-picking set," she said dryly.

"You called that one right. My dad was a cop and he would've taken a piece of my hide if he'd found one in my room." He pulled out a thin, flat-head tension wrench from the case. "Besides, I felt obligated to set a good example for my three younger sisters."

"Do they live here?"

"Hannah, she's the oldest, is a librarian in Honolulu. Sarah's a teacher in Maine. And Lara's the baby. She's a nurse stationed at a CASH—combat army support hospital—in Iraq."

It was the first personal glimpse he'd allowed. Although she had trouble seeing this man living with three sisters, she could hear the affection in his tone.

"You must worry about her."

"Yeah." After a moment's study, he chose a long, thin pick.

"They certainly all moved a long way from home."

"I suspect that was the point."

So much for personal insight.

"Isn't a lock made a SEAL can't open." He stuck the wrench in the lock, then followed with the pick. "We'll rake it first. Maybe we'll get lucky and all the pins will fall into place."

"You're quick." Kate believed in giving credit where credit was due.

"When it comes to stuff like this." He selected another pick and tried again. "Other things I prefer to do real slowly."

His grin was wicked and far too appealing. She was

tempted to warn him that he was coming close to getting shot, but decided the best way was to just play it cool and professional.

"Let's just get inside and check the place out," she said with chilly dignity.

"Yes, ma'am." He didn't smile. But from the amusement in his deep voice, Kate knew he wanted to.

12

THE APARTMENT HAD BEEN TRASHED. PAINT-ings torn off the wall, the canvases slashed; the couch was lipstick-red leather and looked as if it had been expensive. Unfortunately, the cushions had been viciously cut apart, the marks looking as if the destruction had been more methodical than the result of any violent rage.

A small skirted table had been overturned, spilling carved wooden figures, candles, seashells, and shiny stones. A colorful silk, depicting two snakes entwined in an embrace, added to the surreal appearance.

"Do you think the cops did this?" she asked.

"Could've." He pulled another pair of gloves from the pack and handed them to her, then stepped over the stuffing from the couch cushions that was scattered over the wooden floor like fallen snow. "But they'd have needed a search warrant. Which they didn't have."

"How do you know that?" As soon as she heard herself ask the question, Kate knew the answer. "You checked?" Before she'd even shown up at his door to hire him? Once again he'd managed to surprise her. "Why?"

"Let's just say I was curious."

"Let's not. And remember that we're supposed to be a team here, Broussard. Like back when you were in the SEALs."

"Yeah." He rubbed his jaw, and although he didn't flinch, she viewed a flash of pain move across his eyes, revealing that his bruised and battered face hurt as badly as it looked to. "Though I gotta tell you, *chère,* if any of the guys on my team had looked like you, I would've re-upped for another tour."

Flirting appeared to be as natural to Nick Broussard as breathing. There was no reason to take it personally. A man as sexy as this undoubtedly went through life charming women from eight to eighty.

Twenty minutes later, Kate had discovered her estranged sister had owned 140 pairs of shoes, two dozen designer bags, more clothes than Kate could ever imagine owning in her life, enough lingerie to open her own Victoria's Secret store, and more than enough sex toys, whips, blindfolds, and handcuffs to start hosting neighborhood dungeon parties.

"Looks as if she took her work home with her," Nick said as he picked up a black leather riding crop.

"Different strokes," Kate murmured. Then could have immediately bit off her tongue.

He lifted a dark brow at her unintended double entendre, but chose not to comment.

"You know," she said, "speaking of taking her work

home, Dubois wasn't real forthcoming, but he did seem to enjoy letting me know my sister was a prostitute."

"Yeah, I can picture him getting off on that. But what she chose to do for a living didn't necessarily make her a bad person. Just one workin' outside the margins, which isn't that unusual down here. Like I said, people liked Desiree. She was real friendly."

"Sounds as if you knew her well."

"I wasn't a client, if that's what you're implying."

"But you were friends?"

"Is this an interrogation?"

"No." *Yes.* "I'm just trying to get a handle on the situation. You said that in many ways, this is a small town, with everyone knowing everyone else. That makes sense. But I'm getting the impression that your relationship with my sister was a bit more personal."

"Depends on how you define personal. Did she tell me she had a sister? Yeah. Did I know her *maman* was a little shady? Yeah, she'd dropped some hints about that. Did she mention that same mother had recently moved here and married one of the richest and most influential wheeler-dealers in the city? No. Did I ever sleep with her? Hell, no. Does that about cover it?"

She'd pissed him off. Tough.

"For now," she said, annoyed at how the sight of Nick absently tapping the crop's handle against his broad palm sent an illicit thrill zinging through her.

Tara's collection of pornographic videotapes was also extensive, covering just about every kink imaginable, but not unusual given her career choice, and certainly nothing Kate hadn't seen during her days working sex crimes and Vice. And none, she was vastly relieved to see, featuring juveniles.

"All commercial," he said after they'd checked each tape by taking it from its cardboard sleeve. "No home-made movies."

He sounded a bit surprised by that. Then again, although she couldn't imagine ever taping herself making love, Kate decided that any woman who actually owned a copy of *Harlots of Hell—No Boys Allowed* undoubtedly wouldn't have all that many sexual inhibitions.

Kate had never considered herself sexually inhibited. But compared to her sister, she might as well have been living in a convent.

Thirty minutes later, Kate knew her sister's taste in music tended toward hip-hop; her reading material was mostly fashion magazines, with a scattering of erotic novels; but rather than the Playboy Channel, or some other adult fare, her TiVo was set up to record old 1950s sitcoms that reflected an idealized world neither Tara nor Kate had ever personally known.

If the pint cartons in the freezer were any indication, her favorite Ben and Jerry's flavor was Half Baked frozen yogurt. She drank Russian vodka she kept iced and Jose Cuervo margaritas.

Which was more than Kate had known before arriving in New Orleans. But she still had no idea what mess her twin had gotten into that would've gotten her killed.

"I wish I'd known," she murmured, only realizing she'd spoken out loud when Nick stopped skimming through a stack of mail that was strewn over the kitchen counter and glanced up at her. "If I'd known she was in so much trouble. I could've helped."

"You had no way of knowing that. Your sister was headstrong, she. Hard to get Desiree Doucett to listen to anyone about much of anything."

Kate could certainly identify with that. She was also feeling horribly guilty. If only she'd been less stubborn, if only she'd made an effort to reconcile with her sister, Tara might still be alive.

It was growing dark. Sheets of lightning trembled against a vermilion sky curtained with rain.

Trying to sort out what to do next, Kate went over to the apartment window and looked down onto the writhing tangle of tropical plants. A crumbling stone statue stood in the center of the overgrown courtyard; the trio of satyrs chasing a comely nymph through the green, algae-choked water seemed a perfect metaphor for this sin-drenched, troubled city.

"She couldn't have committed suicide," she insisted yet again.

"It's been twelve years since you've seen her." Nick was leaning against the bedroom door frame, thumbs hooked in the front pockets of his jeans. Her illicit gaze followed the direction his fingers were pointing, right down to his groin.

When his penis flexed beneath the worn denim, Kate's pulse shot right off the Richter scale.

"People change," he said in a deep, raspy voice that caressed her every nerve ending and told her that he'd caught her checking him out—and that she wasn't the only one suddenly imagining him doing things to her. Her doing things to him in return. Wild, wicked things.

What was she thinking? She'd come to New Orleans to solve her sister's murder, not to have sex with a total stranger.

It was the electricity in the air that was getting thick enough to drink. It had gotten beneath her skin. She could literally taste it on her tongue.

"Now there's a pithy observation," Kate said, dragging her gaze away before she drowned in those eyes that had darkened to the color of midnight over the bayou.

Outside the window, the smoky neon sign from the strip club next door cast pink and green shimmers onto the rain-slicked cobblestones below. Inside, the burned wax scent of votive candles in red glass, along with another vaguely unpleasant odor hung in the stale air.

"Maybe you ought to embroider it onto a pillow."

"Dubois happen to say anything about you having a smart mouth, *chère?*"

"Actually, he did."

Her back was to him, but Kate had no trouble hearing the humor in his voice. To her mind, there was nothing funny about murder.

"Which I took as a compliment because it goes along with my smart head. Unlike Dubois, who undoubtedly found his shield in a box of Cracker Jacks. Dammit, there's no way, given the condition of this apartment, any cop with half a brain could've called this a suicide."

"So you keep saying."

"Right. And you might as well get used to hearing it, because I'm going to keep saying it until I nail her killer."

"*We* nail her killer. Teamwork, remember," he said as she looked back at him over her shoulder.

"Besides," Kate insisted, "the furniture shoved against the door is proof she was trying to keep someone out."

"Wouldn't be the first working girl to suffer herself some drug-induced paranoia."

Kate wished she'd been surprised to learn that her twin had grown up to be a prostitute. If only . . .

No! She could give in to the dark emotions battering away at her and wallow in guilt later. Right now the objective was to put her sister's killer behind bars. With or without the help of the cops.

"I want her book. If we can get our hands on her client list, we can begin narrowing down the suspects."

"Remy said the cops are lookin' for that," he said with exaggerated patience, grating on Kate's last nerve. "But, being a murder cop yourself, *chère*—"

"It's Detective."

"Being a murder cop yourself, Detective Chère, you oughta know police investigations take time to do right."

Kate snorted. "What you mean is the cops are giving any city hotshots, who may have paid my sister for sex, time to cover their collective asses."

He sighed heavily. Pushed himself away from the door frame and crossed the room to smooth his big hands over her shoulders.

"Hey, darlin'. This is New Orleans." His drawled

Cajun patois was as rich as whiskey-drenched bread pudding. "Folks have a certain way of doing things here."

"The Big Easy."

"That's what we call it, all right," he agreed.

"I meant the movie." She shrugged off his touch. "Dennis Quaid says it to Ellen Barkin."

He brightened at that, his smile a bold flash of white. "You like that movie, *chère?*"

"I hate any movie that glamorizes crooked cops."

He shook his dark head. "You're a hard woman, Detective Delaney."

"I'm a murder cop."

Rational. Logical. Tough-minded. Where others saw shades of gray, she saw black and white.

Cops and killers.

Good versus evil.

As a gust of wind rattled the green leaves of the banana tree in the courtyard, Kate sensed a movement just beyond the lacy iron fence. A man, clad all in black and wearing a brimmed hat that shielded his face, stood on the sidewalk, beneath an oak tree dripping with silvery green moss.

The tree's thick, twisted roots had cracked the cobblestone sidewalk; the limbs Tara had crashed through on her fatal fall to the ground clawed at the window, leafy branches scratching against the glass.

"The landlord said other women have been killed in this building."

"That was before my time."

Broussard was standing close enough behind her

that she could feel the heat emanating from his body, along with musky male sweat and the tang of lemon, which would've seemed incongruous on a man who reeked of testosterone if Kate hadn't known the cop trick of using lemon shampoo to wash the smell of death out of your hair.

"The way the story goes, a young slave was found in the formal parlor, her dark throat slit from one pretty ear to the other."

His hands were on her again, long, dark fingers massaging the boulderlike knots at the base of her neck.

"Later eight other bodies were discovered buried in the garden. They'd all been raped. Brutalized. And each one had a gad cut into their breasts."

He paused, waiting for her to ask.

The silence stretched between them, broken only by the sound of the wind, moaning like lost souls outside the window.

Kate blew out a frustrated breath. "So, what the hell is a gad?"

"A protective tattoo designed to protect the wearer from evil spirits. The guy who built this place was a *bokor*. A priest who specializes in the dark arts, what Voodoo practitioners call the left-hand way. They're not all that common, though we've got a handful of 'em living here in the city."

"Obviously the tattoos weren't much protection."

Having grown up with a mother who staged fake séances, Kate didn't believe in magic, white or black. Or any other woo-woo things that went bump in the night.

He shrugged. "Hard to stop a man with killin' on his mind."

She couldn't argue with that.

"Your sister had one."

"One what?" The rusty gate squeaked.

"A gad."

She glanced up at him. "The police report didn't mention that."

"It'll show up in the coroner's report."

"Dubois still should've put it in."

"Like you said, Dubois isn't the sharpest knife in the drawer."

The man was now in the courtyard, staring up at the window. A lightning bolt forked across the sky, illuminating what appeared to be malevolence in eyes blazing like turquoise fire in a midnight-dark face.

Kate, who'd always prided herself on her control, tensed.

"What's wrong?" Broussard's fingers tightened on her neck.

"That guy in the courtyard." White spots, like paper-winged moths, danced in front of her eyes. She blinked to clear them away. "He's—"

Gone.

Kate stared down into the thorny tangle of scarlet bougainvillea and night-blooming jasmine. The man had vanished. As quickly and silently as smoke.

13

ALTHOUGH NICK SUSPECTED SHE'D UNDOUBT-edly throw herself out the window herself before admitting it, the lady was shaken. Her complexion had been the light ivory of a natural redhead. Now she was the palest person he'd ever seen. So pale he wouldn't have been surprised if he could've put his hand right through her.

She'd also begun to shiver, and although it might have been his imagination, as the bells of St. Louis Cathedral chimed the quarter hour, Nick thought she swayed. For just a moment.

"How long has it been since you've eaten?"

"Eaten?" She repeated the word as if he'd spoken in a foreign language.

"Breakfast? Lunch? Maybe an early dinner?"

Nothing. She was standing there on her own two feet, her eyes were open, and from the rise and fall of her breasts beneath that ugly-as-sin black jacket, she was still breathing. But she'd pretty much checked out.

"Some nuts on the plane?"

"I had a Snickers bar."

"That's something." He supposed sugar and chemicals beat nothing at all. "When?"

"Yesterday." She thought back. "Around noon. I bought one from a vending machine. Along with a cup of coffee."

"Yesterday. Around noon." He shook his head. "Christ, it's no wonder you nearly passed out."

A spark of life brightened eyes that had been spookily distant only a moment before. "I did *not* almost pass out."

It was a lie and they both knew it, but not wanting to waste time arguing, he decided against calling her on it. Instead, he took hold of her arm.

"Let's go."

"Where?"

"To get some food in you."

"We haven't finished searching the apartment yet."

"Take a look around. The place has been thoroughly trashed. If there was anything in here to find, it's already been found."

"I hate it when you're right." She drew in a deep breath that had an interesting effect on her breasts beneath that tidy white blouse. "You mentioned a gad being a Voodoo symbol."

"Yeah." Nick had a sinking feeling he knew where this conversation was headed and didn't like it.

"That would suggest my sister was involved with Voodoo rites."

"I figured she must have had a passing interest in it,

to have that tattoo in the first place. And the shells and wooden dolls lying on the floor point to some ritual work. But we never discussed religion."

Her eyes cleared. Sharpened with renewed determination. "We need to check all the Voodoo shops in the city."

"Do you have any idea how many you're talking about?"

"No. Do you?"

"A bunch." Though, like everything else in New Orleans, fewer than there'd been before the hurricane.

"Well then, we'd better get started."

"First we eat."

"We can eat later."

"Look, maybe you've got some sorta anorexic thing going for you, cupcake, but this body needs fuel on a regular basis. I haven't had anything since lunch, and I'm due. We'll eat," he repeated. "Then I'll take you to the hotel. You do have a hotel room, right?"

"I thought I'd find something when I got here," she said. An uncharacteristic lack of pre-planning, Nick suspected. Which showed how upset she was about all this.

"That's gonna be a bit difficult, given that a lot of the hotels haven't reopened yet, and it's Mardi Gras."

"I forgot about Mardi Gras." Nick was not surprised by that.

"Don't worry. I'll make a few calls, see what I can find. Then, after we get you settled in somewhere, I'll start making the rounds of the shops."

"I appreciate the help. And I suppose I could eat something," she allowed, appearing to know when she'd reached the upper limit of his willingness to compromise. "Then *we'll* start making the rounds of the shops."

Christ, the woman was stubborn. And driven. Then again, could he blame her? Wouldn't he do the same thing if it had been his sister who'd died under mysterious circumstances?

Hell, he'd be shaking the entire city down, looking for answers.

Resigned, he practically dragged her across the cluttered wood floor to the door. "We'll talk about it over dinner."

It was, Kate realized, the closest thing to a concession she was going to get from him. She hadn't missed that way he'd rolled his eyes toward the ceiling—or the heavens—like a man praying for patience. Nor was she supposed to. It had been done for her benefit.

Obviously, given his SEAL and cop background, he was used to being the alpha male. Well, he'd just have to get used to the idea that he'd met his match.

The restaurant was a block away, and given that parking was difficult to find, Kate readily agreed with Nick's suggestion to leave the Hummer where it was and walk.

Charmaine's Place was situated on the second floor of a building that may have once been red, but had faded to a soft rose adorned with lacy wrought iron. As soon as Nick opened the door, the rich scent of Creole spices and crawfish, mingling with the aromas of fresh bread wafting up from the French bakery below, had Kate's mouth watering.

A thirty-something woman, whose white chef's apron couldn't conceal a body that looked as if it'd stepped out of a centerfold, broke into a huge smile as she spotted Nick.

"Hey, sweetcakes, it's been a while." She put down the tray of frothy pink Hurricanes she was carrying, flung her arms around his neck, and kissed him smack on the mouth. "Where y'at?"

"Awright," he drawled, his hands settling comfortably on her hips, seemingly in no hurry to back away. "Where y'at?"

"I'm doin' a helluva lot better than you, it looks like," the waitress said, sweeping a fond glance over his face. "Don't you look like somethin' the *chat* dragged in."

"You should see the other guy," he said, repeating what he'd told Kate.

She trailed a bloodred nail down his bruised cheek. "It'd take more than one guy to cause this amount of damage." Her gaze was concerned.

"It'll heal. They—"

"I know." She sighed heavily. "They always do." Shaking her head, she turned toward Kate. "Hey, *chère*. I'm Charmaine Réage."

"Kate Delaney. So you're the owner?"

"Owner, cook, cocktail waitress, and more often than not, what with it being so hard to get decent help these days, chief bottle washer," she said with unmistakable pride before turning her attention back to Nick. "You wanna eat indoors or out, *cher?*"

"In, I think," he decided, glancing at Kate for confirmation.

"Definitely in," Kate agreed. Although it'd been in the eighties when she'd arrived, the temperature had begun dropping rapidly as the sun disappeared.

"What can I bring you to drink?" Charmaine asked after she'd led them to a table overlooking the street.

"Just tea for me, please," Kate said.

Although there was no way she'd admit it to Nick, she was already dead on her feet. No way was she going to risk alcohol knocking her the rest of the way out.

"And I'll take whatever you've got on draft." He handed Charmaine back the menus she'd placed on the table. "Why don't you just choose what's best tonight," he suggested. "If that's all right with you," he said to Kate.

"Works for me."

The opening course of shrimp remoulade was delicious and definitely lived up to New Orleans's reputation for great food, but Kate couldn't focus on it. Not when her mind was whirling with possibilities.

"We need to talk to people Tara knew," she said after Charmaine had taken away their shrimp plates and delivered two huge platters of crawfish étouffée. "Girls she might have worked with. Dubois actually seemed tickled to pieces to tell me she'd been hooking, but he refused to give me any details, claiming the information was on a need-to-know basis."

"And he didn't feel you needed to know."

"Apparently not."

The étouffée was so hot, Kate was amazed it hadn't set off the smoke detector. She took a drink of ice water, hoping to extinguish the flames engulfing her tongue. "Which pisses me off, because you'd think, especially as shorthanded as the force is right now, he'd be happy to have someone willing to work the case with for free."

"It's a turf thing. How would you feel if Dubois showed up in Chicago trying to hone in on your territory?"

"I wouldn't let Dickhead Dubois look at one of my murder books if he showed up with a search warrant signed by the chief justice of the United States. But I get your point. Which is why I hired you."

"A good decision for more than one reason. Because I not only know where she was working, I've moonlighted at the place."

"You've moonlighted as a male prostitute?"

When that idea caused an unwanted flare of heat, she took another long swallow of water.

"Damn. I don't know whether to be flattered or insulted. Especially after that crack insinuating that I was size-challenged when it came to a certain vital body part."

He rubbed his square jaw. Looked thoughtful, as if he were actually considering the matter.

Since she figured she owed him after that earlier Hummer dig, Kate put down her fork, folded her arms, and waited, allowing him to play the moment out.

"So," he said finally, "I suppose I'm going to choose to be flattered."

"I'm delighted. But to get back to where my sister was working—"

"It's a cruise ship offering gambling trips down to Mexico. The girls are officially hostesses, but everyone knows there's more going on than roulette on board. The guy who owns the place, Leon LeBlanc, is a local wiseguy."

"Surely it's not legal for a mobster to get a gaming permit?"

When her smooth brow furrowed, Nick's fingers itched with the urge to smooth those lines away.

"Even here in Louisiana," she tacked on.

"You make us sound like Sodom and Gomorrah."

She colored a bit at that. A pretty little flush on those cut-crystal, Kate Hepburn cheekbones that chased away the paleness that had lingered even after he'd gotten some food down her.

"Well, you can't deny that the state's never exactly been known for its strict interpretation of laws," she said.

"Which is important to you."

"Of course." Her tone suggested she couldn't imagine taking any other view. "I'm a cop."

She was also a woman. A very appealing woman.

Unfortunately, at the moment she was also his employer. And while he might not be nearly as rigid about propriety as Kate Delaney, one rule he'd always lived by was to never mix work and sex. Which was, of course, a helluva lot easier to stick to when you worked with a team of Navy SEALs.

"Leon runs most of the rackets in the Louisiana Gulf area. The license is technically in his son's name. Since the old man's got so much on his plate, he leaves the day-to-day operation of the casino to his kid, Stephen."

"But you work for him?"

"Probably seventy-five, maybe even eighty percent of cops moonlight," he said. "Back in my dad's day, there were even cops who acted as employment brokers, who'd arrange for the jobs, then take a cut of the pay. I've done some security work at the casino." He wasn't yet prepared to share the entire truth with her. "Found a couple of the employees skimming."

"It doesn't bother you?" Her bright brows dove down toward that cute little crooked nose. "To be working for a criminal?"

"*Alleged*."

It was difficult to keep his tone light when it actually bothered the hell out of him. Even more so since LeBlanc had had him dragged out into the bayou and roughed up. Reminding himself that sometimes the end justified the means, Nick held to the cover story he'd come up with when he'd arranged to get kicked off the force, which would hopefully give him credibility in LeBlanc's eyes.

"He's never been convicted of anything," he said. "And last time I looked, people were still innocent until proven guilty in this country."

"There's a huge difference between innocent and not guilty."

"Granted."

She was looking at him like he was something that she might scrape off the sole of her shoe, making him want to go ahead and admit to his own recent problems with the law. Get it over with now.

Telling himself that she'd already had a lot dumped on her the past twenty-four hours, Nick decided to wait. After all, a bit more time wasn't going to make that much of a difference in the whole scheme of things.

He was also thinking that, as her employee, he had an obligation to tell her about what Tara had been up to. But since Kate Delaney's case, if it even was a valid one, was all tangled up with his, and he wasn't yet sure he could trust her not to go running off and sharing it with the cops—which could, if she told the wrong person, get them both killed—for now he was keeping it to himself.

Besides, if Tara had been murdered, and he wasn't willing to categorically rule that idea out, LeBlanc was the obvious suspect. Until you factored in that it didn't make any sense to hire Nick to find Tara, then have one of his own goons kill her.

Of course, his own guys *had* been looking for her. Maybe they'd coincidentally found her right after LeBlanc had hired him.

Nick had never liked coincidence. Never trusted it. But he also knew, on occasion, it did happen.

So, once he managed to worm his way deep enough into the organization to nail the mobster for Big Antoine's death, he could start peeling the onion to see what other crimes the mob boss was mixed up in.

"So," he said, after Charmaine had taken away their empty plates and brought them each a mug of café au lait and an order of the house specialty dessert, white chocolate bread pudding, "how did a pretty southern belle from Mississippi end up a murder cop in Yankeeland?"

"It's a long story."

"I'm not going anywhere."

"Yes, you are." She glanced down at her watch. "You're going with me to check out those Voodoo shops."

"And we will. But you've gotta admit the contrast is intriguing. Here you've got identical twin sisters. One ends up selling her body to high rollers on a floating bordello while the other becomes a homicide cop in Chicago. What do you figure the odds of that happening are?"

"I've no idea. Not being a gambler myself, I'm not that up on oddsmaking. Having spent so much time in a floating casino, you'd undoubtedly know more about it than I would."

Kate glanced around the restaurant, obviously frustrated. "I know we're in the damn South, but how long does it take to get a check around here?"

She was obviously still on rush-rush big-city time. "Like Charmaine said, a lot of restaurants are still havin' trouble with staffing. Lots of workers haven't been able to make it back to the city. Because their homes blew away. Or got filled to the rafters with toxic, disease-carrying sewage water."

"I'm sorry." She frowned. "I'm really not as self-absorbed and hard-assed as I'm sounding."

"Well, you know, sugar, I wasn't going to mention it, but now that you bring it up, I'll admit that I couldn't help noticing, when we climbed the stairs up to your sister's apartment, that you just happen to have one very fine ass."

She shook her head. "You can't help it, can you?"

"Help what, *chère*?"

"Hitting on anything female."

"Now, that's harsh." He lifted a hand to his chest. "Have you seen me so much as spare a glance toward any other woman in this restaurant?"

"Well, they've certainly all been looking at you. If you were that bread pudding, which was absolutely sinful, by the way, you'd have been a goner five minutes after we'd walked in the door."

"Can't help what others do."

But he was enjoying that little spike of what damn well looked—and sounded—like jealousy. A jealous female was not an indifferent one. Maybe once he wrapped up this case, he'd take the sweet-smelling detective sailing. Go riding the waves. And each other.

"But at the moment, I'm not interested in anyone else but you."

Her lashes were like red-gold spikes against her cheeks as she lowered her eyes and began fiddling with her cutlery. Liking the fact that he could make her nervous, Nick decided to up the stakes. Just a bit. Reaching across the white tablecloth, he skimmed a fingertip down the back of her hand.

"You were telling me about how you ended up in the big city."

She blew out a breath that ruffled her curly bangs and jerked her hand away. "So, you knew Tara and my mother are—were—grifters."

"Like I said, she'd mentioned your *maman* playing a little fast and loose with the law from time to time," he said noncommittally.

"More than a little fast and loose. Grifting was, while I was growing up, pretty much a family business. I was rifling purses by five. Picking pockets by eight."

"Everyone has their talent. Sounds like you were a prodigy."

Which didn't surprise him in the least. He had a feeling that Kate Delaney never did anything by half measures.

She shrugged. "I don't know about that. But Tara's talent definitely was charming people." A smile tugged at the corners of her lush lips, momentarily brightened her eyes. "Mama always said that there wasn't a bird safe in any tree when Tara was around."

"She did have a way about her," Nick allowed.

"Did." She repeated the past tense in a flat tone. The light in her meadow-green eyes was extinguished, like a candle being snuffed out by an icy gust of wind. "God, I can't believe she's gone."

She leaned her elbows on the table and began rubbing at her temples with her fingertips.

"So, tell me some more about you and your sister's childhood."

"Childhood." Her voice was edged with both scorn and sadness. "What's that? I was a sophomore in high school when Mama got arrested for a sweetheart scheme. That's where—"

"A beautiful and usually younger woman or hunky guy takes advantage of a lonely person, usually of the opposite sex, but not always."

"That's pretty much it. Unfortunately, she made the mistake of choosing a pigeon who neglected to mention that his nephew was a Chicago vice cop. When his uncle told him about it, the cop, Dennis Delaney, flew down and raised holy hell, and Mama ended up spending four years in jail. And this is where it got weird."

Like lifting purses at five and havin' a mama who went to jail for grifting wasn't?

"Dennis and his wife had always wanted kids. But she couldn't get pregnant, so they'd taken in a whole string of foster kids from screwed-up families. He offered to take both Tara and me back to Chicago with him. Child Protective Services was understaffed, so they were hot for the idea. Then, at the last minute, Tara decided there was no way she was going to live with a cop, so she refused to leave."

"But you wanted to?"

"I can't begin to tell you how much. I was fifteen years old, and exhausted from living on the edge, never knowing when the cop on the corner was going to slap a pair of handcuffs on me and drag me off to jail.

"Tara was like Mama; she liked the rush of risk. Plus, she always said there was a feeling of control when she could con people into doing exactly what she wanted them to do. Like getting someone to hand over all their money for a psychic reading at a carnival, or short-changing a clerk, or pulling a badger game on some un-suspecting mark."

"I once asked your sister why, with her looks and smarts, she stayed hooking," Nick said. "She told me that she liked being a prostitute because she got high wielding power over rich and powerful men who were used to being in charge of everyone and everything. Said it was better than drugs."

"Obviously she hadn't changed all that much. I'm pretty much a control freak myself—"

"Now, there's a surprise."

Nick received a perverse and dangerous rush of plea-sure for being able to make her lips curve. Even if it didn't last long.

"You should do that more often," he said.

"What?"

"Smile. You really are stunning."

He watched her square her shoulders. Stiffen her spine. The pleasant respite was short-lived. Dirty Har-riet was back. In spades.

"I'll grin like a jack-o'-lantern when we find my sis-ter's murderer. To make a long and shoddy story short, we had a huge fight. She told me I was being disloyal to Mama. I told her she was crazy.

"So, I escaped to Yankeeland, as you so quaintly referred to it, while Tara stayed in Mississippi in foster care. She turned eighteen the same week Mama got released and they moved to Memphis . . .

"Meanwhile, I got to experience life with two good people—"

"Who believed in the solid, nineteen-fifties family values you—and apparently your sister, if her TiVo list is any indication—dreamed of living. And to show your gratitude, you dutifully followed your foster father into the police force."

Her pouty lips firmed. "It wasn't like that. I admired Dennis Delaney. Enough to go to court and legally take his name when I turned eighteen. He was a good man who stood up for people who couldn't stand up for themselves. I thought that was an admirable job and decided a person could do a helluva lot worse than be a cop."

"You're not going to get any argument with me on that one," Nick said mildly, even as he remembered a time when he'd felt the same way about his own father. Before he realized that not every policeman in America returned home from his shift with envelopes stuffed with cash. "So, I'd bet he's real proud."

Once again the light dimmed in her expressive eyes. "He's dead. He keeled over from a heart attack two days before I graduated from the police academy."

"I'm sorry."

"So was I." She glanced down at her practical, leather-banded watch again. "We'd better get going if we want to start questioning those Voodoo shops before they close."

"Hey, you may be from the city of big shoulders, but this just happens to be the city that never sleeps."

"Last I heard that was New York."

"Obviously you've never been here during Mardi Gras."

He tossed some bills onto the table, leaving Kate to notice he'd left an overly generous tip. "Charmaine's a single mom with three kids at home," he said when the restaurant owner tossed him an air-kiss good-bye from across the room. "Her ex is currently in Angola for grand theft auto, breaking and entering, armed robbery, violation of parole, possession of a controlled substance, spousal abuse, and resisting arrest."

"That's quite an impressive yellow sheet. Were you the arresting cop?"

"As it happens, I was. Why?"

"Just wondering." Resisting arrest was a catch-all phrase that could mean a lot of different things.

"It was a righteous bust," he told her, as if knowing exactly the direction her mind had taken. "Was I glad the son of a bitch decided to swing at me after he'd put Charmaine in the hospital with a concussion and a broken jaw and cracked ribs? *Mais*, yeah. But it was his decision to swing first."

"I'm surprised you didn't throw in jaywalking and spitting on the sidewalk."

"Spitting on the sidewalk's not even a misdemeanor in New Orleans. I would've given the other a shot, but I figured there was no point in overkill. Especially since any one of those by themselves would've given him his third strike."

Thus earning him a life sentence.

"Charmaine seems grateful."

Unfortunately, as Kate had learned in her patrol days, not all battered women were so pleased to have their husbands or boyfriends hauled off to jail.

He shrugged his wide shoulders. "I was just doin' my job. And although she's still struggling financially, at least the money she pulls in from this place isn't goin' up her no-good husband's nose anymore."

"Okay."

He glanced down at her. "Okay what?"

"You get points for that one."

He grinned. Put his arm around her shoulder. "That's a start. I think, *chère,* that this just might be the start of a beautiful friendship."

"Don't push your luck," she warned.

But she did not, Nick noticed with satisfaction as they left the restaurant, shrug off his touch.

14

THE FOG HAD ROLLED IN FROM THE RIVER, thick white clouds of moisture that gave the Quarter a mysterious, spooky feeling. It caused sounds to echo: Kate could hear the cheery calliope of a paddlewheeler out on the river, the shriek of a woman's laughter, a sweet, strangely lonely song from a tenor sax.

As if it were the most natural thing in the world, he moved his arm from around her shoulder to her waist.

"These cobblestones are tricky anytime. Worse in the dark. Worse yet, when the fog's in," he said. "Wouldn't want you tripping and messin' up that pretty face."

Although she was more than capable of taking care of herself, the night and the fog and the strange city had her feeling too much like one of those brainless heroines on the covers of those Gothic romances her mother had once devoured like chocolate truffles. The idiots who always seemed to go down into the basement to check out strange sounds with only a candle. Or who'd walk in the fog on the moors when a killer was on the loose. So she let his hand stay where it was.

More laughter floated by on the soft, moist air. Somewhere a dog barked.

"So," she said, "how far to the first shop?"

When he didn't immediately respond, Kate stopped walking.

"Broussard? How far away is it to the first Voodoo shop?"

He sighed heavily. Turned toward her. "Look, we need to talk about this."

She splayed her hands on her hips. "If by talking you mean where you tell me you're going to play the lone-wolf PI while I do my damsel-in-distress act and sit by a hotel phone waiting for you to call in with your report, there's no point in discussing it."

"It's Mardi Gras. Which means the shops in the Quarter will be filled with drunk tourists looking for some kinda forbidden thrill. Most of the ones in the Lower Ninth haven't reopened, and while there's probably some business going on out of selective homes here and there, they'd be hard for two white outsiders to find. We can tackle them in the morning. A few hours isn't going to make a difference."

"You were a cop long enough to know the forty-eight-hour rule," she argued. If a murder wasn't solved in the first forty-eight hours, chances were it never would be.

"Which we're already tipping over," he pointed out. "And you're not going to help anyone if you're too beat to think straight. How long has it been since you've had a decent night's sleep?"

Too long. Long enough she couldn't remember how it felt.

"I'll sleep once my sister's murderer is behind bars."

As she looked up into his frustrated gaze, she heard the clang of a streetcar, the distant whine of a motorcycle.

"Aw, shit!"

It happened so fast, even Kate, who'd worked for five years on the street before making detective, didn't have time to respond.

At the same time, everything slowed down, taking on a slow-motion, life-flashing-before-your-eyes, about-to-die feel.

A helmeted driver on a black motorcycle pulled up beside them. The muzzle of the pistol he was holding in his left hand flashed. There was the pop, pop, pop of gunfire.

Nick dragged her to the ground and threw his body on top of hers.

"Don't move," he gritted, amazingly calm for someone who'd just been shot at. "Not a muscle." Twisting, he pulled out a cell phone and punched in 911.

"This is an emergency," he said when the dispatcher answered. "Shots fired." He was giving the cross streets and a description of the shooter when yet another bullet clanged off a stone wall just above them.

"And whatever you do, don't lift your head," he told Kate.

Lying on top of her, Nick's body was solid and warm and . . . *aroused*?

It couldn't be.

But it was.

And even worse, he wasn't the only one. She'd nearly been killed. Probably would have been if he hadn't somehow foreseen what was about to happen and pushed her to the ground. She should be thanking her lucky stars she was alive.

That's what she should be doing.

Unfortunately, while her mind was scrambling to figure out what the hell had just happened, her body, imprisoned between Nick and the damp cobblestones, was betraying her by thinking how solid—and oh, wow, how unbelievably good—his erection felt pressing against her.

"We've got a drive-by shooting," Nick told the dispatcher with a calm that, if she hadn't been a cop herself, Kate would have found amazing.

Thankfully, he seemed unaware of his body's reaction. And better yet, he also appeared oblivious of her unbidden response.

"Send a car now."

Too late. The motorcycle took off, disappearing into the night with an earsplitting whine that reminded her of the Jet Skis that raced around Lake Michigan every summer.

"Dammit." Nick leaped to his feet, his long legs braced apart, holding the pistol he'd pulled from somewhere in a two-handed grip. "It's too freakin' foggy to risk shooting." His voice was roughened with angry frustration.

He scooped up the phone he'd thrown down when

he'd pulled out his Sig. Then crouched down beside her.

"You okay?"

"Of course."

Sirens screamed through the foggy night. "Stay down," he instructed when she started to stand up.

"I'm as much of a cop as you, Broussard. More, since you're not with the force anymore. And as much as I appreciate you covering my back, I'm perfectly capable of taking care of myself. Besides, the shooter's long gone."

"You're probably right." He held out a broad, dark hand. Kate flinched as he pulled her to her feet.

He turned her hand over. Frowned at her palm. "You're hurt."

"It's only a scrape. Things could've gone a lot worse." Like they both could've died. "How did you know that guy was going to shoot?"

"The red laser light on the front of your blouse."

"My blouse?" She looked down at her chest, as if expecting to see it still shining there.

"Yeah. I guess it's lucky for you I was checking out your breasts when he came by."

"You were checking out my breasts?" *Again?*

"That's not the pertinent question." He didn't, she noted, apologize.

"And the pertinent question would be?"

"You've only been in the city a few hours. Granted, you can be a bit of a pain in the ass, but how the hell did you already piss someone off enough to want to kill you?"

Before she could toss back a stiletto-sharp response, two black-and-whites came screaming up to the curb, sirens blaring, bar lights flashing blue strobes. The cops who leaped out of the car, guns drawn—one the whitest person she'd ever seen, the other African-American—looked unbelievably young. And—oh, great, wasn't that all they needed?—nervous.

"Looks like the cavalry's arrived," he said.

"They're not exactly Starsky and Hutch." Kate decided to table her pique with him until they handled this situation.

"Get down on the ground," the white one's voice cracked as he shouted the command. "On your stomachs, legs spread, hands on the back of your head. And drop the damn bag."

15

KATE UNDERSTOOD THE CITY WAS IN DESPER-
ate need of police, but couldn't they at least let them get
through puberty before sending them out in cruisers?

"I'm getting down on the ground." She repeated the
cop's words, hoping they'd offer some assurance as she
tossed her purse out of reach, then once again lay prone
on the sidewalk. "I assume you know, or at least have
heard of former detective Nick Broussard?"

She tilted her head toward Nick, who was lying beside her. "Oh, yeah," the other cop said. "Everyone's
heard of Broussard."

"I'm Detective Kate Delaney, Chicago, PD. If you'll
just let me get my ID out of my bag—"

"Just stay where you are, ma'am," the first cop said.
"Check the bag," he instructed his partner. "Are we
going to find anything dangerous in there, ma'am?" he
asked. "A knife, needles—"

"I flew here from Chicago today. I know screeners get
a bad rap, but I suspect if I was carrying any weapons, I
wouldn't have been allowed to board the plane."

"You could've bought something once you got to town," the cop argued, proving he had at least one working brain cell.

"Far be it from me to tell you how to do your job, boys," Nick said, his tone as casual as if they were all standing at the bar at some local cop watering hole, shooting the bull. "But while we're discussing the contents of Detective Delaney's purse, the assailant is getting away."

"So neither of you are the assailant?"

So much for that alleged brain cell.

"Dispatch has already been informed that the assailant was riding a Kawasaki motorcycle," Kate told him through her teeth, wishing she could lower her hands. It wasn't that easy lifting her head so she could carry on this stupid, ineffectual, time-wasting conversation. "He might have even passed you."

"The ID reads 'Chicago PD,' " the second cop reported. He was holding his Mag-Lite on the card in her billfold.

A small crowd was beginning to gather. "You might want to pick up the bullets from the sidewalk before you lose evidence to the looky-loos," Nick suggested.

The guy, who reminded Kate of the albino monk from *The Da Vinci Code,* squared his shoulders. "We don't need your advice on how to handle evidence, Broussard."

"May we get up now, Officer?" Kate asked, attempting to forestall the cop from getting into a pissing match with Nick.

"Sure." His words were directed toward Kate, but his heated gaze was on Nick. "Are you hurt, ma'am?"

"It's Detective," she said, hoping to garner enough authority here to keep things from getting out of hand. "And I'm just dandy."

"Do you know any reason anyone would want to be shooting at you, ma'am?" Junior asked.

"None at all," Kate said, not quite truthfully.

She couldn't believe that any of the Chicago cops making anonymous death threats would've actually followed her to New Orleans, but she'd certainly arrested criminals with less motivation for murder.

She turned to Nick. "How about you?"

"Non," he said. "It was probably just a random drive-by. Some gangbanger's initiation so he can join up with his homies."

Another car pulled up to the curb. Kate groaned inwardly as Dubois stepped out from behind the wheel.

"Well, well. Who do we have here?" He grinned as he swaggered toward her, his shirt straining against his broad belly, looking as if he'd been sent in from Central Casting to play a stereotypical fat, corrupt southern cop. "If it ain't the little lady from the big city."

"It's Detective," Kate corrected.

"You know, that's a funny thing." He rubbed his chin. Tabasco-sauce stains dotted his yellow tie. "After you left the station earlier, I happened to be talking with a Chicago cop."

It was his smirk that gave him away. *Just happened.*

Yeah, right. How about he picked up the phone and made the call to check up on her?

"Well, he told me you fudged a bit when you told us you were a detective. Seems you're on administrative leave. So you could testify in a federal case alleging poleece misbehavior."

"It was police *corruption*. And there was nothing alleged about it."

"So you say. But the jury's still out on that, isn't it?" The damn smirk was back. It was all Kate could do not to knock it off his fat face. "Because this is America, land of the free and home of the brave, where suspects are innocent until proven guilty in a court of law."

And wasn't that what Nick had said earlier? Kate knew she'd be more likely to stumble across a blue unicorn in Jackson Square than find a cop who ever believed he might, just possibly, be arresting an innocent person.

Since it was obvious she wasn't going to find out anything about Tara from this Neanderthal, she turned toward Nick, who'd been standing beside her, silently watching the conversation play out.

Kate was grateful he hadn't rushed in to help her out, as if she were some damsel in distress who needed rescuing.

But maybe that was because he agreed with Dubois?

Remy Landreaux, who'd paused to talk to the uniforms after getting out of the unmarked car, strolled over, his expression bland. "Why don't you go get those patrol guys looking for witnesses," he said to his partner, more of an order than a suggestion. "While I have a little talk with the vic?"

Kate could tell Dubois wasn't thrilled about that idea. But Landreaux must've outranked him, because he lumbered off, leaving them alone.

"Helluva partner you've got there," Nick said.

"If you cared about what kinda guy I had to partner up with, *cher*, you should've stayed on the force," Remy said mildly. "So, why don't we take a couple minutes for y'all to give me your statements, and you can be on your way."

The facts of the shooting were cut-and-dried, and both Nick and Kate remembered it exactly the same way. Unfortunately, none of what they remembered was going to prove that helpful in apprehending the shooter.

"There's something else," Remy said as he slipped his notebook back into the pocket of his suit jacket. "Your sister's case has taken on some complications that I'm not at liberty to discuss with you at the moment," he told Kate. "But while you may currently be persona non grata for ratting out your fellow cops—"

"Crooked cops," she corrected.

"Yeah. From what I could tell from the reports Dubois had them fax to him, they look as guilty as sin." He laughed at her obvious surprise. "What, you don't think I can be on your side?"

"Let's just say I wasn't given the impression that NOPD is all that thrilled to have me here."

"Things are complicated," he said, telling her nothing she hadn't already figured out for herself. "But believe me when I tell you that most of the police officers wearing a badge these days believe in an uncorrupted police force."

He slanted Nick a significant look Kate couldn't quite understand. Not helping was the fact Nick's expression gave nothing away.

"And you would be in that majority?" she asked Landreaux.

He nodded. "Absolutely." He tipped his fingers to his forehead in a little salute and started walking back to the car when he turned back to them. "Oh, just remembered." He reached into his jacket pocket again and pulled out an NOPD business card. "I wrote your mama's address and phone number on the back. Just in case you'd like to get in touch with her."

Kate would've rather coated her body with chicken grease and gone skinny-dipping with alligators. But she took the card. "Thank you."

"Hey." His smile was warm and appeared genuine. "We good guys have to stick together."

16

"I PROBABLY SHOULD HAVE TOLD YOU ABOUT that federal jury thing," she murmured.

"We can get into that later."

"Later," she agreed as they drove past what looked to be a convention of Hell's Angels going into the bar where Nick had been caught by undercover cameras taking a bribe.

And wasn't Ms. Black-and-White Law-and-Order going to be thrilled to find out about that?

Nick wondered why, given that there'd never been any love lost between Dubois and him, the dickhead hadn't spilled the beans about him having gotten kicked off the force.

Perhaps he'd decided, after that little news flash about what had happened with Kate in Chicago, to save the bombshell of Nick's public disgrace for some more opportune time.

Maybe using it as a weapon to divide them, when, and if, either he or Kate became a problem.

Nick knew, all the way to the marrow of his bones,

that Dubois was dirty. He also suspected the guy had more than a little to do with Big Antoine's "suicide." But proving it was another matter.

And now, with Kate's arrival on the scene, things could get really complicated.

Especially since it was more than apparent that one or both of them had now become a target.

"I don't imagine, considering the fact that you were just shot at, you'd be willing to just call it a night? Start hitting the Voodoo shops in the morning?"

"Is that what you'd do? If you were working this case alone?"

"Probably not." Since he was already not being one hundred percent honest with her, Nick was willing to admit to the truth about this.

"Well, then." She folded her arms. "Let's get started."

Three hours later, Kate was Voodooed out. Native Charms Botanica was much like all the other shops they'd been in. A plethora of papier-mâché and carved wooden masks hung on the brightly painted walls; the wooden shelves were overflowing with painted rattles, Voodoo dolls, candles, displays of beaded bracelets, religious statues, tarot cards, and bottles of oils.

Kate had never seen so many alligator heads and teeth in one place in her life. Actually, she'd *never* seen an alligator head. Or tooth, either, for that matter. And she could have gone the rest of her life without the experience.

A stunningly beautiful woman with thick black hair

braided in beaded cornrows, and skin the color of café au lait, looked up as they entered. She started to break into a smile as she saw Nick, but when she also caught sight of Kate, her eyes widened.

She broke into a torrent of what Kate took to be Cajun French. Nick answered back, the words rolling off his tongue as if he'd grown up speaking the language. Which he undoubtedly had. He could have been discussing the weather, or the economy, or this year's New Orleans Saints' season; whatever, the deep tones were as warm and smooth as a whiskey sauce on bread pudding—and sexy as hell.

"Kate, this is Téophine Jannise."

He put his arm around the woman, the gesture easy and natural. Kate felt a little stab of something alien and was appalled to realize it felt uncomfortably like jealousy.

"Téo, this is Kate Delaney. She's visiting from Chicago."

"Welcome to New Orleans." She extended a beringed hand. "You're obviously Desiree's sister."

"Yes, I am." Kate didn't see any point in correcting her sister's name.

"How lovely that you can visit your twin."

"She's dead." She hated saying those words.

"*Non!*" Téo's shocked gaze flew to Nick. There was another torrent of French.

"She says your sister was here just last weekend." Then added, "On Sunday," answering the question Kate had just been about to ask.

"*Oui*," Téo confirmed. "She came in looking for some diab oil and St. Expedit root." She frowned. "I told her I would never stock such things in my store."

"Why not?" Kate asked.

"Because they're used by *bokor*. Those who follow the left-hand path."

"Black magic?"

"*Oui*. Though you must understand that all magic, black and white, is not actually magic at all, but merely a way to employ the supernatural powers of the *lwa*."

"Which would be your gods?"

Although it wasn't germane to her goal of finding Tara's killer, Kate had always had a strong streak of curiosity. Which, she figured, was part of what made her a good cop. She honestly was interested in hearing a bit about this alien belief system, if for no other reason than to try to understand her sister a little bit better.

"The *lwa* are not gods, at least in the way a Christian might think of the concept," Téo explained. "They're *mistè*, mysteries that humans can't fully understand, yet we know them as immortal spirits with supernatural powers who oversee all aspects of life, present in all forms of nature: trees, wind, sea, earth. Also, they're present in our ordinary world, in figures, crosses, and other man-made items consecrated to them."

She gestured toward a row of small cloth dolls on a display in the shop window. "In the pantheon of religious beliefs, they fall somewhere between God and humans. They're the link between us and our one God, whom we call Bondye, but he's far too powerful and remote for direct worship. So he created the *lwa* as manifestations of different aspects of himself and allowed them to exist in both worlds as a way for him to communicate with humankind."

"They sound a bit like saints."

"*Oui*." She smiled, obviously pleased Kate had grasped the concept. "They're very much like Catholic saints, angels and devils. Although they behave very much like humans, with all the range of our unruly emotions, and can behave irrationally, which is why it's important to stay on their good side.

"But, other than that, the resemblance is very strong, because Roman Catholicism has been influencing Voodoo customs ever since the seventeenth century, when fearful plantation owners in Haiti forced all the slaves to convert to Catholicism. It did not take long for the two religions to begin to blend, and practitioners simply started using the saints to stand in for their own *lwa*.

"The word *lwa* means law, and in fact the *lwa* represent the cosmic laws, which means black magic and evil spirits are facts of life in the Voodoo religion," she continued.

"For every positive force, there must be a negative force to keep the world in a harmonious balance, and while legitimate devotees of Voodoo know how to work such magic, having taken an oath upon initiation to never cause anyone harm, they don't practice it."

"So all that stuff about putting curses on people and making zombies is just exaggerated movie hype?"

"For the most part. Oh, there will always be those

who use the dark powers as a shortcut to achieving what they want. There are also those who choose to practice it as a way to make money. But they themselves pay a very high price for crossing the divide."

"How?"

Could her sister have been one of these dark practitioners? Was that why she'd been killed? For revenge?

"When a *bokor* purchases the assistance of any dark *lwa*, he enters into an *anajan* to repay the spirit with an expensive sacrifice. Once he makes this commitment, he becomes the *lwa*'s slave for the rest of his life. If he ever tries to break this agreement, the spirit will punish him with death. Or the death of his loved ones."

Kate exchanged a look with Nick, knowing they were thinking the same thing. While she couldn't quite make the leap to believe in supernatural spirits making deals with evil sorcerers and running amok in the world, committing murder and mayhem, Kate had definitely seen enough in her years as a cop to know that evil did exist.

And it was beginning to look as if Tara had somehow gotten herself caught up in something very evil that had proven deadly.

"What happened after you told her you didn't have those items to sell?" she asked, trying to return the conversation to its original track.

"She became very agitated." Téo's lips turned downward in a frown. "Truthfully, she was already very upset when she came in. I suggested a calming potion, but she wouldn't stay long enough for me to mix one up for her."

"We need to know if you have any idea where my sister might have gone once she left your store."

"You must understand what you're asking." The woman's expression turned grave. "Becoming even remotely involved with the dark forces is very dangerous."

"I'm willing to take the chance," Kate said, when what she really wanted to say was, *Why don't you ask me if I give a flying fuck?*

Téo glanced over at Nick. "Can you talk her out of this foolishness?"

"Believe me, if I could, we wouldn't be here."

"There is something you should understand," Téo told Kate. "Besides the *lwa*, there is another category of supernatural beings in Voodoo, endowed with great powers."

She paused.

Kate, who'd always prided herself on being able to read people, couldn't tell if Téo was taking time to carefully choose her words, or if she was being overly dramatic. "And that would be?"

"Twins."

Although she'd been trying to be respectful of this woman's belief system, Kate couldn't help rolling her eyes.

"You may choose to disbelieve. But because you are a twin, my religion considers you sacred."

"Sacred." They'd now gone so far beyond her ability to suspend disbelief.

"Because you are the living, breathing representation of the balance of forces that is the bedrock of Voodoo belief. Together you and your sister form the human and the divine, the mortal and immortal. There are even those who believe that twins are more powerful than the *lwa* because of their union and that they always become *lwa* after death."

"So, what you're saying is my twin sister is now a god?" Next she'd be suggesting Tara was not really dead at all, but only zombietized, or whatever it was called.

"A supernatural being," Téo corrected. "I understand how you, who've not been properly trained in the religion, might doubt this. But if you're going to enter this world, you must realize that there is a much-used Haitian saying: *Maraso yo rasiab.*"

"Which means?"

"Twins don't get along. It's considered normal for twins to hate each other. Which is why when one dies, there are many who will believe it was at the hand of the other."

"My sister and I may not have been close for many years. But there's no way I'd want any harm to come to her. Besides, I was in Chicago when she was killed."

"It wouldn't have been necessary for you to be here."

"Right. Being like some supernatural powerful wonder Voodoo goddess, I could have sent my minions, or flying monkeys, to do my evil work for me."

"I don't believe you could do such a thing."

"You're right. I couldn't." *Wouldn't.*

"But others might. Others who cared for your sister."

"You happen to have any names of some of these *others?*" Nick asked.

"I'm afraid not. Desiree had not been a member of our community all that long. I don't know who she'd made friends with."

"Maybe you can give us the name of some of these dark-hand folks?"

"There is a man in Algiers." She took out a pad of paper and wrote down a name and address.

"Did you tell my sister about him?" Kate asked.

Téo sighed. "I'm afraid I did . . . She was so insistent." A sheen of tears brightened her dark eyes. "So . . . needy."

"Thanks, sweetheart." Nick folded the piece of paper and stuck it into a front pocket of his jeans.

"Be careful," she said, then turned her attention back to Kate. "I understand that you'd probably be uncomfortable having a *desounen,* death ritual, performed for Desiree."

"Uh, yeah. You'd be right."

"I know Desiree was raised Roman Catholic. Will you be having a funeral mass for her?"

The question came from left field. "I haven't given it any thought."

"It would be a good thing. All Voodoo death ceremonies begin with a formal mass. But even so, your sister's journey to Ginen, the mythical homeland of the spirits beneath the primordial waters, can be fraught with danger. For you both.

"Without the proper ritual, a soul can become trapped in the physical realm, forced to wander the earth forever, never finding a permanent home. When that happens, the soul can take revenge on family members for not properly putting it to rest.

"What I said about twins not getting along? There is more you need to be aware of."

She took a small purple satin beaded bag from the shelf and pressed it into Kate's hands. "This is a Paket Kongo. Think of it as a powerful magnet, gathering and concentrating the power of the *lwa*'s protection. This blend of herbs is favored by the Gédé, who oversee everything connected with death.

"Desiree may be angry at you not just because of the lack of burial ritual, but also because of your estrangement before her death."

"Did she tell you that we were estranged?"

"Were you not?"

Kate really, really hated it when people responded to a question with another question. "It had been a while since we'd spoken." And wasn't that a major understatement? "But estrangement might be a bit harsh."

"Nevertheless, with her death your sister automatically became a *lwa* known as a *marasa*. Not only are they very powerful, they can also be very temperamental and tyrannical at the best of times. And dangerous. You must keep this packet with you at all times."

The bag, smelling of coffee and tobacco, and something else that teased at Kate's memory, creeped her out. And that was before she turned it over and saw the skull embroidered on the purple satin.

But not wanting to be rude, since Téo had given

them the first real lead of their case, she reached into her bag for her billfold.

"It is a gift," Téo said. "And the least I can do for the sister of a woman whom I felt would've become a close friend. May I also offer you a few more words of advice before you go?"

"Sure."

"You must honor Desiree with a period of mourning. During this time you should wear purple. Or black."

"Black probably won't be a problem," Nick said.

Kate shot him a sharp look to let him know she was not amused.

"This is important. It shows your love and respect for your sister, and if you neglect this duty, she can bring you great harm." She crossed the room, opened a cabinet, and took out a small, leafy-green plant.

"But even without the ritual, you can still do something to protect your sister, whom I can tell you loved, by putting this sesame plant in her casket. If a black sorcerer digs it up, he'll be compelled to count all the seeds before beginning his magic. But he can only perform his spells at night. And there are far too many seeds to count before daylight."

"Clever."

"There is one final thing."

"What's that?"

"When you meet with the *bokor,* do not accept any gifts from him. Especially a small jar or bottle. This is where he keeps the souls he's captured. Souls he uses to perform his evil tasks for him."

Kate blew out a long breath. "Well, thanks a lot. I appreciated all the information and think we've got it covered. I know Desiree would be grateful."

She handed the potted plant to Nick and shook Téo's hand. Then escaped before the woman could dig some livestock out of one of those crayon-bright cupboards.

17

"ANOTHER OLD FRIEND?" KATE ASKED AFTER another dash through the rain to the Hummer parked at the curb.

"Sort of," he said mildly. "She and my sisters used to play Barbie dolls together. Every so often, they'd have sleepovers."

Kate had no trouble imagining Téophine Jannise mooning over her friends' big brother. She certainly would've.

If she'd felt safe inviting any friends over to the house. Which, of course, she never had. She could still remember the time in the third grade when one of the richer kids had come over after school to work on a joint science project, "Do Rocks Float?"

As it turned out, they did if they were lava, but the project nearly didn't get finished because Antoinette, always looking for a potential mark, had spent so much time grilling the poor girl about her family. Needless to say, she did not come back.

Kate shook off the unpleasant memory. "I realize it's

not polite to make fun of other people's religions, but I'm surprised she didn't give me a rooster or goat to sacrifice."

"Never know," Nick said easily. "Maybe that's where the tradition of a funeral supper first came from."

"I'm going to have to do something about a funeral, too, aren't I?"

The thought hadn't occurred to her until the woman had brought it up. But with their mother off who knows where, it looked as if the job was going to fall to her.

"I can help you with that, if you want. I know this priest who works at a shelter in the Quarter who's a pretty good guy. And a Desert Storm vet."

"He was an army chaplin?"

"A surgeon, actually."

"How does that work? Being a priest and a surgeon?"

"I don't know. He's never shared the particulars."

And, being a guy, and a veteran himself, Nick had probably never asked, Kate decided. "So, how far away is Algiers?"

"It's the part of the city across the river on the west bank. Maybe fifteen, twenty minutes. We'll check it out first thing in the morning."

"Why not now?"

"Because it's late, the neighborhood's dicey . . ."

Kate tossed up her chin. "Like I can't handle a dicey neighborhood? I'm a cop."

"Yeah, I seem to recall you mentioning that a time or two. So, if it makes you feel any better, blame me for not wanting to go there this late at night without a SWAT team backin' us up."

"I think you're forgetting who hired whom."

"That's where you're wrong." He stopped for a red light. "But the thing is, if I let you get yourself killed or maybe drop dead from exhaustion, I don't get paid."

"That's a major exaggeration."

"Is it?"

"Absolutely." No way was she going to admit that the burst of energy the dinner and coffee had given her was wearing off, leaving her feeling on the verge of crashing.

Reaching across the space between them, he skimmed a finger along the soft purple smudges beneath her eye that no amount of concealer had been able to hide. "You're carrying an awful lot of baggage here, *chère.*"

She rolled her shoulders, trying to shrug off an unwanted sizzle of awareness. "I told you, life's been stressful lately. And the light's turned green," she pointed out. "You can go now."

He glanced up into the rearview mirror. "There's no one behind us. How about a compromise," he suggested. "You *have* heard the word, haven't you, Detective?"

Kate angled her head and kept her eyes on his as she answered. "Of course I've heard of it. I'm just not overly fond of the concept."

His lips curved in a smile so devastating, the State of Louisiana should require it to be registered as a lethal weapon. "You ought to give it a try. You give a little, I give a little, and we both get what we want."

His wickedly devilish wink told her exactly what he

wanted. Well, this Cajun Casanova was just going to have to learn that he couldn't always have every damn thing—and every woman—he wanted.

But while she'd never admit it to him, the idea of starting out again in the morning was appealing. Even if she was afraid she'd be kept awake by nightmares of Tara's death.

"Oh, hell, I'm getting a headache from all the damn incense, anyway." She jerked away from his light hold. "But I want to start first thing in the morning."

"Absolutely." He was smart enough not to smirk, now that he'd gotten his way.

Téo watched the man she'd once had a raging crush on and Desiree's twin turn the corner and disappear from view. Then she locked the door and—although Mardi Gras was her busiest time of year, thanks to curious tourists—she flipped the window sign to "closed."

She pressed her fingertips against her eyes, as if she could erase the images flashing behind her closed lids. Took a deep breath.

Then crossed herself, which may have seemed surprising to some people not familiar with her religion, but she'd never believed one had to choose either Voodoo or Catholicism, and neither did the philosophy of Voodoo.

After all, Marie Laveau, New Orleans's famed nineteenth-century Voodoo queen, who served as both hairdresser and spiritual advisor to the city's wealthy whites and Creoles, had not only been born Catholic, she'd gotten married in St. Louis Cathedral, and Father Mignot himself had celebrated her funeral mass.

If only Marie were here today to advise her.

Afraid that there might not be enough magic in New Orleans to protect them all from the storms she feared were coming, Téo went through the beaded curtain into the back room.

"You heard?" she asked.

"*Oui.*"

"And?"

"And?" the man repeated, a bit mockingly, she thought.

"What do you intend to do?"

Toussaint Jannise shrugged and held out his hands, palms up. "It is out of my hands now."

"I warned you."

"You did."

He seemed unreasonably calm for someone whose life was hanging by a very thin thread. Then again, that was always one of the things that frustrated her so. Especially during those times, like now, when he'd get himself into terrible trouble.

He rose from the red velvet settee. Placed his broad hands on her shoulders and pressed his lips against her forehead.

She allowed herself to lean against him. Just for a moment.

As always, his calm soothed.

Was this how it had been for Desiree? she wondered as she felt her heart slow to match the rhythm of his far steadier one. Had she received some comfort before plunging to her death?

"I have to go." He put her a little away from him.

"To Algiers?" She had to push the words past the lump in her throat.

"Everything will be all right." His turquoise eyes, which were such a riveting contrast to a complexion the hue of burnished copper, were tender. "You'll see."

He skimmed the back of his fingers down her cheek.

Téo turned her back, unable to watch him leave. How she wished Desiree hadn't involved her half-brother in her dangerous scheme!

The beaded curtain rattled behind him. She heard the click of the lock opening. Then the door opening. The sound of the rain hammering on the sidewalk outside the store.

Then there was nothing but silence.

And the beating of her blood in her ears.

"Hello?" a deep male voice called out.

Oh, hell. Would it have been so difficult for him to have locked the damn door behind him? She welcomed the flash of irritation; it burned away a bit of her fear.

"NOPD. Is anyone there?"

"I'll be right out."

And weren't the police just what she needed?

Still, it could have been worse. The officer could've come while Toussaint had still been here. And wouldn't that have been a pretty mess?

Téo scrubbed at her wet cheeks with the backs of her hands. Took another deep breath. Said a short prayer to

Ogou Fer, the warrior *lwa,* asking him to empower all those who'd been drawn into this trouble.

Then, although it was a challenge, she pasted a bright, welcoming smile on her face.

"Good afternoon, Detective," she said as she swept through the beads with the grace and power of the runway model she'd once been. "How may I help you?"

18

"SO," KATE SAID, "I SUPPOSE THE NEXT ORDER of business is to find a hotel."

She still couldn't believe she'd just taken off to New Orleans without taking care of that basic bit of business. Which went to show how upset and distracted she'd been lately.

"You're not staying at a hotel."

"Why not?"

"Because unless what happened earlier was just a random act of urban, post-Katrina violence, someone's gunnin' for you. If you think I'm going to leave you alone to let whoever took a shot at you try again, you need to raise your expectation of what you want in a hired gun."

"I'm not hiring your gun. Just your investigation skills."

"Well, lucky for you, you're getting both," he said as he headed back to the marina. "Consider my quick draw a lagniappe. That's—"

"Something for free. I read it in an article in the in-flight magazine."

"There you go. So, until we figure out who's gunning for you, you're staying on *The Hoo-yah*. And while we both know how hot you are to get in my pants, the boat's got two bedrooms. So, unless you decide you want to pay me a little midnight visit, you're perfectly safe."

"Could you be any more arrogant?"

She didn't want in his damn pants. Okay. Maybe the thought had occurred to her. But that didn't mean she was going to act on it.

She rubbed her temples. God, she was so tired. "Okay. But just don't think, because you've won two arguments in a row, that I'm always this easy."

"The thought never crossed my mind," Nick said dryly as he pulled into the parking lot.

"On another topic," he said as they walked down the dock toward the ketch, "that thing that happened earlier?"

"The shooting?"

"No. The *other* thing. When I was lying on top of you."

"Oh." Kate nodded. *"That* thing." That supersize erection that had felt much too good for comfort.

"Danger has been proven to be an aphrodisiac."

"So I've heard." She'd always wondered exactly how those clinical studies were carried out.

"I just didn't want you to take it personally."

"Don't worry, I didn't."

"Take one reasonably good-looking male and one gorgeous, drop-dead gorgeous female, toss in gunshots zinging overhead, shake vigorously, and it's a guaranteed recipe for what happened."

Kate wondered which of them he was trying to convince. "I'll keep that in mind."

His explanation was logical. And Kate had always prided herself on her logic.

"Want a drink?" he asked as they entered the belowdeck salon.

She looked dead on her feet. Nick knew all too well how the rush of adrenaline could drain away and leave you feeling like a wet rag. But still edgy and unable to sleep.

He went into the galley adjoining the salon and opened the refrigerator.

"I've got beer . . . and beer . . . and hey, look at that, more beer. Or, I think I've got a bottle of brandy squirreled away somewhere."

Bingo. There, in the cabinet over the sink, was the bottle of Courvoisier Remy had shown up with the day Nick had opened the agency.

"I wouldn't turn down some brandy," she decided. "But just a bit. Otherwise I'll pass out."

He poured the brandy into the two balloon glasses his longtime friend had also shown up with.

"Passing out might not be such a bad idea, after what you've been through in the past twenty-four hours." He handed one of the glasses to her and sat down in a leather chair facing the sofa.

"Right now, I just want to sit here and sip my brandy and pretend that we're simply two people sharing a nightcap after a lovely dinner. Which seems a lifetime ago."

"Getting shot at does have a way of changing things."

"Tell me about it."

He hit the remote, turning on the CD player. Then groaned inwardly when the vampy voice of jazz great Shirley Horn singing "Soothe Me" came out of the wall speakers.

"Good timing." Kate nodded her approval. "Was that choice just luck? Or do you have the song set up for whenever women visit?"

"Pure luck of the shuffle." No way, in this situation, would he have chosen what was, hands down, the most erotic song he'd ever heard. "I can change it." He reached for the remote again.

"No, don't. I like it." She leaned her head back, closed her eyes, and fell silent. But he knew she was still awake when she took a sip of brandy.

"Soothe me," Shirley was crooning to some unseen lover.

When just watching this woman swallow made him want to press his mouth against her throat, Nick knew he had now officially stumbled into some very deep quicksand.

She reached up and unfastened the clip at the nape of her neck, then ran her fingers through her hair in some female way that caused it to surround her face in a glorious halo of fiery curls.

"Mellow me way down inside," the jazz singer invited.

Nick wanted to be deep inside, all right. But there was nothing mellow about how he wanted to make Detective Kate Delaney feel.

"I was working the OCIU—organized crime intelligence unit." Her tone was flat, almost detached. She leaned back and closed her eyes. Nick figured it was easier for her that way.

Dragging his dirty male mind away from a fantasy of those red silk spiral curls skimming down his body, following the hot, wet path her mouth was making, he forced himself to focus on her story.

"It was part of the terrorist information division, a top-secret division created after 9/11," Kate said. "In the beginning, I was so excited when I won the promotion."

She opened her eyes again. They shone as she thought back on that day.

Do not freaking think about this woman getting excited.

"The unit's mandate was to unearth secrets. And keep them."

"Something, given how you said you and your sister grew up, you were probably real good at," he guessed.

"Yeah. I was."

She was absently smoothing her fingers up and down her throat, a gesture that had Nick wanting to run his tongue along that same path.

"We started out looking for ties to terrorist cells, but within the first six months, we'd begun keeping files on every mover and shaker and politician in the city."

As Nick's gaze followed those slender fingers into the V of the silk blouse's opening, he mentally unbuttoned one more button.

"And you were surprised by this why?"

"How about because I believed we were supposed to be the good guys?" she said in a flare of heat.

"It'd be a lot easier if white was on one side of the line, black on the other," he said. "Good guys versus bad guys, like those spies in *Mad* magazine."

"I was uncomfortable with the situation. So I went to my lieutenant."

"Who treated you to a lecture explaining that we're in a war, the terrorists don't fight fair, and between the damn activist courts and the pinkos in the leftist liberal press, the only way your side had a fair shot to counter the balance and keep America safe was by extralegal means."

"That's exactly what he said. In the beginning, it wasn't all that different from what cops have been doing forever. Like pulling over a gang member you knew was dirty to search his car, and worrying about finding probable cause after the fact.

"I'd never liked that, and refused to do it myself when I was on patrol. But I could certainly understand the theory that a lot of cops believed, that sometimes you just knew that if a guy wasn't guilty for one thing, he'd done something else. And would do a lot worse later on."

"Might as well get a conviction and get the scumbag off the streets."

"That was always the argument."

"Thus making those same streets safe for women and children," he said dryly.

Cops took a lot of crap. Day in and day out. Nick could understand how it'd get old real fast and how a lot of starry-eyed idealists would soon start believing that if they gave some crap back, eventually it'd all even out.

"That's the kind of thinking that can become a problem if the guys at the top of the food chain let it get out of hand," he said. "Which I guess is what happened to your covert unit?"

"It didn't take long for things to go spiraling way out of control," she agreed. "If you were connected with the right people, harmful facts were deleted. Even falsified. If you were seen as an enemy, the opposite happened."

"You could've quit."

"I know. And I probably should have. No, strike that. I *definitely* should have. But I didn't want to let them drive me out of a career I'd worked so hard at."

She took another sip. "There was this mob lawyer we couldn't quite nail. So one of the guys went to his wife with pictures of him having sex with one of his string of girlfriends. She divorced him, got a generous cash settlement, which she immediately hid away in some offshore banks, then turned him in to the IRS."

Kate frowned at the memory as she ran a short buffed nail around the rim of the crystal glass. "Mission accomplished. When I complained about the tactics, the captain told me if I made waves, I'd be back to chasing down rats on the waterfront and arresting transients for pissing against buildings."

"But despite that threat, you still went to the feds?"

"We were fishing for online predators and got a high-rolling political donor caught in our net. He'd been talking dirty to teenage girls in chat rooms. And presumably, if the conversations were any indication, doing a lot more.

"I wanted to do a sting. At least put a tail on him. Catch him at the girl's house, or a motel. But the file mysteriously disappeared one night and he suddenly stopped going online. It was like he'd been tipped off. That went way too far over the line for me, so yeah. I went to the feds. With the copies of the emails I'd downloaded onto a flash drive."

"Thus ending your police career."

"But *I* wasn't the one in the wrong."

"Doesn't matter. You crossed that thin blue line, sugar. Broke the unwritten law about cops not ratting out other cops."

"Even when those cops are breaking the very laws they've sworn to protect?" she asked on a short, hot flare of indignation.

Aw, hell. She still didn't get it. "You're not saying you're planning to go back?"

Didn't the lady cop realize that the odds of her surviving there would be along the lines of bin Laden joining the U.S. Special Forces?

"I want to. I thought I could, in the beginning. The Justice Department attorney assured me that by getting rid of those few bad apples, I could make the department strong again. Stronger, even, than it had been before."

"Wonder Woman lives."

"What's wrong with wanting to make things better? To fix things? That's what cops are supposed to do."

"And you couldn't let the bad guys drive you out. Because then they'd win."

"That's exactly why I wanted to stay." She looked surprised that he'd understand. "But I'll admit it's not real encouraging when you start getting death threats on your answering machine and your picture is put on targets on the police firing range."

"Better your picture getting shot at than your body. Which, need I remind you, was exactly what happened earlier this evening."

She opened her luscious mouth. Closed it again. Then polished off the last of her brandy.

"Surely you don't think someone would come all the way to Louisiana to make good on one of those threats?"

"Anything's possible."

He'd thought that shooter might have targeted her because she'd hit town and begun making waves about her sister's death. Or maybe even because LeBlanc's goons hadn't gotten the word Tara was dead and had mistaken Kate for her twin.

But this news flash about death threats from Chicago cops definitely added a new wrinkle. Especially knowing that Dubois had found out about her testimony.

The guy was incompetent.

He was also as crooked a cop as Nick had ever met.

Could he have come up with a payback plan for her with those corrupt cops back in Chicago?

If there was money in it?

Abso-fucking-lutely.

19

"GOD, I CAN'T BELIEVE THIS IS HAPPENING. I'm thirty-one years old." She rubbed her temples again. "I've been a cop for ten years, and until I landed in the OCIU, I thought of myself as one of the good guys. Every day I strapped on a pistol, put on my white hat, and walked out my door like goddamn Rebecca of Sunnyside Farm, out to protect and serve."

"Sunnybrook."

"What?"

"Though I don't think she ever packed a pistol, it's Rebecca of *Sunnybrook* Farm."

"How would a big manly guy like you know a thing like that?"

"Hannah—the librarian sister?—read it so many times the pages started falling out. My dad was a Vietnam vet who came back from in-country with what people these days would call *issues*. It wasn't always easy around our house, and I always had the feeling she was trying to beam herself into the story."

"That's tough."

Something like compassion moved across her tired eyes. He wasn't surprised when she shook it off, like a batter shaking off a wild pitch. Compassion tended to appeal to a person's better angels, and when that happened, you could go soft.

Which was the one thing the lady didn't need right now.

"Sunnyside, Sunnybrook, whatever." She pressed on. "My point is that until all this shit hit the fan, I'd begin each morning fooling myself into believing that I might make a difference.

"Oh, I knew people don't naturally feel all warm and fuzzy toward cops. When I was assigned to a patrol car, people hated to see me in their rearview mirrors because they figured I had nothing better to do than ruin their day by giving them a ticket. If I walked into a Krispy Kreme and ordered a cup of coffee, right away people'd start making lazy-cop and donut jokes."

"I'm amazed they dared," he murmured.

"They might not have said anything to my face," she allowed. "But I could feel them thinking it. There was this one time I was on patrol along Lakeshore and pulled into the parking lot of the aquarium, and this woman with a kid waved me down."

She was on a roll now, getting all caught up in the frustration of her situation. Nick figured she had another five minutes, tops, before she crashed.

"The kid was about three, maybe four, and pitching a hissy fit because his mother wouldn't buy him a stuffed toy shark. Know what the woman told her son?"

"That if he didn't shut up and behave, she was going to have you arrest him and take him away to jail?"

"Yeah." She shoved her hand beneath her bangs, lifted her hair. "How did you know that?"

He shrugged. "I suppose it goes with the territory."

"But why? Kids are supposed to know that if they get in trouble, they can call a cop. But that little boy was looking at me like I was the Wicked Witch of the West. It's no wonder kids buck authority, with parents telling them shit like that."

Personally, Nick thought kids bucked authority because it was their nature, and part of the growing-up process.

"Helluva life we've chosen for ourselves, huh, Broussard? Even though you've gone private, you're still spending your days hanging out with the lowlifes and the scum of the gene pool."

"It's not written in stone, you know. We could always do something else."

"Sure. I hear the city's short on doctors. You can start doing heart transplants and I'll become a brain surgeon."

"That may be a bit more of a change than I had in mind. Ever think of taking some time off?"

"In case you weren't paying attention to Dubois, I just happen to be on administrative leave."

"That's not time off when you're down here digging into a case that'll probably come back a suicide."

"Like you wouldn't do the same for one of your sisters."

"*Mais*, yeah, I sure as hell would. But maybe, once

we figure out what happened, you should just get away somewhere for a few weeks to unwind."

"Unwind? Like a *vacation?*"

She made it sound like a dirty word.

"Got something against vacations?"

"How about they sound boring?"

"Depends on the company. I picked *The Hoo-yah* up for a song from this surgeon who moved to Arizona, where he wouldn't have to worry about any more hurricanes. I'll hoist anchor and by this time tomorrow we'll be off to Alaska. What do you say, *chère?* We'll watch glaciers crash into ice-blue waters, visit some old gold-rush towns, have some hot sex, check out some totem poles, have more hot sex. Watch whales. Maybe have sex while watching whales."

"You're kidding, right?"

"Okay. We can skip the totem poles."

She was having trouble holding that frown.

"Given that I hate cold weather, I think I'll pass on any state with glaciers."

She did not, Nick noted, discount the hot-sex part of the suggestion. He also figured that her dislike of cold could be another reason, along with the fact that her cop career there was toast, for her not to be in any hurry to go back to Chicago.

"No problem. We'll sail down to Cozumel, then through the Panama Canal, where we can kick back on deck and watch the rain forest go by, have some hot sex, then head up the coast, maybe find a fiesta in Acapulco, and after I rub sunscreen into every luscious pore, we'll let the cliff divers wow us in Mazatlan."

"What are you doing here when you could be sailing the world?"

"Maybe I was waiting for a first mate. And maybe the timing wasn't right."

As she took that in, Kate rubbed a fingertip on the dirty thigh of those ugly black slacks he was going to be glad to see her get rid of.

"Timing is everything," she murmured. "Or so they say."

She wasn't going to ask. But she *was* curious. He was beginning to read her tells, those little giveaway signs that let him know what she was thinking.

Not that she had that many. The lady was good. But Nick, whose life had for the past fifteen years depended on the ability to know what his enemy was up to, was better.

"My dad ate his gun a few months ago," he said after he'd let the silence spin out for a couple minutes. "He left me with some business to clear up."

"And have you? Cleared it up?"

"Just about. I'm working on tying up a few loose ends."

Her remarkable eyes narrowed as, like any good cop would do, she latched onto what he hadn't said. "Was the case cut-and-dried?"

"It closed the same day."

He could see the wheels turning in her head. "But you have doubts."

He shrugged, finding it ironic they'd have this in common. What were the odds of two suspicious suicides in six months? Both somehow connected to Leon LeBlanc?

Slim, but not impossible. Especially since, as he'd told her, in many ways New Orleans was a small town.

"My old man was a marine back in the sixties and early seventies. He saw a lot of combat. In 'Nam, then later as a cop, here on the streets. Streets that can, at times, define *mean*. New Orleans was, after all, the murder capital of the world for most of his years on the force. Big Antoine also had himself a fondness for Jack Daniel's, he, so I suppose anything's possible."

"You don't believe he committed suicide."

"No. I don't."

She no longer looked exhausted. In fact, she reminded him of his old bird dog, Laffite, when the bluetick hound had been flushing out a covey of quail. Her eyes, lit with interest, were as bright as emeralds, and if the lady had had a tail, it'd be wagging.

"Maybe, since you're helping me find out about Tara, I could help you investigate your father's death," she suggested. "Tit for tat, so to speak."

Despite the fact that his father was his least favorite subject, Nick couldn't help laughing. "There's nothing I'd love better than to play with your tits, *chère.*"

The surprised laugh that burst out of her was rich and warm and sexy as hell. Nick had always preferred women who could laugh in bed. Then reminded himself that he was a professional.

And professionals didn't go to bed with clients.

Well, okay, maybe Sam Spade had. And Philip Marlowe. And a lot of those other guys from those cool old black-and-white film noir flicks. Usually the PI was played by Bogie. Of course, the client was always some glamorous dame who was setting him up for the fatal fall.

Which, in this case, just might be worth the risk.

"Oh, hell," she said.

Every cell in his body went on red alert. "What's wrong?"

"I'm about ready to crash."

It was like watching a brightly colored balloon deflate. He'd seen the same thing happen in BUD/S training, when a gung-ho wannabe would suddenly hit the wall and end up ringing out.

"Let's put you to bed."

"Why am I not surprised you'd suggest that?"

The fact that she didn't protest when he took hold of her arm and hauled her off the couch revealed how exhausted she was.

"I meant *alone*. As delectable as you may be, even when you're about as wrung out as a wet dishrag, it could do irreparable damage to my ego if you were to fall asleep while I was making love to you."

"I don't think anyone could dent your ego with a jackhammer." She was weaving on her feet, like a drunken sailor on shore leave. "A mortar."

Also like a drunk, she was concentrating mightily on putting one foot in front of the other.

Step. Sway. Focus.

"Want some help?"

"This boat, as lovely as it is, isn't exactly the *Queen Mary*," she said. "What is it, a fifty-footer?"

"Fifty-eight."

"So, are you suggesting I'm not capable of walking less than sixty damn feet?"

"No. I'm suggesting you look ready to fall on your face."

"If that's your idea of flattering a woman, Broussard, I'm amazed you ever get laid."

"That was meant as fact, not flattery, but hey, if you think you can stay awake while we do the mattress mambo, I'm up for it."

"Be still my heart." Kate patted her chest. "But as romantic as that offer is, I'm afraid I'll have to pass."

Another step. Sway. Focus.

Deciding to take matters into his own hands, he scooped her off her feet and flung her over his shoulder, picking up her overnight bag with his free hand.

"Dammit, Broussard." She stiffened in his arms. "If you think carrying me around like some caveman—"

"Technically, it's a fireman's carry. Not a caveman's."

"I know that."

Her head shot up, throwing off his equilibrium. He put his hand on her butt to regain balance. Then, when that felt a bit too good for comfort, Nick realized this might not be the best idea he'd ever had.

"I was speaking metaphorically," she insisted from her upside-down position.

"You're the one who brought up wanting romance."

"I didn't say I wanted it! I was being sarcastic."

"Yeah, I kinda figured that out." So he wasn't exactly Rhett Butler. But no woman had ever complained before. "Next time, Scarlett, I'll try to be more gallant," he promised as he entered the bedroom.

She lifted her head again. "There's not going to be a next time. And how the hell did you know that?"

"Know what?" He tried to be careful as he dumped her onto the bed, but as boneless as she was from exhaustion, she still bounced twice.

"That Scarlett was my birth name."

"You're kidding."

"Unfortunately I'm not." She braced herself up on her elbows and shook her head.

Her lips turned down in a frown that made him want to take them with his own mouth. And that was just for starters.

"I was originally named Scarlett Kathleen Carroll. Needless to say, I dropped the Scarlett at the same time I changed my last name to Delaney. Tara's wasn't as obnoxious, and as you undoubtedly noticed, she was more flamboyant than me, anyway, so she kept it. Our mother," she said dryly, "took *Gone with the Wind* to heart."

"Apparently."

He stood beside the bed, looking down at her, taking in the tumbled red spiral curls, the deep green eyes, cheekbones that could cut glass, and voluptuous lips, and decided that if she'd been around when the movie studio was conducting that nationwide search to find the perfect Scarlett O'Hara, Vivien Leigh would've been flat out of the running.

"What?" she asked, getting a bit of her sass back.

He rubbed his jaw. "You know, I can understand why you changed it, but it sure as hell does fit."

"That's it. Now I'm definitely going to have to shoot

you." She flopped back onto the mattress as Nick went into the adjoining head to retrieve his toothbrush and shaving kit. "Tomorrow."

It only took a moment. But when he returned, she was standing beside the bed, taking what was known in the SEALs as a combat nap. Her eyes were open, she was staring off into space, and if she wasn't actually asleep, she was seconds from falling on her face.

"Hey," he said gently.

She jumped when he touched her arm. Her eyes widened, filled with what appeared to be fear, and her left hand instantly flew up to a shoulder holster that wasn't there.

"You've got good instincts." Nick knew she hated feeling vulnerable. Suspecting that she'd hate even more having shown any vulnerability, he opted for a matter-of-fact tone. "Cop instincts."

She hitched in a breath and, as he watched, struggled to settle herself. "I wasn't sleeping."

"Did you hear me say you were?" Because it was getting harder and harder not to touch her, he allowed himself to smooth a hand over her shoulder.

"I was about to open my suitcase and got to thinking. About . . . things."

"You've got a lot on your mind."

"I wasn't sleeping," she repeated. "You just startled me."

"It was my fault," he said. "I shouldn't have made a move without letting you know first."

He figured they'd be able to move beyond this moment. He'd apologize for spooking her. She'd get her tough-as-nails cop mojo back, and they'd move on from there.

That's what Nick thought.

Until, dammit, she nervously, unconsciously, licked her lips.

And nearly took his breath away.

"So, with that in mind, I guess I should warn you," he said.

"About what?"

He slid his fingers into the coiled red silk of her hair. "That I'm about to make a move."

Her eyes widened. In the glistening glow of the copper wall sconce, he noticed, for the first time, gold flecks dusting over the emerald green.

"I'm not sure this is a very good idea."

"You're probably right." Not wanting to dwell on the negative, he ran the pad of his thumb over her lips. "But I'm having a damn difficult time thinking of a better one."

She could have moved away. Hell, as a big-city cop, she could've probably done some fancy martial-arts move she'd learned at the police academy to throw him on his ass.

But she didn't so much as move a muscle. Just stood there, watching. Waiting.

So, Nick went ahead and did what he'd been wanting to do since she showed up at his boat this afternoon.

He lowered his head and took her mouth.

20

IT WAS NOTHING LIKE WHAT KATE HAD ANTICI-
pated. There was tenderness where she would have expected power, patience rather than passion.

The kiss was a beguiling whisper against her mouth, soft as thistledown and tasting of cognac. It was only a kiss, she told herself as his tongue traced a damp, beguiling pattern across her lips.

The feathery brushing of lips, the slow stroke of his tongue, the gentle nip of his teeth on her bottom lip was more temptation than proper kiss. More promise than pressure.

Kate knew that she could stop him. Even now, if she stepped away, he would have to let her go. But his mouth was so clever. So tempting.

That his lips would be so clever, and his hands would move up and down her back with such a confident, practiced touch, came as no surprise. Any man who radiated such potent sexuality would've had plenty of opportunity to perfect his technique. What was coming as a revelation was that such a meltingly soft touch could create such scintillating heat.

His mouth tempted.

Enticed.

Seduced.

As rich liquefying pressure flowed through her, Kate let out the breath she'd been holding on a soft, shimmering sigh and twined her fingers together behind his neck.

God, she loved his mouth. Loved. It.

She loved its taste. Its thrillingly clever expertise. She wanted to feel it all over her body, wanted it to do things to her. Wicked, wild, wonderful things. Everywhere. In every way. All night long.

And that was just for starters.

Desires, too long untapped, rose to the surface, drawing her into a world of steamy, potent passion. Kate realized she could easily get lost in this world. Too fast. And too easily.

The problem was, as that same desire tightened her nipples and pooled between her thighs, she couldn't think of a single reason why that wouldn't be a good idea.

Oh, hell. Nick groaned inwardly. Talk about your major miscalculations!

The attraction had been there from the moment Nick had seen her, but no mere attraction had ever made him ache the way Kate Delaney was making him ache. And no sexual desire had ever made him feel as if he were inexorably sinking into that quicksand Big Antoine had warned him about.

Although it had taken every vestige of self-restraint

Nick possessed, he'd started out gently. Lightly. Enough to get her used to the idea, but not enough to scare her off. Or worse yet, piss her off.

The plan was to draw her into the mist, not drag her into the flames. But what was a guy to do when the sexiest female on the planet wrapped her long, slender arms around his neck, pressed her stone-hard little nipples against his chest, and—oh, Jesus—drew his bottom lip into her mouth?

Splaying his fingers against the back of her head, he crushed his mouth against those petal-soft lips, pushed his tongue past her teeth.

It wasn't like she was helpless. If she'd so much as murmured a word of protest, he'd have stopped.

Granted, it wouldn't be easy, he admitted as he pulled her up on her toes and yanked her tight against him. Not with those hot, sexy little sounds coming from her throat. Not when her short, neat nails were digging into his shoulders.

Not when she was kissing him back, her mouth greedily feeding as if his were an all-you-can-eat chocolate buffet.

His senses tangled, Nick could hear the blood roaring in his ears as he ran a hand down her side, skimming over her, exploring the shape of her body while his tongue explored her taste. His fingers grazed the side of her breast, dipped in at her waist, delved lower, over her slim hips.

In turn, she yanked his T-shirt free of his jeans; her hands ran up and down his back, fretting over muscles and tendons, sending every nerve ending in his body into meltdown.

He pushed her back against the wall and moved between her legs, the placket of his denim jeans making a rasping sound against the front of her black slacks.

And still she didn't back away. Instead, wrapping one of those mile-long legs around him, she molded herself against his aroused body.

His mouth raced over her face, along her jaw, down the long silk of her throat, his teeth nipping at the hollow where her neck curved into smooth, slender shoulders.

He ached to touch her. In every way.

Ached to taste her. Everywhere.

Ached with a need so deep and primal it nearly brought Nick to his knees.

She was warm.

She was woman.

And, hot damn, she was willing.

He could have her. Now. Tonight. All night.

And then what, Broussard?

What're you going to do tomorrow? When she'll hate you for taking advantage of the situation? Of her?

Although it was one of the hardest things he'd ever done, rather than pulling her down onto his bed and taking what he needed, taking her hard and fast, consequences be damned, Nick managed, just barely, to surrender the intoxicating warmth of her mouth.

And her oh-so-willing body.

It took Kate a second to realize his hands were no longer on her.

She nearly stumbled.

A strawberry flush rode high on her cheekbones and in the deep V of her blouse, between the buttons Nick couldn't remember opening. Her eyes were bright, as if burning with fever, and her hand, lifting to her throat, was far from steady as her fingers brushed across skin that already bore a faint bruise from his teeth.

"Well." She sounded every bit as breathless as Nick felt. "I didn't realize they had earthquakes in Louisiana."

"They don't."

"Then that was *us*?"

"Yeah. I'm pretty sure it was."

"I think we may be in trouble."

Nick plowed his hands through his hair. "Look, I'm—"

"If you dare say you're sorry, I really will have to shoot you," she said, cutting off his plan to do exactly that.

"You kissed me." She shrugged. "I kissed you back," she added, proving herself the master of understatement, given that she'd come damn close to sucking out his tonsils. "Men aren't the only ones with urges."

She dragged her hand through those tangled bright curls he'd been imagining draped across his thighs. "Just because I'm a cop, that doesn't mean I'm cold, dammit."

"Sweetheart, the last word I'd use to describe you is *cold*. In fact, if you were any hotter, this boat would've gone up in flames."

She didn't deny his appraisal. "Well, now that we've satisfied our curiosity, we can just forget what happened and move on."

"That was one helluva kiss, Detective Chère." Because he couldn't resist the lure of that magnolia-soft skin, he ran the back of his hand down her cheek and enjoyed feeling the heat rise again. "I'm not sure I'm going to be able to forget it that easily."

This time she ducked away from the light caress. "Well, you'll have to try. Because it's not going to happen again."

He watched her square her shoulders, stiffen her spine, and, right before his eyes, morph into that no-nonsense, Joe Friday, Yankee police detective. Which, he told himself reluctantly, was probably for the best.

"I'll give it my best shot."

"You do that. Now, considering you're charging me by the hour, I suppose we ought to call this a night."

Here's your hat. Don't let the door hit you in the ass on your way out.

"Works for me," Nick said. "I'll see you at nine."

"What's wrong with eight?"

He figured she'd just argue if he pointed out that she needed to get a decent night's sleep. "You're not going to find any shops open before ten. Nine'll give us plenty of time for breakfast."

"I don't eat breakfast."

"You should. It's the most important meal of the day. But if you're still serious about not eating breakfast in the morning, you can have yourself a mug of creamy café au lait and watch me eat."

21

DAMN, NICK BROUSSARD WAS, HANDS DOWN, the most frustrating man she'd ever met, Kate thought as he sauntered out of the bedroom. It wasn't that he wasn't being extremely obliging, which he was.

If he'd been telling the truth about that laser on her blouse, he'd also saved her life.

Of course, she was paying for his services. Still, that was a lot more than she'd bargained for when she'd hired him.

But even as she kept reminding herself that she needed him, Kate hated the way he kept steamrollering her, doing whatever the hell he wanted. And worse yet, somehow getting her—a card-carrying, self-admitted control freak—to go along with his plan.

She wasn't used to surrendering power over any aspect of her life to anyone. But she seemed incapable of bucking this frustrating man.

Too much was happening, dammit. Kate was starting to feel on the verge of coming unraveled at any minute. She'd never been one to back away from danger. She was a cop, for Pete's sake.

So why the hell couldn't she handle one slow-talking, laid-back Louisiana lothario?

Okay. What she needed was a good night's sleep. Tomorrow morning, fresh and rested, she'd be able to marshal mental reinforcements. Find her self-control.

At least here on this boat no one was trying to kill her.

Kate still couldn't believe her sister was dead. Maybe they hadn't spoken for years, and maybe that was as much her fault as it was Tara's. But Kate had always believed, in the back of her mind, that she'd have plenty of time to make things right between the two of them. She'd always hoped that one of these days, Tara would escape from under their mother's influence and discover that you really could have a life on the right side of the law.

Of course, she allowed, as she washed her face and brushed her teeth, her own life wasn't so hot right now.

But her recent problems were only a temporary glitch. Something that she would get past, then move on with her life.

She changed into the pair of boxer shorts and oversize navy Chicago Police Department T-shirt she used for pajamas, then climbed into bed. As exhausted as she was from traveling, and all the other events of the day, Kate should have fallen asleep right away. But she couldn't stop her unruly mind from circling back to that kiss.

If such a blood-heating, knee-weakening experience could even be called a mere kiss. Kate imagined entire galaxies had been blown to smithereens with less heat and force.

What had she been thinking? From the moment she'd arrived at this beautiful boat and seen him standing on the dock, backlit by the lowering sun, she'd known he was going to be trouble. Trouble wrapped up in a six-foot-two, buffed, and tan package of bad-boy charm.

She rolled over. Punched her goose-down pillow.

Having been raised in a home where truth wasn't even an occasional visitor, Kate hated nothing worse than a lie.

She never, *ever* lied.

Not even to herself.

Especially not to herself.

She'd been vulnerable. She didn't like to admit it, hated worse *being* it, but there it was. There was no denying the fact.

It wasn't Nick Broussard himself, although he was definitely more of a temptation than most. It was merely that she'd been under a lot of stress. She hadn't been eating properly. Hadn't been sleeping. Factor in her having been celibate for the past six months, ever since her affair had crashed and burned on the pyre of her testimony, and it only made sense that she'd have reacted so intensely.

It hadn't really had anything to do with him personally.

I could have been *any* man.

Okay, maybe not any man. Like she'd rather be smeared with honey and staked out on a killer anthill than have Dubois touch her. But just about any sexually attractive male probably would have garnered the same response.

Well, not *exactly* the same response. Remy Landreaux was good-looking and sexy in a suave, *GQ* sort of way. But she certainly didn't feel inclined to wrap herself like poison ivy around the homicide detective.

Oh, hell. Who was she kidding?

She rolled over again, onto her back, and glared up at the ceiling.

The former SEAL was a walking, talking testosterone bomb of a complication. But she'd never had any problems dealing with complications in the past.

In a way, it was good they'd gotten that kiss out of the way. What was done was done. Now that they'd gotten that sexual tension out of their systems, they could move on and concentrate all their energy on bringing her sister's killer to justice.

Nick wasn't going to be a problem.

Because she wouldn't allow him to be.

That's what Kate told herself.

Liar.

22

THE ST. JUDE SHELTER ON RAMPART WAS appropriately named, given that St. Jude was the patron saint of hopeless causes, and Tara Delaney figured her situation was about as hopeless as anyone's could get.

The only good thing was, according to the small blurb on page 8-B of *The Times-Picayune*, everyone— including, she dearly hoped, Leon and his psychopathic nutcase son, Stephen—thought she was dead. And for now, although she hated the idea of Toussaint grieving about her being gone, she was damn well going to stay that way, for both their sakes, until she could come up with a plan.

She still couldn't believe Kelsey Peters was dead. Kelsey had been the only woman friend Tara had ever had. Which was why when her friend had discovered she was pregnant, Tara hadn't hesitated to let her hide out at her apartment while Kelsey tried to make up her mind what to do.

Not that Tara believed there was any choice. Unless the father was some rich john who'd go totally against type and want to marry the woman he'd paid to have sex with, and raise the kid they'd made together, Kels was going to have to have an abortion.

As she'd tried to tell Toussaint over and over again, every time he'd pressured her to leave the business, Leon had never been one to let his girls walk away. One of the ways he kept them in his stable was by making sure they were provided with the best designer drugs money could buy. Then, of course, there was the debt.

There wasn't a girl on that damn ship who didn't owe Leon LeBlanc at least twenty thousand dollars. Most, like her, owed a lot more.

Leon had not only paid for her boobs and a designer wardrobe Nicole Kidman herself might have envied, he'd also sprung for the plastic surgery that had made her one of the most sought-after call girls on the Gulf Coast.

And, although science hadn't yet gotten to the point where he could clone his best income producers, it was amazing what a good surgeon could create when provided the proper raw material.

To anyone who might have seen them together—and more than one john had paid through the nose for exactly that—she and Kels could've been identical twins. Hell, although Tara hadn't seen her sister in a dozen years, she'd be willing to bet serious money that the resemblance between her and Kels had been closer than that between her and Kate.

Which made sense, since both she and Kels had been created in the same mold by the clever hand of the same doctor.

So now, because of a twist of fate, and a shitstorm of bad luck, Kels was dead. And she wasn't. At least not yet. With any luck, she could keep it that way.

At least long enough to figure out what to do next.

Of course, the mistaken identity didn't have her home free. She knew that once the autopsy report was filed, the truth would come out. Then there was also the little problem that when Kelsey didn't show up for work, Stephen, who ran the day-to-day operation for his father, would undoubtedly start wondering which of his two missing hookers had actually landed in that courtyard.

His goons were probably looking for her at this very moment, which was why she didn't dare try to leave town. Or even check into a hotel.

She could call Nick. But too many cops knew she was Broussard's hooker snitch. They'd probably have the boat staked out, thinking maybe she'd given him the damn videotape. Maybe they were even following him, not that he couldn't ditch a tail. But one of the reasons she was in this fix was that she was too damn impulsive.

She had to be careful.

Come up with a careful, rational, thought-out plan.

And meanwhile, trust no one.

Fortunately, the thugs who did the LeBlancs' dirty work were hired for their brawn, not their brains. She could probably stroll right past them and they wouldn't even recognize the shy, slightly dumpy woman with the short sparrow-brown hair, raggedy nails, sensible shoes, and shit-ugly polyester wardrobe from the Salvation Army thrift shop.

Even Toussaint, who'd been leaving Marie Laveau's tomb tonight when she'd arrived, hadn't recognized her. Of course, that may have been because his vision was blurred by the unshed tears glistening in his eyes. Tears that had almost made her stop and let him know she was alive.

But because she knew he'd feel some stupid caveman obligation to protect her, she needed to keep him in the dark. For his sake. After all, she'd gotten herself into this mess. She was now going to have to get herself out.

Her new look wasn't going to get her on an Oprah makeover show.

Which was the point. Tara wanted to blend into her surroundings.

To fly beneath the LeBlancs' radar.

Fortunately, no one ever noticed a homeless woman.

Well, almost no one.

"You're late," the hottie wearing faded jeans and a green Notre Dame sweatshirt greeted her as he unlocked the door to her knock.

"You going to kick me out for breaking curfew?"

She figured the priest, being a man of God, wouldn't be thrilled to hear she'd been paying another visit to the Voodoo queen's tomb. She also dearly hoped her previous request, which she'd made with Toussaint, hadn't had anything to do with Kels being killed in her place.

"Of course not," Father What-A-Waste said. "Though, if it happens too often, we might have to have ourselves a little chat about following rules."

She tossed her newly dyed hair. "I've never been a real big fan of rules."

"And how is that working for you?" he asked mildly.

She splayed her hands on her padded hips. "You know, Padre, if you weren't a priest, I'd think you were being sarcastic."

"Would you now?" He relocked the door to the street.

She'd realized last night that he wasn't actually locking the women and children in, because the doors could all be easily pushed open from the inside. The goal was to keep out any men who might be in the mood to victimize them.

Which was exactly what Tara was counting on.

23

DAMN IF HE HADN'T BEEN ONE STEP AHEAD OF her all along. Bad enough he'd beaten her—usually an early riser—up this morning. As she stood at the window after her shower, watching Nick pay off the two guys in yellow slickers delivering the world's most nondescript rental car to the marina parking lot, Kate couldn't quite decide whether to be pleased or not.

On one hand, she reminded herself that she was, after all, paying for the man's expertise, and who'd know better how to pull off a covert mission than a special-ops guy?

She was also relieved they wouldn't be riding around in his ridiculous hey-look-at-me-bitches black pimp-mobile.

But she didn't like the fact that he'd kept his plan to himself.

"So whatever happened to teamwork?"

They were definitely going to have to have another talk about his inability to play well with others.

Proving as unpredictable as everything else about

her life these days, the weather seemed to have done a one-eighty from yesterday's sunny and warm. Black-edged clouds rolled across a gunmetal-gray sky that was drizzling rain.

Fortunately, since it had been thirty-five degrees when she'd left Chicago yesterday—had she only been in New Orleans a day? —Kate was prepared for the change in temperature.

"It's raining," she announced when he returned to the boat.

Terrific. As if he hadn't been able to see that for himself while he'd been outside. This wasn't as bad as some mornings-after she'd suffered, but on a scale of one to ten, it still only rated a five on comfort.

"The weather's unpredictable this time of year."

Okay—she considered as he poured coffee into a black mug depicting a gold eagle holding a trident in its claws—maybe it was more a three. At least she wasn't the only one who was conversationally challenged in the morning.

He was wearing the black jeans again, but this time with a black sweatshirt. The sleeves were pushed up, revealing well-defined forearms.

He handed her the mug. Breathing in the rich aroma, she took a tentative sip and burned her tongue.

"Look, about last night . . ."

Buying time, she blew on the coffee, took another, longer drink as she tried to remember the carefully constructed argument against any personal involvement she'd come up with in the shower.

"Which part? Dinner? The shooting? That humdinger of a kiss?"

Humdinger. Well, that was one word for it.

"The kiss."

"Ah." He lifted a brow. "The one that isn't going to happen again." He took a drink of his own coffee. "Unless you've changed your mind?"

"No. I haven't." She decided the little spike of lust that shot through her at the sight of his firm, chiseled lips on the rim of that mug didn't really count. "But I thought, if we're going to be working together, we should get it out into the bright light of day." She glanced over at the rain-streaked window. "Metaphorically speaking, that is."

"Works for me," he said easily. "Because I spent some time last night thinking about the same thing, and well, as gorgeous as you are, Detective, you really aren't my type."

"Well." Kate blew out a breath and reminded herself that she'd always put a high premium on honesty.

She really was serious about avoiding any personal involvement. So why did his assertion sting?

"That's good. Because you're not my type, either." That was absolutely true.

"Well, then." He was leaning back against the counter, long legs crossed. "We shouldn't have any problem, then, should we?"

"Not at all."

He was the most compelling man she'd ever met. The contrast between his black-as-midnight hair and his blue eyes—set in the coppery tan she figured came from living on a boat—was absolutely riveting even before you tacked on the strong blade of a nose, chiseled lips, and square warrior jaw.

"I'm glad we got that settled," she said.

His smile was dry, and openly amused. "And I'm glad that you're glad."

If the sedan had been any more nondescript, it would've been taken for an unmarked cop car.

"Good choice, going for two doors," she said. Four doors definitely would have screamed police.

"I passed camouflage instruction with flying colors."

The idea of yet another Voodoo shop, particularly one that dealt in black magic, was not appealing. Kate reminded herself that this trip wasn't about fun. Besides, she didn't believe in ghosts or ghoulies or anything else that went bump in the night. Which, though she'd never given it any thought before, included Voodoo.

As he drove through block after deserted block that looked spookily like a ghost town, she reluctantly dialed the number Remy had given her for her mother. She'd already tried it this morning, soon after getting up, but the call had been picked up by her mother's answering machine.

It was the same story this time.

"No answer, huh?" Nick asked.

"No, dammit."

"I called the hospital while you were in the shower,"

he revealed. "St. Croix's been moved out of the intensive care, but he still isn't being allowed visitors."

"His accident has got to be a coincidence," Kate said, wishing she could fully believe that. "My mother may not have an honest bone in her body, but she'd never kill anyone for money."

"Doesn't look like the old guy's going to die."

Cops were always observing their environment, looking down alleyways and driveways, checking out the civilians as they drove past. Kate had always thought she was good. Nick was better. His eyes were never still, not in a nervous, unable-to-concentrate way. Rather, they were making quick, thorough sweeps of the landscape, as if he were storing away mental pictures. It took no imagination at all to hear the camera shutter clicking away inside his head.

"You know what I mean."

"Yeah. It could be that she really did take off on a little vacation of her own—"

"And not call the entire time she was gone?"

"Maybe they had a spat."

He slowed down as they passed a slightly overweight, dark-haired woman—clad in an olive-green plastic poncho, brown wide-legged polyester pants, and dirty running shoes—leaving what appeared to be a homeless shelter. One of many Kate had seen in the city.

"The other possibility is that she knew what your sister was up to, your sister's killer came after her, too, and the husband made the mistake of getting in the way. Maybe he tried to protect her."

The same unsavory thought had occurred to Kate. "And she took off running. Unfortunately, that's a scenario I can buy into. And by the way, I couldn't help noticing that you used the term 'killer.' Does that mean you believe me about Tara being murdered?"

"I always had trouble with the idea of her killing herself that way." They stopped at a red light; the woman crossed in front of them. "She was too vain to risk ending up a broken corpse."

"And you weren't going to do anything about your suspicions?"

"In case it's escaped your mind, I'm not a cop anymore. It wasn't my case. I did bring it up to Remy, but she's not the only case he's jugglin' right now, so he's waiting for the autopsy."

"Do you think he'll do anything about it if the cause of death comes back murder?"

"Yeah." Kate wished he'd sounded more positive. "I do." His watchful gaze followed the woman into a market. "But you've got to understand, *chère*, the crime rate's skyrocketing back up these days. And the department's shorthanded, and—"

"And nobody cares all that much about a dead hooker."

"You saying the situation would be that different in Chicago?"

She wanted to believe it would. As many problems as she had with the department, she knew the majority of cops were honest and believed in the adage of protect and serve. The problem was, New Orleans wasn't the only police department that was stretched too thin, especially in these days of shrinking tax revenues and increased spending for Homeland Security.

"No." She blew out a breath. "Prostitutes are pretty much on the bottom rung of the social ladder."

Which was how they'd ended up prey for serial killers, going back to before Jack the Ripper.

Guilt weighed heavily on Kate's heart as she flipped open the phone, and willing to go to any ends—even talk with the woman she'd escaped so many years ago—to learn the truth about Tara's death, she punched the number she already knew by heart.

24

NO DOUBT ABOUT IT. HE WAS FRIGGING GOING insane. Bad enough that thoughts of all the things he wanted to do to—and with—Kate had kept him awake most of the night. The woman was a tough nut to crack. But although she was doing her best to hide it, he suspected that inside that tough shell was a soft-as-buttercream heart.

Which, he reminded himself as he polished off a platter of *calas, pain perdue*, sausage, and fried eggs, was all the more reason to keep his distance.

Despite her claim that she didn't eat breakfast, she had broken down and ordered a plate of beignets after the grandmotherly, seventy-something waitress insisted it was a mortal sin to come to N'awlins and not sample the city's famed deep-fried dough carpet-bombed with powdered sugar.

"You know what's wrong with this city?" she asked.

"That's a loaded question, right?"

"Well, perhaps an inappropriate one," she allowed. "Given its present circumstances." When she licked some snowy-white sugar off her fingertips, Nick forced down an urge to put those fingers into his own mouth. "But I was referring to the fact that there's just too much temptation."

Like the temptation to go back to the boat, sprinkle powdered sugar all over her naked body, then lick it off?

"You sure as hell called that one right, *chère*."

Five minutes later, Kate was standing at the rain-streaked window watching the city of New Orleans disappearing behind them. Despite her reason for being on this ungainly white and red ferry, she began to relax for the first time in months.

"This is nice," she murmured, imagining that on sunny days it would be lovely to be standing below on the car deck, breathing in the scents, feeling the river breeze in her hair. "Peaceful."

When they'd discovered a multicar tractor-trailer accident on the cantilever Cresent City Connector bridge had tied up traffic, Nick had immediately declared plan B to be in effect and driven to the ferry terminal.

Although here, at the curve of the river, where the Mississippi flowed wide and slow, Kate felt a bit of a rush being on one of the largest, most powerful rivers in the world.

"It always has been. And it doesn't really take any longer than the CCC, especially when traffic's all snarled up on the bridge like it is today. People'd probably be a lot less stressed out if they'd just leave their cars home and travel 'cross this way all the time. Though I suppose when they'd end up being forced to wait in long lines all the time, it'd just move the stress factor from the bridge to the ferry.

"When I was a kid, I used to sometimes just ride back and forth, all day long. Since passengers ride free, it was a good way to pass the time."

"And it got you out of the house. Away from your father."

He glanced over at her. "Good guess."

She shrugged, trying not to be pleased by the idea that he probably wouldn't share that little bit of personal information with just anyone. "I did the same thing. Except in my case my hideout was the public library."

Even as she sighed, it crossed Kate's mind that this was yet another thing she and Nick had in common.

Cargo ships were cruising up and down the river; pelicans and seagulls followed the boats, hovering over the water, hoping for a meal.

A white, towering wedding cake of a cruise ship was headed out to sea. Many of the passengers standing on the decks waved gaily at the ferry. Although she'd always suspected she'd find being stuck on a ship for days on end claustrophobic, at this moment Kate found herself wishing she were going with them.

Their destination didn't matter. What she wanted, she'd realized with Nick's offer to just hoist anchor and sail off into the sunset, was to escape her life.

"Do you think those idyllic families that are supposed to represent the American norm really exist?"

"Sure," he said, surprising her. "On television."

Which was obviously why Tara had TiVoed all those shows.

They shared a comfortable silence as the white car ferry continued churning its way across the water. With her mind on families, Kate was thinking how one of the reasons she'd balked at getting married, even though the cop who'd ultimately dumped her had proposed on an almost monthly basis, was that she had no earthly idea how to be a mother. Or, for that matter, a wife.

Which brought to mind another thought.

"Have you ever been married?" she asked.

"Yeah."

"Oh." For some reason that was disappointing. "What happened?"

"It didn't work out."

Once again he was proving a master at withholding information. "I figured that much out for myself."

"You asking as a client? Or as a lovely woman I happen to be sharing a romantic river cruise with?"

"I said it was nice. I wouldn't exactly call it romantic."

"That's because it's daylight. Maybe once we get this case wrapped up, we'll come back at night." He casually slipped a companionable arm around her shoulder, as if it had every right to be there. Oddly, it felt as it if did. "The city lights are real pretty from the water. And stealing a kiss beneath a magnolia moon is a time-honored tradition among New Orleans lovers."

"Sounds as if those lovers are doing something wrong if they have to *steal* the kiss." Her tone was a great deal drier than the weather. "However, you're overlooking one thing."

"What's that?"

"We're not lovers."

"That can be remedied easily enough."

Having always believed that the best defense was a strong offense, Kate turned toward him to assure him that was not going to happen, then realized she'd made a tactical mistake when his hand slid down her arm and settled at her waist.

She was now toe to toe, chest to chest with him.

"Look, there's something you need to get straight."

"What's that?"

"I'm not going to sleep with you."

He had the audacity to flash her a roguish, bold pirate's grin. "Well, now, Detective Chère, if you want the unvarnished truth, *sleeping* wasn't exactly what I had in mind."

She choked back a laugh. He really was impossible.

Impossibly sexy. Impossibly appealing.

"Do you have a pen?"

He reached into a pocket of his black leather bomber jacket and pulled out a blue ballpoint advertising Ship Shape Boat Repair.

"Fine. Then write this down. We are not going to have sex. It's not professional. And while I realize the idea is undoubtedly difficult for you to wrap your male mind around, I'm not interested."

"Okay."

It was really difficult to keep her mind on the subject

when his hand was creating such heat at her waist and he was playing with her hair—which was springing loose from the clip at the nape of her neck again—idly twining it around a long, dark finger.

"Okay?" She narrowed her eyes suspiciously. "That's it?"

"Change your mind already?"

"No," she said through gritted teeth. "I haven't changed my mind. I'm just wondering why you're being so agreeable all of a sudden."

"I thought I'd been agreeable all along."

"Obviously we have a different definition of the word," she said over the loud blast of the ferry's horn, signaling their arrival in Algiers.

"Come to bed with me and I'll show you exactly how agreeable I can be."

The slow, deep drawl lapped against the ramparts of her defenses like a river threatening the levee. Heaven help her, the idea of sex with Nick was far too appealing. And as much as she hated to admit it, she wanted him.

So what? She'd always prided herself on being able to distinguish *want* from *need*; otherwise she'd be eating chocolate for breakfast, lunch, and dinner and ice cream as an in-between-meals snack. A wise woman, one who knew the meaning of self-control, could refrain from giving in to her every craving.

She shifted away. Just a little, breaking the contact between them. "I have a question."

He stuck his hands in the back pockets of his jeans and rocked back on his heels. "Shoot."

"Don't tempt me." She let out a huff of breath and kept her eyes on his. "You already told me I'm not your type." And didn't that still irk her? "So why would you want me in your bed?"

"Actually, if you want to get technical, it doesn't have to be a bed. In fact, watching you eat that beignet this morning, I had this idea—"

"Now, see, that just goes to my point," she snapped. "I've always been good at reading people. I've had to be, because sometimes a cop's life depends on it . . . But here's the thing . . . I don't understand you."

"There's not that much to understand. I'm just a normal guy, *chère*. With normal urges. When I see a sexy, good-looking woman, I want her. Simple as that."

"And you always get everything you want?"

"Not always." He began playing with her silky hair again.

"But most of the time."

"You make that sound like a bad thing."

"Hey, your life is your business." She shrugged. "But I'm a bit more selective."

"I guess that means you don't want to hear the dream I had last night about you and me in the shower on *The Hoo-yah*—"

"That's it." She put up a hand like a traffic cop. "And because I don't want to have to go to the trouble of walking my fingers through the Yellow Pages to find a new PI, I'm going to pretend I didn't hear that."

She turned and marched away.

As he followed her very fine ass down the stairs to

where he'd parked the rental car on the deck, Nick tried to figure out what it was about the woman that had him responding like a horny sixteen-year-old kid hoping to get laid for the first time.

She was undeniably stunning, with her mass of fiery hair, flashing cat eyes, long, slender body, and legs he couldn't stop imagining wrapped around his waist as he pressed her against the tiled wall of his shower for some blazing-hot, wet, and slippery full-penetration sex.

But he'd known other women just as beautiful. Some even more so, and hell, hadn't Desiree looked just like her? Or at least Kate was what Desiree must've looked like before that plastic surgery.

She was smart as a whip, too. Brains and beauty were a major turn-on in any woman; toss in a mystery and some danger, and he'd be forced to worry about his masculinity if he didn't want to do her.

But it went deeper than that, dammit. He liked her. Liked her spunk and admired the way she'd overcome the mess her family must've been. And he could empathize with how difficult it must have been for her to do it on her own. Sure, she might've gotten lucky when that cop and his wife took her in, but she'd done all the heavy lifting on her own.

He was also impressed by her integrity, testifying against those crooked cops, even though she'd been surprisingly naive not to realize how much trouble it was going to get her into. As he thought about the death threats she'd received back home in Chicago, and remembered all too vividly how his blood had gone cold when he'd seen that unmistakable red laser spot on her breast, he experienced an overwhelming urge to protect her.

And to do that, to get enough evidence to put LeBlanc and his goons behind bars, he had to keep a clear head. If he kept allowing himself to get distracted by the sexy, sweet-smelling cop, they could both end up dead.

25

AS DETERMINED AS SHE WAS TO FIND HER sister's murderer, Kate was still charmed as they drove off the ferry.

"That's the courthouse," Nick said when she shared her appreciation of a Moorish-looking building with twin crenellated turrets. "It's the third-oldest continually serving courthouse in the state, going back to 1896. There was another one that stood here in the same place, but it burned down in the big fire of 1895 that pretty much devastated the Point, which is why most of the older houses are double shotguns constructed during the rebuilding.

"The place itself goes back to the original land grant that gave New Orleans to Jean-Baptiste Le Moyne de Bienville. Slave auctions were held here, the French built a huge slaughterhouse, and then, in the eighteen hundreds, most of the people worked in the dry docks, which are still going, the lumber mills, or the iron foundries.

"Later jazz became a huge draw to get people coming across 'da river,' as they called it; and, of course, along with the musicians came the clubs, and a red-light district sprung up to service the sailors and the men who'd come across the river to listen to music, do some drinking and a bit of gambling, and top the evening off with a roll in the hay."

"Wine, women, and song."

"Always a popular combination," he agreed.

"Even these days, if what you said about Tara's true."

"Oh, it's true enough," he said as they passed a large, Gothic-style church just as the bells in the tall square tower chimed the hour.

"It really is lovely," she said as they drove through the neighborhoods of pastel-painted homes. Every so often they'd pass a Victorian with lacy gingerbread detail, or a stately Greek Revival with white pillars, homes that had apparently survived the fire.

"Algiers is one of the best-kept secrets in New Orleans," he said. "And I suspect the folks who live here want to keep it that way. Though, given that so much of the city's unlivable, and Algiers was the only part that didn't flood, they may find themselves growin' faster than they'd like.

"Another problem they've got is that it's not just good guys moving in. Like a lot of parts of the city, it's got some iffy, more and more lawless areas."

"And one of those iffy areas is where we're headed?"

"Stands to reason a guy dabbling in black magic wouldn't exactly live next door to the church."

Although the forecast had called for the rain to let up in the afternoon, to Kate it seemed to be coming down harder. A companionable silence, not unlike the earlier one on the ferry, settled over them, the falling rain and rising fog making the situation seem more than a little intimate.

"Have you been here before?" she asked as he pulled up in front of a building.

The sign read MAIT' CARREFOUR'S HOUSE OF MOJO; the stark red-and-black paint job was a contrast to the pretty pastels of so many of the other houses they'd driven past. "Nope." He cut the engine.

"How did you find it so easily?"

He shrugged. "I pretty much have books of maps in my head. Once I know where I need to be, I can see how to get there."

"That's quite a talent." She also suspected it came in handy when sailing. Especially if he was serious about sailing to Alaska and Mexico.

He shrugged. "I didn't really do anything to acquire it, it's just a quirky gift, though it did come in handy on missions. There were guys who'd accuse me of being a mole with a GPS."

"Not exactly flattering, but I get the idea. Though moles are underground."

"SEALs tend to work at night. So I guess they were going with the blind image."

"Got it." She nodded absently as she glanced around the neighborhood. "I'm used to mean streets, but Tara must have really been upset to come here at night."

"It's not every day a person goes looking for black-magic spells. Even here in New Orleans."

Kate's senses were overwhelmed the moment she stepped into the shop. Like all the others she and Nick had been in, it was cluttered to the point of distraction. Kate decided that was not only part of the ambience but some sort of Voodoo version of feng shui, the difference being that the latter was all about balance, and this, to her unpracticed eye, was all about chaos.

Oddly, although the colors were as jarringly bright as they'd been in the other shops, the mood wasn't anywhere near as cheerful. In fact, she thought as she took in a wall hanging featuring a malevolent-looking, hunchbacked figure with three horns sprouting from his head, it was downright depressing.

"That's Bossu," a tenor voice came from behind her.

Surprised, she spun around and saw a man coming out of the shadows across the room. She would have expected a dark magician, especially one who specialized in Haitian-based Voodoo, to be, well . . . dark. But if he'd had a long white beard instead of this goatee, he could've gotten a job standing in for Santa at the mall.

His hair was a wisp of snowy white, his cheeks brightly pink in a remarkably smooth face, his eyes a light, clear blue. Rather than a hooded robe, he was wearing a red and black tropical-print Hawaiian shirt, white cotton slacks, and . . . Birkenstocks?

"Bossu serves Mait' Carrefour."

"Would that be you?" Kate asked.

His double chin jiggled when he laughed. "No, Mait' Carrefour is the god of the underworld, a magician who rules the night and to whom all requests for dark magic must be made. You might call him the godfather of the dark pantheon."

"Which would make Bossu a demon henchman," Nick suggested.

"That's certainly one way of putting it. Not entirely accurate, but colorful nevertheless. Bossu's often perceived as a three-horned bull, the horns standing for strength, wildness, and violence."

"Sounds like an uplifting guy," Kate said. Was that actually a petrified cat looking down at them with unblinking, glassy yellow eyes from an overhead shelf?

"Violence often serves a purpose or makes a point. Didn't the Bible tell us that Jesus overturned the money changers' booths in the temple? Wasn't Lot's wife turned into a pillar of salt? And let's not forget God sending down that forty-day flood. Not to mention his more recent work."

"You believe Katrina was God's work?"

"No. I, and many others on both sides of the issue, can clearly see Bossu's fingerprints—"

"Or hoofprints," Nick interjected dryly.

"Or hoofprints," the man agreed with a disparate cheerfulness, "all over that catastrophe."

He held out a soft, pudgy hand that looked as if it had never done a day's physical work. "I'm Jean-Renee Bertrand, proprietor of Mait' Carrefour's House of Mojo. And you would be . . . ?"

"Nick Broussard." Nick didn't exactly look thrilled by the prospect, but he shook the other man's extended hand. "And this is—"

"Desiree Doucett's twin, obviously," Bertrand said. Blue eyes twinkled as he took Kate's hand and lifted it to his lips. "It's a pleasure, mademoiselle."

"I'm Kate Delaney," Kate introduced herself. It took restraint not to shiver as those moist pink lips touched her skin. "So you knew my sister?"

"Of course." If he was at all offended by the speed with which she snatched back her hand, his benign smile didn't show it. "Voodoo tends to be an insular community. Plus, New Orleans is very much a small town."

"So everyone keeps telling me. Look, Mr. Bertrand—"

"Oh, please call me Jean-Renee, dear," he said. "We're very informal here."

"Okay. So, Jean-Renee, Mr. Broussard and I are here to ask you some questions about my sister."

"A tragedy," he said. "What happened to her."

"So you've heard she's dead?"

"As I said, we're all very connected, both the light and the dark." He shrugged his well-padded shoulders. "News gets out."

Kate exchanged another glance with Nick and knew they were on the same wavelength. Only last night, Téo, if she could be believed, hadn't known of Tara's death. Apparently, the woman who'd seemed so shaken by the tragic news hadn't waited to share it.

"I suppose so," she said. "It was suggested that you might have been one of the last people to see her alive."

"Was it?"

Okay. So he wasn't going to be as cheerfully cooperative as he'd first appeared. "Yes, it was also suggested that she may have come here looking for ingredients to perform black magic."

"Diab oil and St. Expedit root," Nick elaborated.

"Yes, she was here last Sunday evening. And she did purchase those things. Along with some others."

"Did she say what she wanted them for?"

"Of course. As an *oungan,* or priest, part of my responsibility, along with acting as a spiritual intermediary between the *lwa* and my people, is to serve as a psychological advisor and all-around advisor.

"I could not have properly advised Desiree had I not known what problem was bedeviling her."

Bedeviling being the definitive word.

"What was her problem?"

"Someone was trying to kill her."

His mild, matter-of-fact tone while discussing potential murder was every bit as chilling as that mail-carrier-eating serial killer's had been. Kate had to resist rubbing her arms as her blood went cold.

"Do you happen to know who that someone might be?"

"No. She chose not to share that information."

"Did you believe her claim?" Nick asked.

Bertrand shrugged again. "It was enough that she believed it."

"I guess the spell didn't work all that well," Kate said. She hated this guy who was as much a charlatan as her own mother. "Given that she's dead."

"The *lwa* often act in mysterious ways."

"Yeah, I've heard that, too," Kate said, unable to tell if he was being ironic or serious. "Did it occur to you that perhaps you ought to advise her to get additional help?"

"From whom?" he asked. "The police?" Left unstated but hovering heavily in the incense-scented air was the question: *In this city?* "Even if she had been able to get someone to listen to her, the police department has more important things to do than act as bodyguards for any single citizen."

"Granted, but it seems that as her spiritual advisor"—Kate heaped an extra helping of scorn on that description—"you could have done something more positive than increase my sister's paranoia and depression by suggesting her answer lay in black magic."

He sighed. Heavily. The benevolent Kris Kringle face revealed annoyance.

"Black magic does not necessarily cause negative emotions. On the contrary, I've seen more discord coming from those who loudly proclaim to anyone who'll listen that they're white magicians.

"It's the white magicians, after all, who are out to save the world, to force their ideas of harmony, love, and balance on the universe."

"Gotta hate love and harmony," Nick said.

"I have nothing against those who attempt to become harmonious and loving within. It's not my way, but I also believe everyone must have the right to follow his or her own spiritual path. So long as they do not try to impede others from doing the same thing.

"It's the white-light meddlers who wage war against everything and everyone they don't like who cause the problems.

"It's naive to worship, as they do, balance in all things. This, by definition, gives equal power to those dark forces, such as death. Black magic advances life *over* death, seeing death as something that must be defeated for the sake of the living.

"The left-hand way, which I follow, involves looking around our world with clear eyes, with intelligence and wisdom, and seeing what is right and what is wrong. Black magicians take responsibility for each and every action and, equally as important, each and every inaction we take.

"The idea of karma, so espoused by white magicians, is, if you'll excuse my profanity, bullshit. It's an opiate for the powerless, how they trick themselves into believing that those who have harmed them will somehow get their due."

He looked up at Nick. "You were in the military, were you not?" On a roll, he did not wait for a response. "Imagine where our world would be if our government had just sat back during World War Two, and said, 'Oh, dear, that evil man Hitler is gassing millions of innocent people, but attacking him back will create more imbalance in the world, so the best way to handle it is to sit back and wait, and hopefully, he'll receive his just rewards in the afterlife.'

"Or if we'd just said, 'Naughty Japan for bombing all our ships and attacking our sailors. You pissed us off with that one, but we're feeling very balanced because karma's going to take care of you, by golly.' "

"That's overstating the point, but I get where you're coming from," Nick said.

Kate could tell Nick was uncomfortable agreeing

with anything Bertrand was saying. And wasn't that just like a sociopath to find the one inarguable fact to build his entire position upon? She'd seen Antoinette do exactly the same thing time and time again.

"But," Nick continued, "there's no way you're going to get me to condone revenge killings or vigilantism."

"We need to stand up for ourselves. And protect what we hold dear," Bertrand claimed. "Because the truth is, no one needs to give the devil his due. He just takes it."

He turned back toward Kate. "That's why I gave your twin the herbs and charms necessary to wage war against those who had already declared it on her. It was no different from giving her a gun or sending her to self-defense training to learn how to physically protect herself."

"You mean you *sold* her the charms."

"You don't need to make it sound as if I were pushing drugs or dealing in white slavery," he said, clearly affronted. "I sold nothing illegal. Unlike other members of the clergy, we *ougans* don't draw salaries. Yet, like those others, we have often trained all our lives for the priesthood and it's our full-time job. Just as the relationship between the people and the *lwa* is one of give and take, so is that between devotee and priest. Followers of our religion understand that."

Even if you're too stupid to get it. He didn't say the words, but Kate heard him loud and clear.

"May I give you a little personal advice?" he said.

"Sure."

Kate wasn't interested in anything this man might have to say that wasn't germane to her investigation, but she'd learned that sometimes, if you just let a person talk, some valuable bit of information would slip out.

"You must make sure that you honor your twin more properly in her death than you did during her life. She is, after all, a *marasa* now and it's quite possible that she's angry at you for not protecting her."

If he was looking to prick her conscience, he'd just hit a bull's-eye. Of course, he wasn't telling Kate anything she hadn't been telling herself since Detective Landreaux's call.

"That would've been a little difficult to do. Since I didn't even know she was living in New Orleans." Kate's tone sounded defensive to her own ears. "Or that she was in trouble."

"Some might suggest you should have known. Given that you were twins." His smile had chilled considerably, lacking even an iota of warmth. "Two sides of the same soul. Light." He lifted his right hand, palm up. "And, of course, Desiree would have been the dark." The left. "Together you make up the balance all those damn white-magic practitioners are always seeking."

When he took off on another lengthy diatribe about how his way was the true way, Kate didn't need a crystal ball to see that the only thing he was willing to talk about was the so-called superiority of his crazy woo-woo Voodoo religion.

She might have stayed to press him further, but she had the very strong impression that the unpleasant man really only knew what he was telling her: that someone had threatened Tara and she'd been desperate for help.

"What a fun guy," Kate muttered twenty minutes later as she and Nick stood again at the window of the ferry that was making its return trip across the river. "Santa Claus meets Alice Cooper. With a bit of *Rosemary's Baby* thrown in."

"New Orleans has always been known for its originals," Nick said. "Though the guy's admittedly a piece of work. But I didn't get the impression that he knew any more about what Tara was afraid of than he told us."

Just as he had on the first trip, he slipped an arm around her shoulders. Kate knew she was giving him mixed signals, but it felt too good to shake off.

"I had the same feeling," she said. Outside, the fog was rising off the river, so thick and so white it was like looking out the window into a cloud bank. "Though, if he did know who was after her, he might not tell us, because then, if she was hurt, and the attacker wasn't smote by the black spell, it'd show what a fraud Voodoo hotshot Jean-Renee Bertrand really is."

"I take it you don't believe in Bertrand's black magic?"

"I don't believe in any magic, black or white."

Kate had had a great many of her bedrock beliefs turned upside down recently, but about this she was on firm ground.

"So, I guess I wasted my money on that bottle of Love Potion Number Nine."

"I guess you did." A smile tugged at her mouth. Tired of fighting it, fighting him, she let it go free.

"Oh, Jesus." He splayed a hand against his chest,

over his heart, and staggered against the window. "I think maybe we oughta stop by the ER on the way back to the house."

"What's wrong?"

"I feel a fever comin' on."

She lifted the back of her hand to his forehead when she realized it was just an act. "Real cute, Broussard."

He caught her hand on the way back down, laced their fingers together, and drew her closer with just that light touch. "You ever see a lightning bolt?"

"Of course."

"Come out of a clear blue sky?"

"Not that I recall."

"Well, that's pretty much how I felt when you flashed that smile at me. I swear, sugar, it was enough to bring any man with blood still flowing in his veins to his knees."

The compliment shouldn't have given her so much pleasure.

It shouldn't have.

But, dammit, it did.

"It was just a stupid smile."

She tried to remember the last time a man had looked at her the way Nick was looking at her. With both hot lust and easy humor in his eyes.

"And the *Mona Lisa* is just a painting. And the Hope diamond is just a chunk of coal. And the . . ."

His voice dropped off as he glanced past her, over her shoulder. "Hell."

He muttered a French phrase that Kate couldn't understand. At the same time, he cupped her chin in his fingers and treated her to a warm, melting, lover's gaze.

"What's wrong now? I swear, Broussard, if this is another of your seduction ploys—"

"We've got company." His eyes were warm as they roamed her face. His voice was low, but edged with warning.

"Oh?" She'd been a cop long enough not to turn around. But every nerve ending in her body went on red alert. "Who?"

"Remember when you said something about my bruises and I told you that you should see the other guy?"

His thumb stroked her lip. To anyone watching, they'd appear to be merely two lovers caught up in each other, oblivious to the world around them.

"You first lied and said something about running into a door."

Wanting to do her part, she played along by lifting her hand to his shoulder. And tried not to notice that even as serious as things had suddenly become, that feathery caressing touch was still leaving sparks.

"But yeah, sure, I remember," she said.

It had, after all, only been yesterday. Which was actually amazing, since she felt as if she'd been here in New Orleans for much, much longer.

"Well," Nick said, "you're about to get the opportunity."

26

"OKAY," HE SAID, CONTINUING TO LOOK DOWN at her as if wishing he could drag her off to the nearest bed, "here's what we're going to do."

He nuzzled her neck, his mouth next to her ear. "We're going to make our way over to the stairs."

"I can do that."

"Then after a few steps, I'm going to kiss you. Like that's the reason we left. To find some privacy."

"Okay." Her blood was pumping hot and fast in her veins. Partly from adrenaline, but also, she had to admit, from the prospect of kissing him again.

"Then you're just going to hold on to my hand and stay close. Unless bullets start flying. If that happens, I want you to take cover and do whatever the hell you need to do to stay safe."

"While you're fighting off the bad guys like Davy Crockett at the Alamo?" She turned her head, pressed her lips against his jaw. "So, Kemo Sabe, what ever happened to teamwork?"

"Every team needs a leader."

She touched his face. He truly had a beautiful face, even with those bruises, which were beginning to yellow. "Which would be you?"

"The logical leader in this situation"—he braceleted her wrist with his fingers, turned her hand, and planted a kiss in the center of her palm, creating a spark she felt all the way to her toes—"is the person who's actually had combat experience."

And that was what they were talking about, Kate realized. Combat didn't necessarily take place only in the jungles or Middle East deserts. It could happen right here in American cities, with the collateral damage being civilians.

Such as her sister.

"Which would be you," she repeated, leaving off the question mark this time.

"Which would be me," he agreed.

Lacing their fingers together, he began leading her across the floor.

"Want to tell me what this guy looks like?" she murmured.

"Remember the TV show *The Incredible Hulk?*"

"Sure. Where poor Bill Bixby's Dr. David Banner would turn into Lou Ferrigno whenever he got mad."

"That's him. Think the Hulk. If he weren't green. But uglier."

"Well. At least he should be easy enough to spot." And hit, if the worst-case scenario occurred and they needed to shoot him.

"Do we have a plan?" she asked. "Or are you winging it, almighty leader?"

"There's always a plan. Since the odds of him just happening to be on this ferry at the same time as us are slim to none, I have to assume that he followed us. Which means, despite my clever rent-a-Ford sleight of hand, he knows which car is ours."

"Makes sense."

"So, we're leaving it behind."

"We're walking off?"

Maybe Julia Roberts could escape that way in *The Pelican Brief*, but that movie had been fiction.

"Hell no. That kind of stuff only works in the movies."

Later, when she wasn't about to put her life on the line yet again, Kate was going to have to think about how, although just yesterday she wouldn't have believed it possible, she and Nick were often thinking the same thing.

"I know you've got this macho Superman image thing going. But in case you haven't noticed, neither one of us can really fly."

"It'll be okay," he assured her. Then he leaned down again, brushing a kiss against her temple. "Trust me."

As lovely as his lips felt on her forehead, Kate pulled her head back so she could look him straight in the eye. "I do."

And wasn't that a surprise.

They'd made it halfway down to the deck when Nick stopped.

"Wait a minute," he said, loudly enough for anyone

following them to hear. "There's something I need to get out of my system."

With that, he yanked her against him and went in for the kill. So to speak.

Without wasting time with seductive preliminaries, he caught her chin in his hand and slammed his mouth over hers.

Even knowing it was coming, that it was merely an act, Kate wasn't prepared for the breath-stealing, teeth-grinding kiss that shot through them both like rocket fire.

Going up on her toes, straining against him, she opened her lips to the hard thrust of his tongue.

"Well," she said when they'd finally come up for air. "That almost makes running for our lives worthwhile."

"Stick with me, *chère*," Nick said as he put his arm around her, holding her close, shielding her from the Hulk, "and I bet we can do a whole lot better once we get back to the boat."

Tired of insisting they weren't going to have sex when they both knew it'd be a lie, Kate didn't say anything.

Outside, on the deck, the fog was thick and white and wet. If being at the window upstairs had been like looking into a cloud bank, this was like *walking* into one. It was wet and cold, and if Nick hadn't been holding her hand tight, Kate wasn't certain she'd even be able to see him.

Meanwhile, the rain continued, hammering on the deck and the roof of the cars, which in a way was a good thing, since it meant that the Hulk wouldn't be able to hear them. Of course, they wouldn't be able to hear him, either.

Nick led her through the double rows of cars to the front of the line.

"Since when did everyone on the planet decide to get a freakin' SUV?" he muttered.

"Interesting observation from a man who happens to drive the most humongous SUV on the planet," Kate murmured.

"I told you, it's all about image."

"Right."

"Don' worry, sugar," he assured her as they went around to the other side of the boat to try the cars over there. Kate still wasn't sure what he was looking for, but he definitely seemed to have something in mind. "You'll see soon enough I don't need to compensate for anything in that area."

He was openly displeased with the car parked at the front of that line.

"Damn. A minivan?"

"It's not an SUV."

"Just as friggin' useless," he muttered, moving down the line.

"How about this?" She pointed toward a tomato-red Toyota Corolla.

"It'll do, if push comes to shove, but . . . Hooyah, baby."

He stopped beside a large white BMW four-door sedan with a gold package, pulled out his handy-dandy lock-pick set, and within seconds had the trunk open.

"Milady, your carriage awaits."

"We're going to get in the trunk?"

"Well, I was thinking about just settling down in the back and enjoying the comfy soft-as-a-baby's-bottom leather seats and spacious legroom. But then I decided that there was an outside chance that just maybe the driver might notice us."

"But what's going to keep us from suffocating?" she asked as she climbed in, grateful he'd managed to find one with a relatively roomy interior.

"This model's only a year old. It'll have a safety release," he assured her as he joined her in the trunk. "I've been here, done this, in Azerbaijan."

He pulled the trunk lid closed, plunging them into darkness.

"Azerbaijan?" German technology seemed all it was cracked up to be; the seal was so tight, the only light came from the illuminated yellow release handle. "I don't want to know, do I?"

"No." Nick took out his key chain, attached it to the handle, and pressed on a small flashlight, which brightened things up a bit. "You don't."

Obviously there were several variations of "don't ask, don't tell" in the military. And she'd just bumped into a SEAL one, having already figured out that even if she did ask, Nick wouldn't tell.

The BMW's trunk might have been far more roomy than the red Toyota's, but those engineers definitely hadn't designed it to hold two adults. They were pressed together like the proverbial sardines in a can, not that Nick was complaining.

Christ, she smelled good! Robert Duvall might love the smell of napalm in the morning, but Nick would take the fresh, clean scent of Kate Delaney's hair any morning. Or afternoon. Or night. Especially night.

"The Hulk's going to be furious when he finds out he's lost us," she said. He could hear how pleased she was about that.

"Not as furious as LeBlanc's gonna be."

"You're sure he's the one who sent the Hulk?"

"Believe me, *chère*. I'm sure." And didn't he have the bruises to prove it?

"Is that your phone in your pocket," Kate drawled in a damn fine version of Mae West's comment to Cary Grant, as Nick's phone vibrated, "or are you just happy to see me?"

"A little of the first, a whole lot of the second."

He rolled a bit to his side, managed to squeeze his hand between them—which allowed him to cop an accidental but not unpleasant feel that had his gut tangling in a knot of sexual awareness—pulled his vibrating cell phone off his belt, and checked out the illuminated display.

"Hey, Remy." Not wanting to alert the Hulk, in case the thug was walking between the cars, searching for them, Nick kept his voice low, as close to a whisper as he could without giving his former partner cause to wonder what the hell was going on.

"Hey, Nick," the familiar voice said. "I've got some news for your client. Is she there?"

"Damn. We've got really bad reception here. Is it urgent? Or can I call you back when I get in better tower range?"

"Sure, it'll wait, but—"

"Thanks, *cher*. Talk to you in five."

Nick closed the phone.

"What is it?"

When that sexy breath in his ear had him wondering about the chances of a trunk quickie, Nick decided he was now not only in quicksand, he was on the verge of sinking in over his head.

"I don't know." He turned his head, putting them nose to nose. Tilting his head ever so slightly, he made it lips to lips. "He said he had news."

"Good or bad?"

God. Her breath was sweet from the sugary beignets she'd eaten. And warm. The thought of those sweet, silky lips on his body, moving down his chest, over his stomach, which was knotting even tighter at the fantasy, then lower still, taking him deep, nearly undid him.

"Didn't say."

He might be a SEAL. But he was also a man. A flesh-and-blood horny man who couldn't resist plucking at those amazing lips.

"Remy's always been one to hold his cards close to his chest, he."

Not wanting to accidentally leave the phone behind when they bailed, Nick managed to clip it back onto his belt. Which, speaking of chests, involved getting his hand between their bodies again.

When his fingers grazed her tightened nipples, he knew he wasn't the only one turned on.

"You know," he murmured as he circled her mouth with the tip of his tongue and drew forth a shuddering sigh, "this is one helluva lot more fun than the last time I climbed into a car trunk."

"So long as you're willing to overlook the risk of suffocating."

Even as the logical cop pointed out the practical downside, the sexy siren living inside the tidy, efficient body twined her arms around his neck. And began moving her hips in slow, insistent mind-blowing circles against his groin.

"This is crazy," she said.

"Hell, we're all born crazy, sugar. The trick is to stay that way."

Sweet bleeding Jesus. If she kept that up, his mind wasn't the only thing that was going to blow.

He knew he was playing with dynamite, but that didn't stop him from shoving his hands beneath her black jacket and down into the waistband of today's snug black slacks. How many pairs of these things did she have, anyway?

Nick decided it definitely said something about the inner woman that she could be so damn sexy while hiding her body behind that fugly suit.

On the other hand—and hey, wasn't there always another hand?—perhaps that all-cop-all-the-time camouflage had kept other, less observant guys from realizing that there was a living, breathing wet dream living inside all that black serge.

And, hot damn, weren't her panties just proof of that?

"You're wearing a thong." And didn't that news flash set every hot hormone in his body to singing the Hallelujah Chorus?

"It's not easy being a murder cop." She sounded a little dazed by the pheromones that were bouncing around the enclosed interior like crazed pinballs.

Join the club, sweetheart.

"Especially in the brawny, mustachioed world of CPD. It helps to have a secret reminder that I can be a woman and still do my job."

"Your secret's sure enough safe with me, sugar." He cupped a bare cheek in each hand. "But I gotta tell you, you're not going to find me complaining if whatever bra you've got on under that sweater matches these itsy-bitsy teensy-weensy panties."

"That's for me to know." She trailed the back of her fingers down his cheek, around his jaw. "And you to find out," she challenged saucily.

Nick had never been one to back away from a challenge. And he wasn't about to begin now.

Even if making out in a car trunk while a possible hired gun was out there looking for them was one of the riskiest damn things he'd ever done. Given his fifteen years pulling off clandestine missions in countries that the majority of Americans couldn't even pronounce, let alone find on a map, that was saying something.

Then again, it wasn't as if they had all that much else to do at the moment.

"Well, now, you know, I'd love to do just that." He placed a wet, openmouthed kiss against the warm, silky hollow of her throat and felt her pulse leap. "But the problem is, my hands just happen to be a little busy right now." He squeezed her butt to demonstrate his point.

"Oh. Well." She blew out a breath. Seemed to consider the matter. Then he felt her smile against his mouth. "Maybe I can help you out with that."

He nearly wept as she leaned back, breaking that glorious contact of her breasts plastered against his chest.

When she lifted the sweater, weeping was the farthest thing from his mind.

Hot damn. Her breasts gleamed like pearl; the delicate lace cupping them was cotton-candy pink, worlds away from the charcoal-gray sweater and funeral-black suit.

"Well, that answers the age-old question."

When she slowly, provocatively licked her lips, he nearly creamed his jeans.

"What question is that?" Damned if it wasn't a purr. From his murder cop! Talk about your still waters running wild and deep.

"There is, indeed, a God."

When a quick, pleased laugh burst out of her, she quickly covered her mouth with her hand. But the laughter still shone, star-bright, in her gaze.

"Flatterer," she accused.

"It's the truth. You are, hands down, the sexiest woman I've ever met."

Years of middle-of-the-night missions had his eyes accustomed to the dark. Even without night-vision goggles, Nick could see nearly as well in pitch-dark as he could in daylight.

Which was how he was able to tell the exact instant reality threatened to rear its ugly head.

She didn't say she didn't believe him. She didn't have to. The bright flame in her eyes flickered.

Hell. No way was he going to let it go out completely.

Nick wondered if that out-of-the-blue insecurity came from having grown up with Desiree and her grifter mother, whom Nick had never met. But if Antoinette St. Croix was anywhere near as outwardly sexual as her daughter—and the fact she'd gone to prison for pulling sweetheart cons suggested she probably was—that could have left Kate feeling like the family's ugly duckling. Which was, of course, flat out laughable.

But Nick understood how she might feel that way, having accepted a long time ago that his own rocky upbringing had left scars that didn't show on the outside. And although they never spoke about it, at least to him, he suspected the same could be said for his sisters.

As much as he would've happily kept both his hands on her silky-smooth, tight butt into the next millennium, Nick caught hold of her wrist with his left hand and pressed her hand against his chest.

"Feel that." His heart was beating like the rotors atop all those helos that devastated the beach with a pyrotechnic attack to a Wagner sound track in *Apocalypse Now.* "*You* do that to me. Whether you're wearing cop clothes, Victoria's Secret's scantiest, or nothing at all."

"You don't know what I look like without clothes on."

"Well, now, that's a situation I intend to rectify as soon as possible." He moved her hand lower, to his groin, where his cock was pressing painfully against the metal teeth of the zipper. "Meanwhile, check out what else you do to me."

"No one has ever talked to me this way before." Nick had to clench his teeth when her caressing touch moved slowly, wonderingly, over the throbbing erection that felt on the verge of tearing through the heavy denim. "Or made me feel this way."

"Are you saying . . ."

No. No way could a woman this hot be a virgin.

"Oh, I've had sex before," she said, validating his instincts.

Her sweater was still up, gathered at the crest of her breasts; when she shrugged, he said a silent prayer that it'd stay there.

Proving that God was on his side, at least for the moment, it did.

"And for the most part it's been okay, but not exactly a blow-the-top-of-your-head-off experience. More . . . well, you know. Something to do before going to sleep." Another shrug. "Like brushing your teeth."

He nearly laughed his disbelief but managed to keep it in, partly to avoid being overheard, but mostly to protect her feelings.

"Wow. Have *you* hooked up with the wrong guys."

"Tell me about it."

She had not taken her hand away. Nick was torn between fearing he'd have a meltdown if she didn't stop stroking him that way, and wanting her never to stop.

"My last lover was one of the detectives I testified against. He'd also been my partner on the task force for over a year. Needless to say, my getting involved in that federal investigation pretty much put a stop to that relationship."

"Yeah, Joseph Shinski. I read about him."

"When?"

"Last night. I Googled you," he admitted. "After you went to sleep." And he couldn't. "And before you start complaining about any perceived invasion of your privacy, I wanted to get a sense of the case. To see if any one of those cops was behind the shooting."

"That's a stretch."

"That's pretty much what I decided. But I don't think we should rule the possibility out."

"The cop in me agrees. The woman is creeped out by the idea. Anyway, the guy before Joe was a country songwriter. He wrote a song about me that George Strait almost recorded."

Almost being the definitive word, Nick thought.

"That was right before he left town. With my stereo, all my CDs, and my juicer."

"Your juicer?"

"He was on a raw-food diet."

"Well, hell, that was your mistake. Any guy who isn't

man enough to enjoy a bloody Angus ribeye couldn't begin to keep up with you."

Nick had never thought of himself as a possessive man. Since his work as a SEAL wasn't real conducive to long-term relationships, he fully expected the women he slept with to feel the same freedom to move on in the morning.

But for some reason he'd have to think about later, once he satisfied this sexual ache that was becoming more and more painful by the minute, he hated the idea of Kate being with any other man.

Oh, not in the past. That was then. This is now. And could he come up with any more clichés? The point was, those same instincts that had kept him alive for fifteen years in the military, and six months going undercover to find Big Antoine's murderer, were telling him that once he got the sweet-smelling, sexy Kate into bed, he wouldn't be in a hurry to let her go anytime soon.

Meanwhile, what would it hurt to give her a little taste of what he had in mind? Just to show her how worlds away it was going to be from brushing her teeth. All he'd have to do is move his hand from her curvy little butt around to—

Hell. Outside the trunk, the captain blew the boat's cacophonous horn, announcing the ferry's arrival back in New Orleans.

He sighed. Timing, always integral to any mission, was critical. And right now, it wasn't proving to be on his side.

27

DAMN, DAMN, DAMN! ALTHOUGH EVERY LOGICAL bone in her body was telling her that it would be the most outrageous, foolhardy thing she'd ever done, Kate had been on the brink of seeing exactly how far she could get Nick to take things.

Even as he withdrew his hand from her pants, he left heat behind. She could swear she could still feel the imprint of each of his fingers on her bottom.

Regretfully, she yanked her sweater back down. The bra he seemed so enamored with felt too tight, the lace scratchy against her ultrasensitive skin.

The fog, combined with the insulating properties of the BMW, kept Kate from hearing the passengers returning to their cars, but she could feel the motion as the doors opened and the owners of the car climbed into the interior. The doors closed with the same solid-sounding *thunk* the trunk lid had made.

"Get ready," Nick murmured against her ear. "It won't be long now."

"How long do you think it'll take the Hulk to realize we're gone?" she whispered.

"So long as the fog hasn't blown away while we've been in here, I'd say long enough for us to get off. Odds are he was in line behind us."

The motion of the ferry stopped, suggesting they'd reached the Canal Street terminal.

"What if he's waiting at the car for us to come back?"

"He might be. But here's the deal. Unless he's the very last car on, he's not going to be able to stand there and wait for us. People are usually more laid-back down here, but the aftermath of Katrina has created a lot of short-tempered folks."

The engine started up with a throaty purr. Nick had to raise his voice to be heard over it.

"Bad enough that our car's going to be holding them up; they're not going to be at all happy if a second car is abandoned and in their way. Someone on the crew will make him get in his car. If he doesn't want to cause a scene, which I'm suspecting he won't, he'll go ahead and try to get back on later and search the boat."

"How do we know he's alone?"

"We don't. But I didn't see any of the other guys who dragged me out into the swamp."

"They took you into the swamp?"

Apparently she found this more shocking than murder. She also slammed her mouth shut so hard he heard her teeth clunk together.

"Sorry," she murmured. "I didn't mean to be so loud.

It's just the idea of you being taken out there with all those poisonous snakes and alligators . . ."

He felt her shiver. And found himself enjoying the thought of her being concerned for him.

"You've been watching too many horror flicks," he said, smoothing her hair as the car began moving forward. "The swamp is a beautiful, delicate thing."

"I'm sure that's true."

She still sounded a bit doubtful, but he understood her fears. To most Americans, bayou country may as well exist on another planet.

"And I also understand about how everything serves a purpose, so I'm glad the alligators aren't endangered anymore," she said. "But I have to admit being in the camp that believes God created alligators and snakes so we could have great shoes."

That was one more thing he liked about her. Any woman who could keep her sense of humor when stuck in a dark car trunk, while being stalked by someone who might be trying to kill her, was his kind of woman.

Kate could feel when they'd left the ferry. Felt the BMW pick up speed as it headed down Canal Street, away from the terminal.

"There should be a light in a minute," Nick said. "Cross your fingers." He'd cracked the trunk lid to look out, and apparently the light was green, because the BMW didn't stop. Kate was just beginning to wonder how far it intended to go when it slowed. Then stopped.

Nick grabbed her and gave her a quick, hard kiss that ended far too soon.

"What was that for?" she asked as her head spun.

"Because, *chère*, you are one lucky charm." He went back to looking through the crack. "We're about to go into Harrah's parking garage."

"The casino?"

"Got it."

The car stopped. The engine was turned off. Doors opened and shut with a nice solid *thunk*. Then beeped as the alarm was set.

Kate could hear the excited voices and the clicks of heels on concrete as the gamblers headed off to the tables. Since their car had provided escape, she hoped the gamblers' luck would be as good as hers and Nick's had turned out to be.

They waited another few minutes, just in case someone had forgotten something and decided to come back.

Nick was the first out. Then, hoping someone else wouldn't come into the garage, she took his hand and let him help her out of the trunk.

Her legs wobbled a bit, as her foot had fallen asleep after being folded under her for so long, but it was a small price to pay for avoiding the Hulk.

"I assume you have a plan C?" she asked.

"Well, we could always borrow one of these cars."

"You mean steal?"

Only the fact that he was team poker champion allowed him to keep a straight face. Good-bye, adventurous Ms. Suck Face in a Thong. Hello, Detective Black and White.

And the really weird thing was that he was getting a kick out of both of them.

"We wouldn't keep it, if that's what you're inferring."

"Why don't we just take a cab?"

"And risk someone calling the dispatcher, looking for us? I don't think so."

"Not anyone can just call up and get that kind of information."

"A cop can. Dickhead Dubois, in particular."

Unsurprisingly, she didn't have a ready response for that. However, not willing to fold her hand, she tried a different tact.

"Stolen cars tend to be reported."

"Which is why we're going to switch the plates."

He stopped behind a shiny black SUV that was the car of choice of Hollywood A-listers, rappers, and sports stars. Hell, even Tony Soprano tooled around New Jersey in one. Which partly explained, Nick supposed, why the model always made the top-ten list of stolen cars.

"Please tell me you're joking."

"Avoiding being killed isn't exactly a joking matter."

He pulled a Swiss Army knife out of his pocket and opened it to the screwdriver. It took him about twenty seconds to get the Texas plate off. Which definitely suggested he needed to either get back to training or hang up his fins for good.

Then he went two rows over, found another Texas vehicle, this one a rusted-out beater, and replaced its plates with the SUV's.

"Okay," Kate said. "I'll give you points for picking the same state, but what if the driver happens to notice the tag number's not the same?"

"The odds are against that." He got the beater's plate back on in under fifteen seconds, which made him feel a bit better. "Do you know your number?"

"Of course."

Of course she would. "That's 'cause you're a cop. Most people don't ever look at their plates."

"I cannot believe I'm doing this," she muttered as she climbed into the passenger seat.

"Think of it as an adventure. Something to tell our grandkids."

Okay, now wasn't that a Freudian slip? He could feel her tense beside him and knew she'd caught it, too.

Deciding he'd only get himself in deeper if he tried to correct the statement, Nick got to work on the interior. Every model car was different. Some had the cover to the key ignition in the steering column, others behind the dash. After locating it, he used the Swiss Army knife screwdriver again to remove the switch the key operated.

Except now he didn't need the key.

"All right," she admitted. "I'm impressed. Still horrified to be a party to a car theft. But impressed."

"We aim to please. Fasten your seat belt." He pulled his own over his chest. "One thing we definitely don't need is getting stopped for a seat-belt violation."

They were just pulling out of the garage when a tow truck passed, heading in the direction of the ferry terminal.

"I'll bet that's picking up our old ride," he said.

"Probably. Won't they connect the car to you as soon as they run those plates?"

"That'd be hard to do. Given that I didn't rent it."

"Who did?"

"Martin Lamoreaux. An architect from Blue Bayou, Louisiana, up here in the big city, looking to get in on the reconstruction boom."

"Did the U.S. Navy teach you to lie? Or is it a natural-born talent?"

He could tell she was less than impressed. There were times, and this was one of them, that Nick felt as if he were on a mission with Jiminy Cricket.

"Tell you what," he said as the Escalade idled at a red light. "Next time I'm in some godforsaken armpit of a country where any American automatically has a big red bull's-eye on his back, I'll just explain that I'm a member of the United States of America armed forces, there to bring freedom and democracy to their fucking oppressed people. How's that?"

"You don't have to be sarcastic." Her voice was coated in enough ice to cover Jupiter several times over.

"Sorry. But it might help if you remember that you were the one who was shot at last night. The one whose sister just happens to be dead, whether by her own hands or . . . damn."

"What?"

"You got me so hot earlier, I forgot to call Remy back."

He reached for his phone. And without warning, the world exploded.

28

THE FIREBALL ROCKED THE SUV, THE EXPLO-
sion strong enough to nearly overturn the vehicle. The
resultant flash of light was so blindingly bright, Kate's
lids closed instinctively.

"Aw, shit," Nick groaned.

Kate opened her eyes as he scrubbed a hand down
his face.

"You don't think . . ."

Her voice broke off, trapped by the horribly painful
lump in her throat, as she turned and looked out the
rear window to see a towering plume of smoke rising
from the ferry terminal.

"Yeah," he said grimly, "I suspect that was meant
for us."

"Oh, my God."

She was a cop. Although she'd never fired her gun
anywhere but the police range, she'd seen death. Up
close and personal.

But this was too up close. And way too personal.

"There would've been people on the boat."

"Some," he conceded. "But not as many as there might have been. They probably didn't let anyone board until they got the car off, so it would've been just the crew."

"*Just* the crew? We have to go see if we can help."

"Dammit, Kate—"

"We both have EMT training. If people are injured, it's our moral responsibility."

"Even if it means getting killed? What if the guy stayed around to witness his handiwork?"

"He probably did. But if he was willing to shoot us in public, he could've done it on the ferry. We need to help."

"Hell." Instead of continuing away from the river, Nick made a U-turn as sirens began screaming. "This is so not a good idea."

It could have been worse. Thanks to the rain, those walk-on passengers forced to bide their time until the car could be moved off the ferry were waiting inside the terminal, which had protected them from flying glass and pieces of steel.

Drivers and passengers had gotten out of the cars waiting in line and were staring at the ferry with unified expressions of disbelief.

Kate breathed a sigh of relief as she viewed the tow truck still waiting to be brought on board. And on the deck, three men clad in rain gear were spraying foam at the blazing hunk of steel.

"I don't think they need us," Nick said as they cruised slowly by the scene.

"No. It appears not. Everyone certainly seems calm."

"I suspect if we'd been here fifteen months ago, we'd have seen an entirely different reaction. My guess is that those folks who've had to deal with the hurricane and the aftermath have probably developed a fatalistic view of life."

"I suppose so." She thought about that. "Have you seen that behavior before? In war zones?"

"And during natural disasters, yeah." The sirens were getting closer. "Are you satisfied?"

"I suppose so." She leaned back against the leather seat and willed her heart to settle to something resembling a normal rhythm. "He could have killed so many people."

"Unintentionally. There's no way he could have known the car would be left on the ferry. And there was no point in blowing it up if we weren't in it."

"He could've been trying to send a message."

"If he wanted to send a message, he would've called Western fucking Union. No, the bastard made that bomb to kill. It was probably on a timer set up to allow for the boat's docking, because if he blew it up while it was out on the river, he'd go up, too."

"I don't understand." She was starting to put the pieces together, but there was one niggling piece that didn't quite fit. "Why would anyone go to such lengths to kill me? If he's the same person who killed Tara, she must have been involved in something really serious."

While taking her shower that morning, Kate had wondered if her sister could have been killed by a lover.

After all, boyfriends and husbands were the first suspects police always looked at. For a reason. Because they were, more often than not, the guilty parties.

Then she'd wondered if Tara could have been killed by her pimp. Heaven knows, if she'd stayed true to form, it would not be a great stretch to believe she'd been holding back money. And Kate had certainly seen prostitutes killed for less reason than that.

She also could have been doing tricks on the side in her apartment. Which, again, wouldn't have been real popular with her pimp. But it also could've put her at risk with some whacked-out john.

As a black-and-white police car screamed past them on the way to the terminal, followed by a fire truck, the missing piece clicked into place.

"You know, don't you?"

"Know what?"

"Why Tara was killed."

She'd expected him to lie. Once again he surprised her.

"I have an idea. But nothing concrete."

She folded her arms, welcoming the irritation that steamrollered her earlier horror. "And you were going to share your idea with me when?"

"Later."

"Anytime in this decade?"

He shot her a look. "Anyone ever tell you that you're kind of sexy when you get sarcastic, *chère?*"

"No. But that may be because not every man has sex on the brain."

"Sounds as if some guys need to prioritize. And yeah, I was going to tell you last night. But you looked wiped out. So I figured it could wait. Then I was going to tell you on the ferry, but the Hulk showed up."

"So you figured it could wait."

"Until after we got off that boat in one piece, *mais*, yeah." He glanced up in the rearview mirror. "I had every intention of telling you tonight."

"Why don't you tell me now?"

"Because right now I have to call Remy. Because I doubt he was calling just to shoot the breeze."

Without giving her a chance to argue, he pulled the phone off his belt and thumbed in the auto-dial.

"Hey, *cher*. So, what's up?"

Nick Broussard was the best she'd ever seen at hiding his thoughts. But she was pretty good at watching for tells, too. And it was only because she was watching him so carefully that Kate caught the slight lift of his dark brow.

"Okay. Yeah, I'll tell her. I'm sure she'll want to be there."

"Where will I want to be?" she asked as he snapped the phone closed.

"Your *maman*'s house."

"She's back?" Kate couldn't decide if she was glad about that or not.

"So it seems." He thrust a hand through his hair, looking, for the first time since she'd met him, uncomfortable. "There's something else."

"They've got Tara's autopsy report back," she guessed.

"Not yet. Remy said they're pushing the doc and they're hopeful they'll be getting it sometime late afternoon. Tomorrow morning, latest."

"Then what is it?"

"They picked up your shooter."

"You're kidding." Having witnessed the condition of the city, she'd had the feeling last night's attack was destined to get buried in some file cabinet, never to be looked at again. "Who?"

"Oh, the guy who actually pulled it off was just some low-level wiseguy. But the thing is, he was professional muscle."

"So who hired him?"

"You're not going to like this answer."

"News flash, Broussard. I don't like getting shot at, either. So why don't you fill me in? Or do I have to call Detective Landreaux myself?"

"Okay. According to this guy, and it hasn't checked out yet, but it would be unlikely for him to have been able to just pull the name out of a hat, the guy who paid him a thousand bucks up front, with another fifteen hundred to be paid when the job was done, was Joseph Shinski."

29

"JOSEPH SHINSKI?"

My Joe? Kate was glad she was sitting down. Because the shock was so great, she wasn't sure her legs would have held her.

"Apparently so. Seems you weren't exaggerating when you said you had lousy taste in men. Present company excluded, that is."

"Is Detective Landreaux positive? I mean, I know Joe was furious at me, but to hire a killer—"

"Is extreme," he said. "But not impossible. Hell, you just happen to be in the city that got its nickname, the Big Sleazy, the old-fashioned way. By earning it.

"In fact, there was a really bad period of time from '92 to '95 when no less than sixty NOPD cops were charged with a variety of crimes. One female cop even landed in prison for the murder of another cop in the strong-armed robbery of a local restaurant."

"But how would Joe even know how to find anyone like that here?" As soon as she heard the words leave her mouth, Kate knew how naive they sounded. "I guess it's not that difficult for one crooked cop to locate another."

"They're like a fraternity."

"Sounds as if you know a lot about the subject."

Including the statistics, which she found a little strange. Then again, the city's police department's bad behavior had been all over the news after Katrina; it wasn't impossible to believe that those statistics he'd just cited had been reported by local media.

"It's not exactly a secret," he said, confirming her thoughts.

"So, are they going to arrest Joe?"

"Like I said, according to Remy, they haven't finished checking it out yet. Obviously they're trying to keep the investigation low-key, because they don't want word to get out to Shinski so he can take off, but he expects the guy to be picked up in the next day or so."

"That is so hard to believe."

Her hand was not as steady as she would have liked. In fact, it was shaking like a damn leaf as she lifted her fingers to her temple, where a killer headache was threatening to blow off the top of her head.

"Like I said, I know Joe was furious at me, but—"

"Furious enough to threaten to kill you?"

"It was just his temper talking."

I could fucking kill you, bitch, was actually what he'd said. But Kate didn't feel Nick needed to hear the details.

"You said, and some of the articles written about the case stated, you got other death threats."

"Yes. I did. But I would have recognized Joe's voice."

"Doesn't mean he wasn't in on it. Or maybe he was working on his own, and paying some other guys to make the calls from throwaway phones."

The same way he'd allegedly paid that motorcyclist to shoot her? Kate wondered.

"I suppose anything's possible," she said glumly. "And you know, as ridiculous as it sounds, I can't decide what's pissing me off more. Getting shot at. Or having been stupid enough to sleep with a guy who's now trying to kill me."

"You made a mistake." Nick shrugged. "So did he. The difference is, you're going to get on with your life. He will, too. But his life for the next several years will be behind bars. In solitary confinement in a maximum-security prison."

Just when she thought things couldn't get any worse, Nick proved her wrong.

"There's something else."

"Yeah, I know. My mother. And as much as I'm so not looking forward to it, I appreciate your former partner letting me be there when he questions her."

"Makes sense, since as a grifter, she's made a life-time career of lying, and even though you've been apart for a lot of years, there's a good chance you're still a lot better at reading her tells than Remy, who's never met her, will be."

"She's especially good with men," Kate confirmed. "Or at least she used to be."

"That's what I figured, given those sweetheart cons.

But I wasn't talking about her. I meant there's something I need to tell you about the Hulk."

"What about him?"

"I'm pretty sure he was after me."

"I believe we've determined that."

"Yeah. But here's the thing."

He shoved a hand through his hair. He was clearly uncomfortable. Which, Kate suspected, was a first for him.

"I'm not positive, since I've got a few irons in LeBlanc's fire, but I'm guessing he sent his goon to kill me because of your sister's and my relationship."

Tara was wiping off the countertop after lunch when Father What-A-Waste, aka Father Michael Xavier Gannon, aka Father Mike, came into the kitchen.

"That was a great meal," he told her. "Best crab cakes I've ever had. And bein' from South Carolina's Lowcountry, I've tasted a lot of crab cakes."

"The breading probably made it too heavy on the carbs." She wrung the dishrag out and hung it over the faucet to dry. "And the pie would've been better if I'd had real key limes, instead of the ordinary store-bought ones." She shrugged. "But you've got to work with what you've got."

"And isn't that the case?"

He turned a wooden ladder-back chair around and straddled it. "I appreciate you taking over the cooking."

"It's no problem. It makes me feel good to be useful."

That was the first absolutely truthful thing she'd told

him since arriving here the night Kels had been killed. She'd always loved to cook, having taught herself out of necessity. Kate, who'd never been the slightest bit domestic, could've happily existed on cornflakes three times a day.

As for their mother, well, Antoinette had always had a great many more important fish to fry.

"Well, everyone else is a lot happier, since most of the time they were stuck with me, and my culinary skills mostly consist of spaghetti with jar sauce and peanut butter sandwiches."

"Yeah. I saw all those jars. If another hurricane shows up, you're pretty much prepared to ride it out on PB&J."

"As I said, while I have many talents, cooking isn't one of them."

His grin was quick and warm and, dammit, as unconsciously sexy as hell. In fact, it was partly that he didn't seem to have any idea of the effect it had on women that made it so fucking sexy.

Father Mike was, hands down, the best-looking man Tara had ever met. And considering how many men . . .

Don't go there.

Anyway, this priest named for an archangel brought to mind a fallen angel, one who might have washed off the ceiling of St. Louis Cathedral. Lush black hair framed a narrow, aesthetic face; his eyes, set above high, slashing cheekbones, were a riveting, intense, almost neon blue, and his beautifully sculptured lips had been designed to tempt both sinner and saint.

Technically, Tara had no proof about his appeal to saints. But she could definitely, categorically state that he was damn tempting to this sinner.

"Anyway, that got me thinking," he said. "I have this friend, Chelsea Lamoreaux, who owns a restaurant over on Royal."

"Good for her."

She'd heard of Chelsea Lamoreaux. Who hadn't? Not only was the blonde drop-dead gorgeous, she was part of New Orleans society, one of those blonde Garden District trust-fund bitches who were obviously all frigid, if the fact that so many of their husbands were willing to pay Tara for sex was any indication.

Not that she'd met Mr. Lamoreaux. But just because he didn't appear to dip his wick away from home and hearth didn't mean that his wife wasn't like all the others.

"What with so many workers scattered after Katrina, she's been shorthanded."

"Lot of that going around."

"I was thinking that as much as I'd hate to lose you, St. Jude's is, after all, meant to be a temporary solution. To give women and children a chance to get back on their feet."

"And I appreciate it, Padre."

"Well." His smile lit up his eyes like sunshine on a mountain lake. "Now that we seem to have a mutual appreciation society going, what do you think?"

That you're absolutely delicious and if I hadn't already given my heart to Toussaint Jannise, I could eat you up with a spoon. That's what I'm thinking.

"About what?"

"She's desperate for a dinner chef. She's been doing all the cooking herself, which pretty much has her working from dawn to nearly midnight, which is not the best thing for her little girls."

Tara remembered seeing the Lamoreaux girls' first communion picture in the paper a few months ago. Though she normally didn't have any interest in kids, the fact that they were twins had captured her attention and made her think about how much she missed Kate.

Their dresses had been white lace, covered with seed pearls, and with their tulle veils they'd looked like miniature brides. They were smiling at the camera as if they didn't have a care in the world, which they probably didn't.

Tara had fucking hated them.

"Life's a bitch"—she slammed the cupboard door a little too hard after putting away the salt and pepper—"and then you die."

"Well, that's a pessimistic view."

"Maybe you ought to come down from your fucking celibate religious ivory tower and look around once in a while, Padre," Tara said in a flare of temper. "There's not a whole helluva lot to be optimistic about out there."

"You're a glass-half-empty person, then."

"Now, see, that's where you're wrong." She leaned back against the counter and folded her arms over her heavily padded chest. "I'm a glass-bone-dry girl."

"And isn't that a shame?" Was that compassion in his

gaze? Or pity? Whichever, she hated it. Just like she hated him. "Because you deserve far better."

He stood up, turned the chair around, and slid it back under the table. Then dug deep into the pocket of his faded jeans and pulled out a slip of paper, which he held out to her.

When she continued to stand there, her face an expressionless mask she'd learned to wear early in life, he reached out, took her hand, pressed the paper into it, then folded her fingers to hold it tight.

"There's her number. Like I said, she's there most of the time and is waiting to hear from you.

"Give it some thought," he said mildly. "I think if you quit beating up on yourself and give yourself the break you—we all—are entitled to, you'll see that it's a win-win situation for both you and Chelsea.

"And if you're worried about her being one of those icy, stick-up-the-ass, judgmental society types, you're wrong. Because not only did she establish this shelter, and continues to fund it—"

"Takes a lot of work to write out a tax-deductible check," Tara muttered. And was a Catholic priest even allowed to say *ass*?

"That tax-deductible check helped give you a place to crash when you're obviously running away from something—"

"I am not running away."

"Let me finish."

The whip crack of authority in his voice surprised Tara. She opened her mouth to challenge him, but the sudden blue heat crackling in those Paul Newman eyes had her shutting it again. No one but Stephen LeBlanc had ever talked to her that way. And his sharp words were usually accompanied by his fists.

"Chelsea was born rich, true enough. But that's no more reason to hate her than it is to hate others for being born poor. Or black. Or gay. The point is, she could just spend all her time shopping and getting her nails done and jetting off to Saint-Tropez. But instead, she views her wealth as an obligation.

"Which is why, the first year St. Jude's was open, I've been told she was here every day. All day. Cooking, painting, just listening to women's stories and letting them know she cared.

"She has also, by working the phones and through her network of equally wealthy friends, single-handedly managed to place more of our residents in livable wage jobs and homes around the city than most of the local charities combined.

"So, give it some thought. Some real, serious thought, and try not to let your pride and whatever other reason you have for beating up on yourself get in the way. Because it's obvious that if your life were going all that well, you wouldn't be here.

"Maybe this is your chance to turn things around. Give her a call," he repeated. "Give yourself a chance."

He left the room, stopping in the doorway. Then glanced back over his shoulder.

"And if you do decide to go for an interview, dump all that damn fake padding. It looks ridiculous, and if you think it's keeping men from looking at your body, you're flat out wrong. Because all it does is make a man wonder what the hell you look like under those ugly Salvation Army clothes."

With that he was gone, leaving a thunderstruck Tara to stare after him.

30

"I THOUGHT YOU SAID YOU DIDN'T SLEEP WITH my sister."

"I didn't."

"But you had a relationship?"

"Yeah." He sighed. Could this situation get any stickier? "Not every relationship is about sex. Even those involving sex for sale. She was my CI."

Silence settled over the SUV, broken only by the swish of the wipers across the windshield and the sound of the rain hitting the metal roof. Nick could practically hear the wheels turning as she processed that information.

"Being a confidential informant can be dangerous," she said finally.

"That's why we try to keep them confidential."

"I'm well aware of that." Her voice had an edge to it, revealing a simmering temper. Her breasts, beneath that gray cashmere sweater, rose and fell as she drew in a deep, calming breath. "You were investigating her boss?"

"LeBlanc and his kid. The one I told you about who

runs the ship operations on a day-to-day basis? The night Desiree—Tara—was killed, Leon had his goons drag me off *The Hoo-yah*, throw me in a boat, and take me out to this camp he's got hidden in the bayou. That's when he hired me to find her."

"Why would you need to find her?"

"Because she'd gone missing. He said she had something of his. He wanted it back."

"Something he was willing to kill for?"

"Maybe."

She shot him a look. "What do you mean *maybe*? He tells you that he wants you to find my sister because she took—which is undoubtedly a euphemism for *stole*—something of his. You said yourself that the man's a gangster. A guy used to settling problems with violence. Who sent the Hulk to beat you up."

"As soon as I found out she was dead, I went to LeBlanc's fancy high-rise office in the CBD. He insisted he had nothing to do with her taking that dive out the window. Which doesn't mean he wouldn't lie, but I got the feeling he was telling the truth.

"And while I hate to give him credit for anything, I don't think the bruises are his fault. I got the impression the Hulk was doing a little freelancing on his own time."

"Why?"

Nick rubbed his bruised jaw. "I guess, just maybe, it could've been something I said."

"And that something would be?"

"Well, some events of that night are a little foggy,

given I'd been drinking and they kind of rang my bell, so I've got some residual memory loss, but I seem to recall asking the Hulk what, as an alien outsider, he thought of the human race."

"Wow. Smart move, Broussard."

"Hey." Nick shrugged. "Who'd guess that a guy who makes his living as an enforcer would have such thin skin?"

"And now yours is a Technicolor shade of yellow, purple, and blue, with just a lovely shading of green." She brushed a finger over the bruises. "You're lucky he didn't throw you overboard to the gators."

"Don't think he didn't threaten. But that's my point. If he didn't kill me earlier this week, why would he want to now?"

"Maybe because of what you know about the case? Which you still haven't told me?"

"That's because I honestly don't know what Tara was up to. All she told me was that she had some videotape that was going to make her a fortune. She was going to auction it off to the highest bidder."

"Expecting LeBlanc to be one of the bidders?"

"That'd be my guess. Another guess would be that what was pissing him off so bad was that the tape belonged to him in the first place."

"A tape of her having sex with some big shot, do you suppose?"

"Works for me."

Especially after Nick had seen the still shots, which looked to be taken from a video of him and Tara, and realized that he'd been taped, as well. Obviously that night he'd gone to her apartment in response to a call that she just had to see him. He hadn't been there two minutes when she'd started climbing all over him.

Nick still hadn't figured out whether Tara had been in on that con. Or whether LeBlanc had gotten that camera into her apartment without her knowledge, just to keep tabs on her.

"Do you think they were also running a blackmail con?" she asked. "Get some footage of a visiting bank president, Joe Blow from Podunk, Idaho, screwing a hooker, then offer to sell it to him as a vacation souvenir?"

"So as not to embarrass himself at the bank, or risk Mrs. Blow divorcing him and taking all the community property and IRAs?" he asked. "Yeah, I'd say that was a good possibility. But the thing is, the guy would have to be a pretty big fish, because down in this part of the country, getting caught screwing a beautiful girl, even if she was a pro, wouldn't be any big deal.

"In fact, if a New Orleans banker proved himself in the video to be a studly swordsman, he might just raise his local profile several points down at the club."

"Just good old southern boys having fun," she muttered.

"Hey, I'm not saying I feel that way. I'm just sayin' some people do."

"I know." She made a derisive sound. "It's not that different back in Chicago."

Although she was proving herself tough as nails, and

earning his admiration as well as his lust, Nick knew all this had to be hard on her. Having been a cop all those years—and a damn good one with some commendations to boot, according to the articles he'd unearthed on the web last night—she'd be accustomed to death, even when it involved murder and mayhem.

But it was different when it involved family. Even family you had managed to convince yourself you'd made a clean break with. Because, as he'd discovered himself the hard way, no matter how you fought against them, blood ties could be chains that you were forced to drag through life.

He'd never liked his father. Maybe if he'd met him before the war, things might've turned out different. Maybe not. Maybe his *maman* had just been trying to put a pretty spin on a marriage that should've been declared dead at the altar.

Or even before, when that rabbit had died, which had resulted in the shotgun marriage in the first place.

There were times over the years when Nick had tried to give Big Antoine some credit for having married the sweet and pretty girl he'd gotten pregnant in the backseat of his Dodge Charger that hot summer night they were parked out on Bayou St. John.

He'd wondered if frustration at the prospect of spending the rest of his life with a girl he'd only been on three dates with might have made his father resentful and angry.

But that was just another paper tiger of an excuse.

Same as Vietnam.

The probability was that Big Antoine had been a son of a bitch before the war and an even bigger one afterward.

He was a wife batterer, a bully, a drunk, and a crook.

But none of those things were death-penalty offenses.

He was also blood.

And blood stood for blood. If not, who the hell would?

He reached over and took hold of her tense, cold left hand.

And wow, wasn't she having herself a dandy visit to Mardi Gras? Maybe after they dragged her through the emotional stress of meeting with her convicted-felon mother—who may or may not have been involved in the near fatal accident suffered by her much older, very wealthy husband—they could stop by the tourist bureau and give them a quote for the city's new PR blitz about how much fun there was to be had here in the Big Easy.

He wanted to tell her not to be so hard on herself. That she wasn't responsible for the entire fucking world. She wasn't even responsible for her sister or her mother.

But he knew his words would ring false. Because they always did whenever he tried telling himself the same thing.

"We're going to get him, *chère*." He squeezed her hand reassuringly. "Whoever killed your sister. We're going to nail his balls to the jailhouse door."

Her eyes were tired, a little red-rimmed, and showed the strain she'd been under since long before she showed up on his dock. The earlier adrenaline rush from the ferry and the car bomb was wearing off, and he could recognize the signs of fatigue settling back over her like a wet blanket.

The lady had been on one helluva roller coaster. Unfortunately, he feared it was going to get worse before it got better.

She managed a smile. It wasn't as bright or as sassy as some she'd shared. But it still had the effect of making his heart roll over in his chest.

The fact that he'd been semihard for the past twenty-four hours didn't surprise Nick. He'd been attracted to her since she'd shown up at his dock.

What he wasn't used to was the effect Kate Delaney was having on his heart.

She touched something in him. Something he hadn't even known existed.

And dammit if it wasn't scaring the big bad SEAL more than a nest of al-Qaeda terrorists.

31

IT HAD ONLY BEEN TWENTY-FOUR HOURS SINCE her plane had landed at New Orleans's Louis Armstrong Airport. But it seemed she'd been in the city at least a week. Kate couldn't remember being so exhausted at any other time in her life. Not even during that hot summer six years ago when she and her partner had been parked out night after night, staking out a guy they were convinced was the Miracle Mile Murderer, a serial killer who'd been raping and killing real estate agents who showed pricey apartments.

They'd eventually caught him. But she'd gone into serious sleep deprivation and it had taken her two weeks to get her body back on track.

And even then, she hadn't felt as drained as she did right now.

Yet strangely, at the same time her brain was crashing, other parts of her body were all too vividly alive.

"What time are we supposed to meet Landreaux?" she asked.

"He said three."

"Are we going to the station?"

"*Non*. Your *maman*'s holding court at her house. Remy said something about having tea."

Kate merely rolled her eyes. There was nothing she could say to that. Obviously her mother was currently playing the role of lady of the manor.

"Did he mention how her husband's doing?"

"Yeah. He's on the mend. The doc said if all's well, he can probably go home next week."

Dealing with Antoinette was difficult in the best of circumstances. Dealing with her mother under a possible murder indictment would probably be the straw that'd break the camel's back.

"Has Landreaux gotten a chance to interview him yet about what happened?"

"He tried this morning." They'd reached the marina. Nick parked and they began walking toward the dock. "Apparently the guy can't remember a thing."

"Convenient," Kate muttered.

"Yeah, that's pretty much what Remy thought. Me, too, though, like I said, I still have some gaps about what happened the other night. Maybe they'll come back. Maybe they won't. Maybe St. Croix's will, too."

"And maybe he's merely protecting his wife."

"I've seen crazier things happen," he said as they boarded the boat and went belowdecks. "You hungry?"

Amazing. Just looking at him looking at her that way, as if he'd been starving all his life and she was a whiskey-sauced bread pudding, was enough to cause a surge of lust to curl low in her abdomen, pool hot and wet between her legs, and make her breasts feel all tingly again, the same way they had felt back in the trunk.

"You've no idea."

His laugh was rough, ragged as he pushed some tumbled hair away from her face. "You really are stunning."

A thought, unbidden, and decidely unwanted, flashed through her mind. "So was Tara."

"True enough, I suppose." He bent closer. His lips touched hers, plucking enticingly. "But she was more plastic. Literally. Like a life-size Barbie-doll version of a real woman."

Her lips were tingling beneath his mouth. That now familiar cloud was drifting over her mind even as she tried to focus on what he'd just said.

"We were identical."

"Not recently." He traced her lower lip with the tip of his tongue.

She pulled away. "She'd had plastic surgery?"

"Yeah." He spread his fingers against the back of her head and coaxed her lips back to his. "I thought I'd told you."

"No," she moaned as his hands moved over her shoulders and down her back, settling on her hips.

He pulled her closer, pressing her intimately against his chest, his thighs, his stony erection.

"It's sort of a branding thing the casino has." His deft, clever fingers unfastened the gold clasp at the nape of her neck. Then tangled in the hair he'd released. "All the girls get work done so the high rollers can fantasize doing movie stars. Your sister was pretty much a dead ringer for Nicole Kidman. And do we have to talk about this right now?"

"No." Even as the heat radiating from his body was making her dizzy, Kate moved against him, spreading the warmth.

"Good."

He thrust both his hands into her hair. Instead of the quick, hot ravishment she'd been expecting, he seemed content to merely nibble at her lips forever.

If he was trying to sexually frustrate her, he was succeeding.

If he was trying to kiss her senseless, it was working.

"Nick." Her arms wrapped around him, her hands fretting up and down his back as her lower body moved restlessly, insistently against his. Didn't he realize she was burning from the inside out? "Please."

She couldn't recognize her own voice, which was so hoarse and ragged with need that it could have belonged to a stranger.

"You're in the South now, *chère.*"

Seeming determined to set the pace, he kissed her forehead. Her cheeks. The bridge of her nose. Her chin.

It was the same thing he'd done when he'd kissed her senseless in the BMW. "I don't know how those Yankees make love to a woman." His lips skimmed a trail of fire along her jaw, tasting, teasing before returning to her lips.

"But you're in the Big Easy now. We—"

"Do things differently here." Her whimper of feminine acceptance melded with his deep growl of masculine need as his tongue accepted the invitation of her parted lips.

"Exactly." His teeth closed over her earlobe, his hands slid beneath the sweater to stroke her body. Exploring. Possessing.

Her breath grew ragged. So did his as he returned to her mouth to kiss her slowly, deeply, using his lips, his teeth, his tongue, until she was sure she'd melt into a pitiful puddle of hot need.

"Tell me what you want, sugar."

He cupped the weight of a breast in his hand. Tugged the lace cup down. When he scraped a work-roughened pad of his thumb against a nipple, her body arched upward, offering more.

"You." The ragged word was half plea, half demand. "I want you."

He drew his head back and flashed her a swift, wickedly carnal smile.

"Sweetheart, I thought you'd never ask."

Kate felt a sharp sense of loss as he took his hand from beneath her sweater and shaped her shoulders.

"Problem is, you're wearing too many clothes."

"So are you."

Wanting to drive him as crazy as he was driving her, Kate skimmed a fingernail down the front of his jeans and experienced a delicious thrill when she felt his penis grow even thicker, longer beneath her touch.

"Let's take care of that." He pushed her suit jacket off

her shoulders and down her arms, letting it fall to the floor. "I think you ought to give some serious thought to burning that, *chère*," he suggested as he kicked it aside. "I can't decide whether it reminds me of a prison guard or a nun. Or maybe a guard in a convent."

"Well, that's flattering."

"I said the *outfit* is ugly. You, on the other hand, are sex personified. Hell, darlin'—lift up your arms, okay? so we can get this sweater off you—if it'd been up to me, I would've had you in my bed two seconds after you showed up at *The Hoo-yah*."

He caught the bottom of her sweater and pulled it up over her stomach, her breasts, her head.

"Hot damn," he breathed as his hot and hungry gaze nearly scorched the scrap of lace bra. "As good as you looked in the dark, you are fucking fantabulous in the light of day."

"You're not so bad yourself, sailor," she said. "But I want to see more."

He'd taken his jacket off and tossed it onto a chair as they'd entered the salon. Now she tugged his sweatshirt off, allowing flesh to meet flesh.

"My turn." He unhooked her slacks, sent them sliding down her legs to pool on the floor. Then nudged her down onto the leather couch so he could take off her shoes.

He skimmed a finger up the inside of her thigh. "So lovely."

Excitement crackled up her skin like flash fire. When she unconsciously fisted her hand, Nick slowly uncurled her fingers and pressed her palm against his chest.

"Feel what you do to me, darlin'."

His heart was pounding like a jackhammer.

Enthralled that she could elicit such a response from him, Kate slid her hand down his rib cage, exploring this phenomenon further.

When she bent her head and pressed her mouth against his hard, flat stomach, she felt the muscles clench.

She unzipped his jeans, freeing his penis. He was hard as marble, but much, much warmer. Kate tested his weight and thickness and felt the tumescent flesh stir beneath her stroking touch.

Feeling a surge of feminine satisfaction that she was responsible for such obvious desire, she bent her head and touched her lips to the smooth, straining tip.

He bucked beneath her intimate kiss, a growl rumbling deep in his throat. Encouraged, she ran her tongue along its length and was about to take him fully, deeply into her mouth when he fisted his hand in her hair and lifted her head.

"If you keep that up, we'll end this in about ten seconds flat."

"I wouldn't mind."

Her fingers continued to stroke him as her eyes offered him a blatant feminine dare. Kate wanted him. Now.

"Well, now, darlin', I'm real sorry about that."

He grabbed both her wrists in one hand and pushed her gently back against the arm of the couch, holding her hands together above her head. "Because I want to take my time."

She squirmed beneath his restraint. Her blood warmed. "Do you always get everything you want?"

He flashed a rakish, pirate's grin. "Today I do."

Lying down beside her, he trailed his hands down her naked flesh, fondling her aching breasts, scraping a thumbnail over her nipples, creating a spiral of warmth down her spine.

After her body had warmed to nearly the boiling point, he continued his sensual torment by trailing his mouth over the fiery trail his hands had blazed.

He sucked on her nipples with a hot, hungry greed, creating a primal pull deep in her feminine core. He bit her shoulder, nipped at the tender cord in her neck, then closed his teeth around an earlobe and tugged.

He kissed her stomach. The sensitive hollow between her pelvic bones. Tugged the tiny thong panties down her legs, then created a hot, wet path through the nest of bright curls between her thighs with his tongue.

All the time she writhed restlessly beneath his erotic touch.

When his lips plucked at the source of all that moist heat, her body bucked, arching unashamedly.

"Please."

Kate knew she was begging. But felt neither embarrassment nor shame. Her clitoris was swollen, throbbing with need. The wild, out-of-control trip-hammer beat of her heart was echoed between her legs.

"Nick." Her voice was half gasp. Half sob. "Hurry."

But still he took his time. She tossed her head back and forth as his tongue slipped into her and his teeth began nibbling on ultrasensitive flesh.

"Please," she moaned again, "hurry."

"Don't worry, *chère*. We'll get there." He put his hands beneath her bottom, lifting her hips, pressing her harder against his mouth as he feasted on the hot juices flowing from her.

The pleasure/pain continued, spiraling into a tighter and tighter coil. Just when Kate thought she couldn't take any more, he replaced his tongue with first one finger, then two, reaching deep inside her, stretching her, rasping delicate inner tissues with clever strokes.

He covered her mouth with his, allowing her to taste herself on his lips. Then held her tightly against him, his tongue tangling with hers inside the moist cavern of her mouth as his hand moved between them, his thumb parting the sensitive pink flesh, searching for the hard nub above her vaginal lips.

When he found it, he pressed down. Hard. At the same time, his fingers thrust even deeper. Harder. Faster.

Kate cried out his name as she came.

Nick held her, kissing her lightly, soothingly as her shattering orgasm slowly ebbed.

She was limp. Boneless. The boat could have been on fire and she wouldn't have been able to move from this spot.

"Oh, my God," she managed to gasp. "I think this is where I tell you that I've never, ever felt that way before."

"Well, hang on, darling. Because that was just the

beginning." He touched his smiling mouth to hers. "A little something to take the edge off."

Proving himself true to his word, he took her higher, bringing her to climax again and again, until Kate would have sworn she had nothing left to give.

And even then he proved her wrong.

Nick finally claimed ultimate possession, surging into her, and although she would have thought it impossible, as she tightened around him, drawing him deeper, Kate felt him grow even larger. Harder.

He called out her name and went rigid, his back arched, the muscles of his neck standing out in stark relief. She felt the convulsions deep inside her at the same time she gave in to yet another, stronger release of her own.

Groaning, Nick collapsed onto her. When he would have pulled out, Kate wrapped her arms around his back and her legs around his thighs, unwilling to surrender the glorious feel of him deep inside her.

His lips were pressed against her damp hair and he was murmuring soft words she didn't need to speak French to understand.

32

ANTOINETTE ST. CROIX LIVED ON AUDUBON Place, the most exclusive street in the leafy-green environs of New Orleans's Uptown area, where the movers and shakers, many of whom could trace their roots back to the 1700s, dwelt in mostly isolated splendor.

"Your *maman* definitely landed in some tall cotton, she," Nick said after giving his name to the uniformed watchman in the guardhouse. "Right after Katrina, most of the houses around here, which didn't get flooded, bein' as they're on high ground, had private former special-ops guys guarding them. One owner even heloed in an Israeli team made up of former Mossad officers."

"This can't be good," Kate said as the heavy iron gate rumbled open.

"Maybe she married for love."

"Right."

"Sounds like you don't believe in it."

"For some people. But my mother already has a lifelong love affair going. With herself."

"People can change."

Kate snorted. "Yeah, right. Just wait until you meet her. Then let me know what you think."

Unlike the charming Creole houses crowding the sidewalk in the French Quarter, the mansions of Audubon Place were set far back from the street. Partly, Kate suspected, for privacy, and partly to show off the professional landscaping.

Nick parked behind his partner's beige Crown Vic, which couldn't have looked any more like a police vehicle if it had neon signs plastered to the doors, flashing "Attention Criminals! Unmarked Cop Car!"

The large, three-story Greek Revival house was constructed of white stucco-covered brick, its facade shining like alabaster in the gleaming late-afternoon sun.

A raised parapet created an effect of even greater height while ten massive, three-story-tall Ionic columns supported the great roof.

On either side of the main structure were two-story wings that duplicated the mansion's architectural style, while a white wrought-iron fence surrounded a lushly manicured front lawn that could have doubled as a putting green.

A huge marble fountain claimed the center of a flagstone courtyard beside the towering front door, which looked as if it had once belonged to some European monastery. In the center of the ornately carved door was an iron knocker fashioned in the shape of a lion's head.

Nick pressed the doorbell. A moment after it had rung out in a peal of Westminster chimes, an attractive young man, dressed in a black waistcoat, black slacks, a starched white shirt, and black bow tie opened the door.

"Welcome, Ms. Delaney. Mr. Broussard," he greeted them. "Madame is expecting you. She's with the detectives in the drawing room."

Drawing room? Kate exchanged a look with Nick, who shrugged. They were both obviously out of their league.

The interior of the mansion was dominated by a massive entrance hall with gleaming white Corinthian columns lining the silk-draped walls. A magnificent floating stairway curved up to the second floor, drawing a visitor's gaze toward a towering ceiling embellished with plaster medallions. In the center of the ceiling, cherubs with gilded wings frolicked among fluffy mural clouds lit by a crystal chandelier that had to be eight feet tall.

"Madame?" Kate murmured as they followed the butler across a mile of marble floor. "Wow, not only are we no longer in Kansas, Toto, we've just gone off the planet."

"It's impressive, sure enough," Nick said. "I never would've guessed you could buy a house like this by selling cars."

His tone was dry, indicating that he didn't believe it possible any more than she did. Whatever her mother was up to, Kate realized she must've pulled off the long con of the century. But this time, unless St. Croix was deaf, blind, and senile, her mother may have bit off more of a mark than she'd be able to chew.

The drawing room had the ambience of a baronial castle. Heavy, gilt-framed paintings hung on gold silk-draped walls; satin-upholstered French period furniture rested on an Oriental carpet that could have covered an NBA basketball court. A stone fireplace, tall enough for a man to stand in, took up the far wall.

"Darling!" Antoinette's naturally southern accent was more rounded, and a great deal more cultured than it had been back when she'd been dragging her daughters around the carnival circuit, telling phony fortunes as the Mystical Zelda. "Thank God you've come!"

She hadn't aged a day. If anything, she looked every bit as young as she had that day fifteen years ago when she'd been led out of a Biloxi courtroom in shackles.

Her hair, a smooth and shiny streaked blonde, fell in waves to her shoulders, her lips were colored a soft pink, and not a line or wrinkle marred either her forehead or the skin around her eyes. Her flowered silk dress, which brought to mind Monet's gardens, swung like a colorful bell and rustled as she glided across the carpet.

The femininity that surrounded her had Kate, who'd put her suit back on after that mind-blowing sex with Nick, feeling a lot like a mortician.

"I'm so glad you've come."

Her eyes, which Kate remembered as being hazel but were now—thanks to contacts—Elizabeth Taylor violet, glistened with a moist sheen. She dabbed at the moisture with a linen handkerchief, reminding Kate of when they'd used cheap toilet paper because boxes of tissue were too expensive.

Having seen her mother pull out the waterworks on demand, Kate wasn't buying her tears now.

"Family needs to support one another during tragic times such as these."

She pressed her powdered cheek against Kate's as she hugged her. Kate, who kept her arms stiffly at her sides, couldn't name the floral perfume, but she'd bet it was expensive.

Apparently realizing her daughter was not going to return the embrace, she released her and extended her slender hands toward Nick. A diamond the size of Alaska on the ring finger of her left hand caught the light from the chandelier overhead, splitting it into rainbows.

"And you must be Mr. Broussard. It's a pleasure to meet you. I'm sorry for your recent troubles and am sure, given your sterling military record, it must all be a dreadful mistake."

Recent troubles?

"Thanks." Studiously ignoring Kate's sharp, questioning look, he took both her outstretched hands in his. "I'm pleased to meet you Mrs. St. Croix. I only wish it was under more pleasant circumstances."

"Thank you. It is a very difficult time for me. What with my precious baby's death. And my husband's dreadful accident."

A difficult time for *her*.

Hadn't it always been this way? Antoinette was,

hands down, the most narcissistic individual Kate had ever met. And given that most criminals could be poster children for narcissism, that was really saying something.

"Could I get you a drink, Nick?" Antoinette asked.

"No, thank you," he said politely.

"Do you happen to know what Tara was up to that might have gotten her killed?" Kate asked.

"I've already told Detective Landreaux"—she flashed a tragically wobbly smile toward the detective, who gave her a professionally reassuring smile in return—"that my youngest daughter hadn't shared any personal information with me." Sitting down in a damask-draped wing chair, Antoinette crossed her long, still excellent legs with a swish of silk. "I do know she was about to quit her job as a hostess on that casino ship."

Hostess. Now, wasn't that a euphemism?

Deciding that even if she did know anything, her mother wouldn't share, especially with a cop in the room, Kate turned toward Nick's former partner.

"Nick said the autopsy's almost completed?"

"We should have it any time," he said. "If not by eight, which is when Doc usually tends to close up shop, first thing in the morning."

"So I'll be able to identify my sister's body?"

"Oh, you don't have to worry about that," Antoinette said blithely. As if belatedly realizing her smile, again directed at Remy Landreaux, was inappropriate under the circumstances, her expression instantly turned beautifully tragic.

Her mother had always been able to turn emotions on and off like a light switch. Making Kate wonder if she actually had any true feelings.

"I've already identified our dear Tara."

"You went to the morgue?"

"No. Detective Landreaux wanted to spare me the emotional hardship of going to that dreadfully depressing place." Her lips quivered. She dabbed at her eyes again. Took a deep, shuddering breath. "So he brought me a videotape."

Kate narrowed her eyes and turned back to the detective. "Is that standard operating procedure in New Orleans?"

"Not always," Remy Landreaux responded easily. "But, as Nick undoubtedly has told you, we're operating under less than ideal conditions, especially once FEMA closed down the temporary morgue they'd built and mothballed all their high-tech equipment. Which forced the coroner to temporarily move to a funeral home.

"Meanwhile, most everyone in this city is suffering some level of post-traumatic stress, so we're more than willing to go the extra step to make a difficult process easier on victims' families, whenever possible."

That made sense, Kate allowed. It also left her feeling a little guilty for having been so cynical. Not all New Orleans cops were dickheads like Dubois. Who she was grateful she wasn't going to have to deal with today. Landreaux had, after all, stepped in and had been trying to help her from the beginning by sending her to Nick.

They would have made a good team, Kate decided. Nick's raw yet amiable masculinity, which undoubtedly worked well when dealing with New Orleans's large working-class base, and the other cop's suaveness would undoubtedly be able to win cooperation from the Garden District types.

Of course, neither man would have a bit of trouble with females on either side of the cultural divide.

"Besides"—Antoinette broke into Kate's thoughts— "you wouldn't have been able to recognize your sister, anyway. Given how long it's been since you'd seen her. And people change over time."

"Yeah, I heard Tara changed a lot," Kate said dryly.

She wondered if mother and daughter had gotten a family rate from that plastic surgeon. Antoinette was certainly a walking, talking billboard for Botox and the benefits of preemptive face-lifts.

"Will you be staying in town long, dear?"

"Until I find my sister's killer."

Kate thought her mother paled a bit beneath her expertly applied foundation. "Surely you don't think she was murdered?"

"Yes," Kate said, shooting a look toward the detective, who was probably one of the few cops she'd ever seen who actually looked as if he belonged in a room like this. Despite all the edgy vibes shooting around the room, he looked as cool and aloof—and watchful—as a cat. "I do."

"Oh, my," Antoinette breathed. "I hope that won't hold up Thursday's interment. You've no idea how difficult it is to get a caterer at such short notice. Fortunately, it's after Ash Wednesday. I can't imagine what we would have done if Tara had died a few days earlier."

"Yeah, that would've been real inconsiderate of her." Kate was remembering why she'd jumped at the opportunity to escape to Chicago. Wished, certainly not for the first time, that she'd been able to convince her sister to come with her.

"You will attend, won't you? I managed to get her a tomb in Lafayette Cemetery Number One, which is, of course, a virtual who's who of New Orleans society. They also filmed scenes from *Interview with the Vampire* there."

"Well, I'm sure my sister would be tickled pink to hear that," Kate said dryly. "So, how's your husband?"

"He's doing much better, thank the Lord." Kate had to fight against rolling her eyes as her mother made the sign of the cross against the front of the silk flowered dress. "I was so horribly afraid I was going to lose my soul mate."

Soul mate. Sure thing, Mom.

"We need to talk," Kate said. "Alone."

She looked over at Remy Landreaux, who was still watching them.

Most people would never take him for a cop. To the average Joe Citizen, the detective might look as if he'd just stepped off the pages of *GQ*, all pressed and polished, with his tawny tan and sun-gilded hair. But to those who knew what to look for, his steady, gunmetal-gray eyes gave him away.

She suspected that, as with Nick, not much got by him.

"While Kate and her *maman* are catching up, maybe you and I can put together what we know," Nick suggested to Remy. "See if together we might be able to put this puzzle together. If you're done here?"

He was about as subtle as an Abrams tank. But it worked. Remy Landreaux stood up, shaking imaginary wrinkles out of his custom-tailored dress slacks. His wry smile told Nick he knew exactly what he was doing, but was willing to go along with it if it helped wrap up his case.

As if summoned by an invisible bell, the butler arrived with the detective's jacket and walked the two men to the door.

"Okay." As soon as they were alone, Kate spun on her mother. "What the hell were you and Tara up to?"

"I don't know what you mean." A manicured hand flew to Antoinette's breast.

"I mean, unless she got a personality transplant while she was having all that plastic surgery done, my sister would not have killed herself."

"You don't know that. You've been off living your own life. Without any concerns for the mother and sister you left behind."

"Yeah. You look like you've really been suffering." Kate waved a hand around the opulence. "So what kind of scam are you running on St. Croix?"

Her mother jumped to her feet. Hectic red flags flew in her cheeks. "I'll have you know I love my husband."

"Right. And hey, while I'm buying that, maybe you've got a levee you want to sell me?"

"It's true."

Kate folded her arms. "You don't even know the meaning of the word."

"I do, too." Tears sprung to those thickly lashed eyes.

"Go ahead. Turn on the damn waterworks. But all you'll end up doing is melting your mascara."

If her mother thought she was going to tap-dance around the issue, Antoinette had another think coming. "Because guess what, I know you. You don't have an honest bone in your body."

"I'll admit that I may have had a few faults—"

"A few? That's like saying Ted Bundy had a few problems keeping girlfriends," Kate shot back.

Her mother might have appeared to have metamorphosed into a southern society matron, but she'd always had a core of steel. And a heart every bit as cold and hard.

"You needn't talk to me like that." She tossed up her chin in a gesture Nick would've recognized right away. "I might not have been the most maternal person in the world. But I tried, as best I could, with the resources I had as a single parent, to be a good mother."

Kate opened her mouth. Closed it. Shook her head.

Did her mother have even the faintest connection to reality?

"You taught me to rifle purses before I was in kindergarten," Kate said through clenched teeth. "In what fucking child-rearing manual did you find that little gem of parenting advice?"

"You needn't curse, dear. It's unnecessary. And unattractive. And I wasn't as fortunate as *some* people. I wasn't fortunate enough to go to college. Having two children to raise while I was still in my teens."

"You were twenty."

"Nineteen when I got pregnant."

Kate couldn't argue that one. Nor did she want to get into an argument about birth control and safe sex, because it would just lead them off track.

"I put myself through Loyola with loans and work-study. And you're right. I was fortunate that there were ways not to get pregnant."

Like celibacy for her first three years at the Jesuit college in Chicago, but she wasn't going to share that with her mother, either.

What was interesting was that Antoinette had kept up with her. She'd like to think it might have been because she'd cared. But the truth was that she'd probably just wanted to keep tabs on where her eldest-by-five-minutes daughter was in case she ever needed to hit her up for money.

"And isn't it disappointing that you're not doing anything with that fancy degree?"

"I became a cop."

She chose not to add that Nick had pretty much nailed why. She'd wanted, in some small way, to try to pay back the man who'd saved her life. Saved her from turning out like her mother. And, oh God, like Tara.

"Any high school graduate can be a cop. Why, I'll bet they even take people with GEDs. And really, dear, don't you think I know why you decided to go into law enforcement?"

Kate knew she shouldn't bite. But she couldn't help herself. "Okay. Why don't you tell me."

"Because you wanted to get back at me."

"You have to be kidding!" Kate's barked laugh held not an iota of humor. "Christ. You've always thought everything was about you. I became a cop because I watched my father—"

"Dennis Delaney was in no way your father," Antoinette shot back derisively. "He was the man who sent your mother to prison."

"Because, excuse me, my mother was a damn criminal! Who was more than willing to lead her own children right into her own sad and shabby life."

"You girls loved the drama. And when most children were eating at McDonald's, you just happened to be dining at some of the finest restaurants in the Gulf South."

Despite the seriousness of the argument, Antoinette's ruby-red lips curved into a faintly reminiscent smile. "Do you remember that Easter brunch when I wore the empathy belly under the maternity smock?"

"And pretended to faint, and Tara screamed bloody murder, and while both of you held everyone's attention, I lifted billfolds from purses." It was the day she'd told Nick about.

"We left that restaurant with nearly a thousand dollars. Which paid for a vacation in Hollywood."

Where Antoinette had stood in Judy Garland's footsteps and had been thrilled to discover that she wore the same size—five and a half—as those famous ruby slippers.

Kate didn't really remember that part of the trip, having been much more enthralled with Disneyland's Jungle Cruise, but her mother had told the story so many times she could picture it in her mind.

In fact, the mental image was so clear that two years ago when a thief had broken into the Judy Garland Museum in Grand Rapids, Minnesota, in the middle of the night and stolen one of the six pairs of the slippers created for the movie and insured for a million dollars, Kate had actually wondered if, just maybe, her mother had been behind the theft.

"We were kids," she said. "We had no way of knowing right from wrong. Especially when you made it a game."

"It's very sad."

Antoinette reached into a drawer in a hand-carved table and took out a gold cigarette case, the kind you only saw movie stars using in 1930s and 1940s movies. She lit a cigarette with a matching gold lighter, drew in a deep breath, and let out a sigh on a plume of blue smoke.

"What's sad?"

"That you've grown up to be so rigid. When I remember you as such a happy little girl."

"I don't want to talk about this anymore."

"Fine. Why don't you tell me about your very delicious Nick Broussard?"

"He's not *my* Nick. And there's nothing to tell. I

needed a PI to help me prove that Tara didn't kill herself. Detective Landreaux recommended his former partner. End of story."

"Now who's the liar?" Antoinette's sly smile was that of a cat who'd just come across a succulent bowl of rich sweet cream. "Have you slept with him yet?"

"That's none of your business."

"Ah. I knew it." She nodded, pleased with herself. "I am, after all, psychic."

"A phony psychic," Kate corrected.

"If you don't choose to believe, that's your business," her mother said airily. "But the chemistry between the two of you is more than a little apparent. Yet you were still comfortable in each other's space. Which tells me that you've scratched the itch at least once."

She flicked a gaze over Kate's face. "From that visible beard burn on your face, I'd say rather recently. Perhaps even right before you came over here."

"Again," Kate said through gritted teeth, "any relationship I may or may not have with Nick Broussard is none of your business."

"Of course you're entitled to your little secrets, darling. We all have them."

She paused, a significant beat. Knowing her mother as well as she did, Kate waited for the other shoe to drop. It didn't take long.

"Including your Nick. I suppose, given that you're so close, he's told you about his little problem with the police department?"

"I know he left. To open his own investigative agency."

"He left," Antoinette agreed with a nod of her sleek blonde head. "But it wasn't exactly of his own choosing. And the agency came after he was thrown off the force for corruption."

"I don't believe that."

Nick might play a little fast and loose with the rules. But corrupt?

No way.

"Why don't you ask him?" her mother asked.

Her smoothly modulated tone was mild. But the gotcha look in her pansy Liz Taylor eyes told Kate she was enjoying her daughter's discomfort. Once again the cat image came to mind. But this time she imagined her mother as a sleek Siamese toying with a mouse. The mouse, of course, being her.

"I will."

Her mother was a textbook pathological liar. She was also, like all successful grifters, an expert at knowing exactly which buttons to push.

"But for now, I want to know what you know about Tara."

"Not a thing. Really," she insisted. "Except that she was always my problem child. Always needing attention."

"Maybe because she never got any from you. "

"That's a cruel thing to say."

"Sometimes the truth hurts."

"She had problems. Mental problems."

"What kind of mental problems?"

"She'd get depressed."

What a surprise, living with this woman.

"Once, when she was twenty, she tried to slit her wrists. She was hospitalized for three months."

"I'm sorry." Which didn't even come close to describing how sorry.

"As I said, she was a difficult child."

"I meant I was sorry for her. Was she on antidepressants?"

"Off and on," Antoinette said, dismissing the subject with a wave of her hand.

"Did you know what she was doing for a living?" Kate asked.

"She was a hostess on the Crescent City Casino ship."

"She was a hooker."

"Prostitution's illegal."

"Like everything you've done to make a living all your life isn't?" Kate blew out a frustrated breath. "Look, I'm sick to death that my sister was hurting and I wasn't here to help her. But I don't give a damn about what she was doing to earn a living except for the fact that it couldn't have helped her self-esteem, and I'd think that having sex for money would be horribly depressing.

"But unfortunately, it's too late to do anything about that now. So, what I came here to find out is if you knew about that videotape."

"What videotape?" Her violet eyes widened innocently. Which, of course, didn't mean a damn thing.

"The tape she was using to possibly extort money from Leon and Stephen LeBlanc."

The color drained from Antoinette's face. "She couldn't have thought she could ever pull off such a reckless scheme!"

"Nick says she was."

"Leon was dangerous enough. But at least he's fairly civilized. From what people tell me. But Stephen." She shook her head. "The word on the younger LeBlanc is that if he's not a psychopath, he's at least a sociopath."

"I suppose it takes one to know one."

"How sharper than a serpent's tooth it is to have a thankless child." She took another shaky puff, then stabbed the cigarette out in a crystal dish. "Martin doesn't like me to smoke," she revealed. "I've been trying to cut back, but this has been such a dreadfully stressful time."

"Speaking of your new husband, what con did you play to land in this place?"

"What makes you think I ran a con?"

Kate's only answer was a long, hard look.

"Well, that answers that," Antoinette decided, dropping the southern country-club accent. "You really *are* a cop."

"Yes. I am."

"At least you *were*. From what I hear, you've had a few problems yourself back in the Windy City."

Do not let her draw you into another endless argument you can never win.

"Your husband can't be a stupid man." Kate doggedly stuck to the topic. "He's going to find out what you did. Whatever it is."

"No. He's not." Her hands trembled as she shook another cigarette out of the case. "Because I'm going to fix it."

Oh, hell. "I don't want to hear this, do I?"

"You're the one who insisted," her mother reminded her on another stream of smoke.

"It all began when I met this lovely young man who worked as a title clerk at the office of Motor Vehicles . . ."

33

"SO," KATE TOLD NICK AS THEY LEFT THE HOUSE, "what she and that guy from the OMV were doing was essentially stealing the cars' identities by stealing the identification numbers from luxury cars and SUVs and putting them on stolen vehicles."

"Which was essentially laundering the hot cars," he filled in. "Once they had a legitimate VIN number, they'd be easier to register."

"I suppose I shouldn't be surprised you'd know about that. Given that we're still driving around in a stolen SUV."

"Yeah, I'm not wild about that idea, either. But if it makes you feel better, as soon as we get back to the marina, I'm going to call a tow truck to take it back to the casino."

"I'm glad to hear that. But what's changed?"

"While you were having that little chat with your mother, Remy told me they picked up the Hulk."

"Really? Wow. That was quick."

"They got lucky. The firefighters saw him watching

the burning car with a bit too much interest. Let's face it, we had a break; the guy's not real hard to miss."

"Well, that's true enough. So why was he trying to kill us?"

"Actually, Remy's pretty sure he was after *me*. And it's a long story I promise to share as soon as we're back on *The Hoo-yah*."

"Does it have anything to do with you leaving the police force?"

So much for choosing his own time and place, Nick thought with an inner sigh. "Your mother didn't waste any time."

"She's always been big on controlling the situation."

As was her daughter. Nick figured that must've been one helluva conversation the two of them had had.

"I got kicked off the cops." There. It was out.

"For corruption?"

"That was the charge."

"But not the truth."

He looked over at her, met her steady gaze. "It was the truth as far as it went."

He watched her processing that. "But it wasn't the whole truth and nothing but the truth," she said.

"No."

"I knew it."

"That's it?" Surely Detective Law and Order wasn't prepared to drop the subject that easily?

"For now." She placed a hand on his thigh. "Of course I want to hear the story. But you told me you'd tell me when we got to the boat. That's enough for me."

"It's a complicated situation." Nick wondered what he'd ever done to get so lucky to meet this woman, who didn't trust easily but for some reason trusted him. "Meanwhile, you were telling me about your mother. Who, by the way, isn't exactly Donna Reed."

"Noticed that, did you?"

"I didn't have to be a detective to spot the clues. It also explains a lot about your sister. And makes me admire you even more. It couldn't have been easy. Raising yourself while trying to be a surrogate mother to your twin."

"It was the way it was." Kate shrugged. "We've both seen kids grow up in a lot worse situations. At least we always had food and a roof over our heads. We might have had to move in the middle of the night because we were scamming the landlord for the rent. But nothing was so bad that we could even qualify as associate members of the endangered-children-of-the-world club.

"Anyway, Antoinette and her boy toy were part of a national ring that trolled mall parking lots, car dealerships, and online auction sites, finding cars that matched the ones they'd already stolen."

"Which, with the help of corrupt title clerks like the boy toy, who'd forge the signatures of owners who'd applied for duplicate titles after their VINs were stolen, essentially changed auto theft from a street crime to a white-collar offense."

"Exactly. Which is a lot more difficult to catch. Not to mention prosecute. I'd already heard about it before Antoinette got involved. There was one group in the

Southwest, Operation Road Runner, that allegedly cloned cars worth eight million dollars."

"Not exactly kids going joyriding on a Saturday night," he said.

"Tell me about it. A lot of the cars with the altered VINs are sold to other criminals. But lots of private buyers, auto auction houses, and car dealers can end up being duped. So, essentially, you could buy a car from say, St. Croix Mercedes, only to find out later that it had actually been stolen from some guy in Wisconsin. Or even Canada."

"And that's where St. Croix came in."

"Exactly. The Louisiana wing of the group needed a dealership to launder their hot cars through. St. Croix was the obvious patsy. His kids are grown and scattered around the country. He was widowed five years ago, so he'd been living alone all that time. And my mother, you may have also noticed, is not without her charms."

"She's attractive enough. In a Flashy CZ sort of way." He reached out and squeezed her thigh. "Unlike her daughter, who's the true gem in the family."

Color, the bane of all redheads, rose in Kate's cheeks. "That's a very nice thing to say."

"It's easy to say. Because it's the truth . . . So, did Antoinette get St. Croix mixed up in the VIN ring?"

"If she's to be believed, and that's always a crapshoot, because there are times I think she doesn't even know when she's lying, he doesn't know a thing. She says that although she arranged to meet him on purpose when she went to buy a Mercedes, she honestly did fall in love with him. Enough that she told the guys running the show down here in the Gulf that she was dropping out. That she wasn't going to put her husband's business, his reputation—which apparently is golden down in this neck of the woods—and his life in jeopardy."

"And I'll bet they were just tickled to pieces about that."

"Tickled enough they tried to kill him."

"The plan being that your mother would inherit the dealership. And they'd be back in business."

"Exactly." Kate nodded. "Of course he was a fool not to make her sign a prenup, but—"

"He loved her."

"Yeah. So here's the thing: Antoinette, for the first time in her life, finds herself on the horns of a moral dilemma. Choice number one is that she can dump the life of crime and live happily ever after with the love of her life."

"Which is going to be hard, given that her former band of merry men are trying to make her a widow," Nick said. "Lucky he's a tough old bird."

"Isn't it? So, her other choice is to keep on keeping on, knowing that eventually she'd get caught and the man she loved would lose his business, his reputation, and probably all his lifelong friends. And maybe even his children and grandchildren."

"At worst, he'd end up in prison," Nick said.

"Exactly. Like I said, she's never been one to weigh the right and wrong of a decision, and this one didn't look as if it had an easy answer."

"She could always offer to buy her way out of the partnership."

"That was precisely what she did."

"Paying your way out of a jam is the logical thing to do, I suppose."

"Logical if you're a crook, perhaps," she muttered.

Nick loved that her mind didn't work that way. She was smart as a whip, but she was always going to be a black-and-white kind of girl. Having met her mother, he understood why.

Morality, for Kate, had to be a constant, as fixed as the North Star. If you started cutting corners, you'd find yourself drifting. Then forever lost.

Which made it even more amazing that she was willing to give him the benefit of the doubt before she'd even heard his side of the story.

"Of course, that led to another problem," she said. "The ringleader wouldn't trust a check from her. Or a cashier's check, which, while safer, still could be forged. And they definitely didn't trust a wire transfer."

"No honor among thieves." Sometimes the clichés really were true.

"Exactly. Which is why they wanted cash. A *lot* of cash. Like the five hundred grand they figured her change of mind was going to cost them."

"Not many people have that much cash beneath their mattress."

"Granted. And she could've had the money wired from her offshore bank. But these days transactions like that have to be reported. No way is some local banker just going to hand over a mid six figures in cash. If she even tried to do that, she'd get the attention of the police—"

"Who'd find all that very odd behavior for a woman whose husband is lying in the hospital in a near coma after a hit-and-run."

"She'd look guilty as sin," Kate agreed. "So, she figured she didn't have any other choice but to go down to the Caymans herself."

"She was still taking a helluva risk bringing it back into the States. If customs had caught her, she'd really have been in hot water."

"She knew that. But she was counting on getting a male agent."

"Upon whom she could use her not inconsiderable charms."

"Exactly."

"Well. That's quite a story. And the really weird thing about it is that I sorta believe it."

"The even weirder thing is that I believe it, too. My mother"—Kate told him nothing he hadn't figured out for himself—"has never exactly been on a first-name basis with the truth . . . I do have a request."

"What's that, *chère*?"

"I realize you're not a cop anymore, but perhaps you know someone, maybe Remy, who can try to work out a deal for her? Maybe give her immunity if she agrees to testify against the guys running the show?"

"I know a few people. I'll see what I can do."

"Thanks. I know I shouldn't be cutting her any slack, but—"

"Like it or not, she's still family," Nick said gently. "And it's not like she killed someone. Besides, you never know. This might be the start of a good thing. Her finding redemption. Sort of like Paul on the road to Damascus."

"Right," Kate scoffed. "My mother has always been able to play just about any role. But a saint is a real stretch."

34

KATE LIKED HER LOFT BACK IN CHICAGO. SHE loved the openness of it. The high ceilings, the view of the lake, the hustle and bustle of the city.

But she would have traded it in a heartbeat for Nick Broussard's gleaming white ketch.

She didn't have to pretend to be impressed with the two staterooms, each with its own head, one with a full tub and shower, the other with a shower; the spacious salon boasting a state-of-the-art entertainment center; or the galley fitted out with a refrigerator-freezer, propane stove, eye-level oven, and a microwave. There was even a stackable washer and dryer.

But the pièce de résistance was the diesel fireplace in the main stateroom.

"It's probably overkill," Nick admitted as he turned it on to demonstrate. "But it's also nice on cold, rainy nights."

Like tonight, she thought. "I don't think it's overkill at all."

And wasn't it too easy to imagine herself lying in

Nick's arms in that wide, king-size berth while rain pelted the overhead deck and a warm fire blazed.

"It truly is a stunningly beautiful ketch."

She dragged her gaze from the sinfully enticing bed and looked around at the rest of the room. Unlike a lot of boats she'd been on over the years this one had wide windows that allowed the daylight in, avoiding any claustrophobic submarine feeling.

"It must have cost a fortune, though."

She wondered how, on a military salary, he'd been able to afford it. And was surprised when she didn't experience even a niggling of suspicion.

"Like I said, I got it for a song from a doctor who was having himself a hurricane sale. It helped that I'd sold my thirty-five-footer I was living on when I left San Diego."

"Thirty-five feet is still a nice-size boat."

"She was a dandy," he agreed. "And a long way up from the fifteen-foot sloop I'd picked up at a bargain-basement price from a guy on my old team whose wife decided their growing family needed a minivan more than a sailboat."

"I suppose I can understand that," she murmured as she ran her fingers over a wall. The golden light from the setting sun made the hand-rubbed cherry gleam like polished glass.

"When we left my mother's house, and you told me that the Hulk had been arrested, and we weren't in any more danger, I was seriously considering coming back here and getting very, very drunk," she admitted.

"That's always an option. And I can understand how you'd feel that way," Nick said. "But since I have the feeling that I've had a bit more experience in that area than you do, I should warn you that there's a price to be paid."

"Isn't there always a price," she murmured. Then sighed. "And I need to know what Detective Landreaux told you about Tara. But first I want to go to bed."

"You've had a stressful few days. Finding out about your sister dying, coming here, getting shot at, cars blowing up, those troubles with your *maman*. Wouldn't be any surprise that you'd start to wind down. A nap before dinner will probably do you a lot of good."

"Or, you could make love to me."

"*With* you," he corrected.

"Whatever," she said as she began to attack his belt buckle. "Just so it ends up with you inside me."

They came together, falling onto the bed, where they tangled the sheets and sent pillows falling onto the floor.

Clothes were torn off, scattered to the four corners of the room. Her sweater landed on a chair, his jeans ended up on top of the TV, followed seconds later by Kate's slacks.

They rolled over the mattress, rough, relentless, tugging at the rest of their clothes, breaths labored, quick gasps turning into low moans.

His hands were everywhere, tangling in her hair, stroking her moist flesh, moving between her legs, where she was hot and wet and ready for him. His teeth scraped against a nipple, causing her to suck in a quick, harsh breath, then moved on to nip at the distended nub between her slick, quaking thighs.

Kate caressed him in turn, reveling in the hard play of muscles beneath dark flesh, exalting in a feminine power like nothing she'd ever known as his stony sex swelled to fill her hand.

He was so hot. So hard. His mouth. His hands. His body. Kate touched and tasted and found him magnificent.

The light had gone, but Nick had no trouble seeing her in the glow of the gas fire. Could see himself backlit by the flames reflected in the jet pupils of her catlike eyes.

Nick wanted her. In every way a man could want a woman he was falling in love with. He wanted to pleasure her as he'd never pleasured any other woman. Wanted her to experience delights she'd never felt with any other man.

God help him, he, who'd never wanted to feel tied to anything or anyone, wanted to possess Kate—body, mind, and soul.

He was nearing desperation when he remembered— shit—that, not having had sex since he'd bought *The Hoo-Yah*, although he'd dutifully kept a rubber with him, he'd never moved any into the bedside drawer.

"The condoms are in the head," he said as he reluctantly extricated himself. "Don't go anywhere."

"I wouldn't think of it. But don't take too long." She flashed him a wicked siren's smile. "Or I may have to start without you."

He retrieved the box in record time and ripped a package open.

She leaned up on her elbows, watching as he stood beside the bed and rolled the latex condom down the length of his erect and straining shaft.

Just looking at her looking at him that way, the lust battering away at him mirrored on her own flushed face, almost had him losing it right then and there.

As if able to read his mind, she went up on her knees, wrapped her arms around him, and pressed her mouth against the moist, hot flesh of his stomach.

Then grabbed his hips, pulled him down onto the bed, and straddled him.

"I have a confession," she said, just before she crushed her mouth to his and kissed him. Hard. And deep. And long.

"What's that?" he asked when they finally came up for air. The hot and hungry kiss had wiped every coherent thought from his mind.

"I think you've turned me into a sex addict. All I seem to be able to think about is ripping your clothes off and getting hot and naked with you."

"Don't feel like the Lone Ranger." His hands skimmed down her back. "Because the entire time we were at your mother's, all I could think about was how good you'd feel bucking beneath me on her fancy Oriental rug."

"And isn't that easy for you to say," she complained without heat. "Since I'd be the one with rug burns on my butt."

"I'd have kissed them and made them better."

"If we're ever in that situation, I'll hold you to that. Meanwhile . . ."

When she wiggled her body against him, Nick imagined he could see the flare of sparks. "Do I still feel good?"

"What the hell do you think?" He pressed her hard against his groin.

A grin tugged at her voluptuous lips. Her long legs were tangled with his. "I think we both feel pretty damn good."

"Me, too. But if you don't want this to end before it begins," he warned, "you're going to have to hold still."

"I'm sorry, Nick." The laughter in her eyes said just the opposite. Not only was she not sorry, she was having a dandy time torturing him. "But I don't think I can do that."

Leaning forward, she skimmed her tongue playfully over first one flat male nipple, then the other, stimulating nerve endings Nick had never known he possessed.

"I'm sorry," she said when his hips bucked at the nip of her teeth. She trailed a fingernail down his torso. "Did I hurt the big brave SEAL?"

"Actually," he managed on a groan as she blew a soft, warm breath against his stomach, causing it to clench, "I think you may just be killing me."

"Don't worry, Nick." She wove her fingers through the crisp, dark hair below his belly. "I promise to be gentle."

She slid down his body, her teeth nipping at the insides of his thighs, her hair draped over him, silk tongues of red flame, the same way it had been in all his fantasies. And last night's dreams.

Her scent swam in his senses. Her touch set his blood to boiling.

Nick's breath was gone. His mind reeled.

It was torture.

It was bliss.

When he didn't think he could last another second, he thrust his hands through her tumbled hair and pulled her back astride him, grasping her slender hips with a force he knew would leave bruises.

But even then she insisted on setting the pace as she straddled him, slowly lowering herself over his straining cock, a torturous millimeter at a time.

Her moist feminine folds clutched at him. Released. Clutched again.

Understanding her need for control, Nick decided that if he had to grit his teeth until they flat out crumbled to dust, they'd do this her way.

Instead of emotionally removing herself from the act by closing her eyes, she kept her burning gaze on his, maintaining a connection that went beyond that of their bodies, that was much more complex than merely what fit where.

She lifted herself up again, her hot, damp flesh—oh, Jesus—just brushing the swollen tip of his cock.

"You like that," she said with a knowing smile as it leaped to attention beneath her stroking touch.

"Like doesn't begin to describe it," he managed in a strangled tone as he struggled not to swallow his tongue.

She was every temptress ever born: Eve, Delilah, Salome stripping off her seven veils to win the head of the Baptist. Nick couldn't imagine any male ever denying this woman anything.

And although he knew she'd deny it for fear of not appearing tough enough, she was also the most caring, emotionally generous woman he'd ever met.

And even if neither one of them was prepared to admit it out loud yet, she was his.

As he was hers.

His fists grabbed up handfuls of tangled sheet.

Her body grew hotter. Wetter.

"But as good as it is, anytime you want to go a little deeper . . . oh, *mon Dieu*," he moaned as she lowered herself again, her inner muscles tightening. Milking him. "That's it, *chère*."

He'd never begged for a woman in his life. Never had the need to. But he'd beg, plead, hell, he'd go out naked onto the dock and howl at the goddamn moon if she'd only finish him off before he exploded.

"You're so big," she said in a breathless little "Happy Birthday, Mr. President" Marilyn Monroe voice that, even as fake as it was, inflamed him further. "I don't know how I can possibly take such a—"

"You can." Pressing his heels against the mattress, he lifted his hips up, straining to fill her. "I promise."

He dug his fingers into either side of her waist and felt her tremble with anticipation. "Have I ever lied to you?"

"Not that I know of." Devil woman that she'd become, she reached between them and took him in her hand. "Then again, SEALs are trained to lie." She was enjoying it. Enjoying her power. Enjoying him.

"Only to the enemy. And believe me, sweetheart, I'm feeling really friendly toward you."

"Ditto." Her curved fingers stroked him, from root to tip. Then back down again.

"But in the interest of honesty," he said, groaning, at the point where he could no longer decide whether to beg her or curse her, "if you keep pumping me like that, we're either going to have a launch any second, or you're going to kill me."

"Well, I certainly wouldn't want to do that. Because I have plans for you, Nick Broussard."

She finally took him all the way in, hot, soft female against hotter, hard male.

Then she began to move, meeting him thrust for thrust as he surged upward and into her again and again.

Harder.

Deeper.

In.

Out.

Faster.

His stomach clenched. His thighs actually trembled, which was a first for him. But he didn't have time to think about it as the explosive climax shot up his spine, blinding him as Kate drove them both over that dark edge.

35

"WELL," KATE SAID. SHE WAS COLLAPSED UPON his chest, her lips buried in his throat, her legs splayed on either side of his thighs.

She felt drained.

Boneless.

Glorious.

"That should've done it," she said.

"Done what?"

She arched her back and nearly purred like a cat as Nick trailed a lazy hand down her back.

"Gotten you out of my system."

"Ah." He nuzzled her neck. "And did it?"

Because he felt so good—too good—she rolled over onto her side. "It should have," she hedged.

He braced himself up on one elbow and looked down at her. "But?"

"You've gotten under my skin. And, I think, in my blood." And, dammit, her heart. "Sort of like a virus."

"Well, that's complimentary." The warm amusement in his eyes suggested he hadn't taken offense.

"I didn't want this," she insisted tightly after he'd returned to bed after dispensing with the condom. "I didn't need it. I've got too much on my plate and the timing—"

"Sucks." He ran a palm over her shoulder.

"Yeah. It does."

"But that doesn't seem to matter, does it?"

"No." Amazingly, even after that hideous meeting with her mother, Kate felt better, happier even, than she'd ever felt in her life. "Do you believe in fate?"

"Honestly?" Nick's stroking touch moved down her arm, his fingers linking with hers. "I'm not sure." He lifted their joined hands and nibbled on her knuckles. "Having been in situations where any chance of survival looked damn iffy, I definitely believe in luck."

"I know the feeling. But fate's somehow different. I mean, think about it. Six months ago, you were in Afghanistan. I was in Chicago. There was no way we should've met."

"None at all," he agreed.

"Yet here were are. Together—"

"Naked—"

"As two jaybirds," she said. She caught his wrist and moved his hand between them, sighing happily when his fingers cupped her breasts. "That seems sorta like fate."

"Or luck."

"Luck works for me." She twined her arms around his neck.

He cupped her butt again. Drew her closer. "So, what would you say to getting lucky again?"

She laughed, feeling ridiculously and uncharacteristically carefree. "I'd say *mais,* yeah, *cher!*"

"So," she said, much, much later, after he finally shared what he'd been keeping from her while they fixed supper in the galley, "when you told me you had some loose ends to clear up after your father's death, the particular end you were talking about was the fact that you don't believe he killed himself?"

"I know damn well he didn't," he said.

Kate, whose culinary skills pretty much boiled down to being able to dial a phone for takeout, was fascinated by his swift economy of movement as he cut some leafy-green celery, green pepper, onion, and shallots into perfect little squares.

She'd never had anything resembling a domestic moment with a man. Now, clad in one of his shirts and the pair of panties she'd rescued from atop a picture frame, she found herself enjoying working together.

"And no, I don't have any proof. But I knew it was staged the minute I got the call."

"The same way I knew about Tara."

He looked so damn delicious in those low-slung jeans with the top button undone and bare feet. Who knew a guy's feet could be so sexy? And how was it that she wanted him again after they'd practically set this boat on fire and she'd come so many times even she'd lost count?

To keep from jumping his oh-so-fine bones, she concentrated on peeling and deveining the shrimp, which was turning out to be a bit trickier than it had sounded when she'd volunteered.

"He might've been crooked." He took a swallow of beer and checked the butter he had melting in a copper-bottom pan. "He might've been a mean drunk who was quick with his fists. But he damn well wasn't suicidal."

"So you weren't surprised to learn he was on the take?"

"*Non.*" The butter sizzled as he scraped the chopped vegetables into the pan. "You sorta get that idea as a kid when your dad comes home from work with pockets full of cash."

"I suppose that would be a good clue. It's funny, isn't it? That we both had dishonest parents?"

"Maybe we're back to that fate thing." He topped off her wineglass, then added tomato puree to the mixture.

"Maybe," she murmured. "And I can understand why you felt you had to come back to New Orleans to find out the truth. The same way I came to track down Tara's killer when it became obvious that the police were going to take the easy way out and not investigate the case." She took a sip of the crisp straw-colored wine he'd bought on the way back to the boat.

"I can even see why you joined the force, so you could get to know all the players up close and personal and sort out the good guys from the bad guys so you could start making a suspect list.

"But what I don't get is why you set yourself up to be caught collecting bribes when you knew that with all the media focus on the cops after Katrina, no one would be able to sweep your behavior under the rug."

She'd no sooner spoken than the answer hit home.

"That's why, isn't it? It's so much more difficult to get away with being crooked these days, you couldn't infiltrate yourself into the group by penny-ante stuff. You had to make a big splash to get noticed."

"Very good. You must be a—"

"Detective. Yeah, yeah, we've been through that before." She waved away his intended joke. "But wasn't it hard to do?"

"Actually, it was easy. There are still joints so used to paying cops for protection, no one hesitated when I suggested they wouldn't get hassled about certain *irregularities* if they contributed to the police widows and orphans fund."

"That's another thing straight out of the movie. Dennis Quaid justifies taking his cut because he's using it to put his kid brother through college."

"Yeah." He grinned. "I thought it was a nice, creative touch."

She shook her head. Studied him over the rim of her wineglass, unable to pigeonhole him.

"But didn't it bother you?" she asked seriously. "Having your reputation ruined like that?" She'd worked so hard to create a reputation that was 180 degrees from her mother's.

"Not really. I left here when I was seventeen, so it's not like I even had much of a local reputation to begin with."

"But you said it's a small town. That everyone pretty much knows everyone else."

"That's true enough. Remy and I grew up together; I first kissed the woman I later made the mistake of marrying at her sixth birthday party at Lake Pontchartrain park, and got into my first fistfight with Dubois when I was nine."

"Oh, please tell me you beat the shit out of him."

"Actually, it was the other way around." He took the shrimp she'd peeled and added them to the pot. "I was nine. He was twelve, big for his size—"

"Like he isn't now?"

"Big like chunky, not blubbery. He was also a bully. And, even then, a dickhead. Next time he came after me, I was ready with a baseball bat. If you look real close, you can see the scar on his forehead just above the corner of his left eye. He pretty much left me alone after that.

"But to get back to your question, given the choice between havin' my name sullied a bit and allowing cops who've sworn to protect and serve get away with cold-blooded murder, especially the murder of one of their own, no matter that he might be a bad apple, well"—he shrugged—"it was pretty much a no-brainer."

"Wow." She blew out a breath. "So much for doing things differently in the Big Easy. You're as black and white as I am, Broussard."

"I hadn't thought of it that way, but—"

"You are." She laughed, enjoying the idea. Enjoying the moment. And the man. "God, who would've thunk it?"

"Hopefully not the bad guys."

She sobered fast. "Do you have any idea who they are?"

"I know Dubois's in on it. And his nephew, George, who works burglary/arson and probably has under-the-counter deals with half the pawnbrokers in the city. Then there's John Flournoy, who used to work out of the Lower Ninth but was promoted to deputy chief of the Criminal Intelligence Bureau."

"The guy in charge of intelligence is crooked?"

"Sound familiar?"

"Yeah, just a bit," she said dryly.

"The difference is that from what you told me, and from what I read about the Chicago case, the guys you testified against were mostly just guilty of abuse of power."

"Like that's not enough?"

"Sure, it's bad." He added lemon juice, salt, and pepper to the simmering mixture. "But down here it's more about lining pockets."

He took another, longer swallow of beer. "A lot of the crooked patrol cops haven't come back. But there are enough left that I've no doubt business is going on as usual. Everyone's just being a lot more low-key about it now. A few days ago, I thought I was close to connecting the dots, but then . . ."

"Tara got killed. And you lost your informer. Your connection to LeBlanc. And whatever he was so determined to get back, which may have had something to do with your father . . ."

"I was trying not to put it quite that bluntly. Given your loss and all—"

She put her fingers against his mouth. "We each lost someone. Were they flawed? Sure. You bet. But like you said, that doesn't mean their lives didn't count. That whoever killed them shouldn't be held responsible for their murders. And if this guy LeBlanc was to blame, well, I've got a stake in this as well, which means I need to meet him."

"He's fucking dangerous."

She laughed at that idea. "And that's supposed to scare me off? I come from the city that gave the country Al Capone, Bugs Moran, and Sam Giancana."

"They weren't around in your day, but I get the point." He nudged her knees apart, moved between her legs. "You eat bad guys for lunch—"

She tilted her head, met his mouth. "And send them up the river for life plus ten." She sighed when his fingertips skimmed sparks over her breast. "That's probably why the cops trashed Tara's apartment."

"That'd be my guess." His clever hands, which had wielded that knife so deftly, were now busy on the buttons of her shirt.

"Do you think they found whatever it was?"

"No way of telling." He slid the shirt off one shoulder. "But I'm working on a new plan to find the smoking gun." Her pulse leaped when he nipped at her neck. "To let them think I know more than I do."

"Putting yourself at risk," she pointed out in a ragged moan as he pushed the shirt the rest of the way off.

A mist was floating over her mind, making it more and more difficult to keep her mind on the conversation. Her body softened. Moistened. Tingled with anticipation.

"No risk." His lips plucked at hers. "No reward." He lifted her off the stool, his hands beneath her butt. "And speaking of rewards."

She twined her arms around his neck, hooked her ankles together behind his back. "Won't dinner burn?"

Like she cared, when he was pressed against her, all hard and male, and wow, so hot she could feel him through the denim. But he'd gone to so much work to cook for her, she felt she at least ought to pretend to care.

"Depends on how long you need this to take."

Holding her tight, his mouth on hers, kissing her deep and deliciously, he walked the few feet to the galley table and sat her on it.

She laughed as she shimmied out of her drenched panties. "Oh, maybe like a minute will work for me."

What was it about Nick Broussard that she couldn't get enough of him?

"Roger that." He shoved the jeans down his legs, pausing only long enough to pull a condom from the pocket.

He was naked beneath those discarded jeans. Naked and gloriously, magnificently aroused. And, Kate marveled, as he sheathed that beautiful stony length, he was hers.

"I like a man who comes to the party prepared." She grabbed his hair, pulled his mouth down to hers.

"And I like a woman who's always ready." He pressed his palms against the insides of her thighs, spreading her legs apart.

She was hot. And so wet he was able to slide smoothly, perfectly into her.

"Ah, *mon ange*," he breathed. "You feel so good."

Her senses swam. Her mind shut down. If she could have spoken, she would have told him that he felt better than good. But all she could manage was a low, ragged moan.

"I could stay inside you forever." He put his hands beneath her, lifting her tighter against him.

No way was she going to complain about that idea!

Kate scissored her legs around him, her hips bucked, urging him on, as he thrust, withdrew, then thrust again, deeper, harder, his powerful stroke making her come again.

Kate heard a scream and realized it had been ripped from her own throat. Colors exploded in a brilliant kaleidoscope behind her eyes, blinding her as the climax slammed through her, made even more powerful by the knowledge that Nick was experiencing it, too.

The colors, fading to a rosy pink and hazy blue, floated peacefully, lazily, in her mind. Nick was half standing, half sprawled on top of her, his mouth against her throat.

She had no idea how long they'd been lying together that way. It could have been seconds. Minutes. Hours. She'd be more than happy to stay this way forever.

The kitchen timer he'd set when he'd put the rice on

to steam started to ding. She laughed and felt Nick's answering laugh deep inside her.

"Do you think that means we're done?" she asked.

He lifted his head and kissed her, a long, deep kiss she could feel all the way to her bare toes. "Not hardly."

Kate felt a sense of loss as he pulled out of her.

"But I need to feed you." His eyes warmed as they met hers, and held. "Keep up your strength." He ran a palm down her body, from her breast to her knees. "For everything I have in mind to do to you—with you—tonight."

The idea, along with the heat in his gaze, made her shiver. "Promises, promises." She flashed him a coy look of her own, amazing herself. If there was one thing Detective Kathleen Delaney did not do, it was coy.

"You're not exactly a teenager anymore, Broussard." She guessed he was probably all of thirty-three. "While I'm just reaching my sexual peak." Which might have just flown by unnoticed if she hadn't met her sexy Cajun ex-SEAL. "Are you sure you're capable of keeping up with me?"

He threw back his head. Washboard muscles she could have done laundry on rippled up his torso as he let loose a deep, rich, self-satisfied laugh.

"Don't you worry that pretty red head, *'tite chatte*," he said. "Because I guar-an-tee it."

A stuttering February sun was shining into the window when Kate woke the next morning. Although she still hadn't made any progress regarding Tara's death, her life had changed amazingly in just a few short days.

She had no idea where her relationship with Nick was headed. But, for the first time rather than feel the need to control every aspect of her life, she was willing to just go with the flow and enjoy being with him.

"It's New Orleans," she murmured as she ran her hand over the pillow that carried his sexy male scent. "Folks have a certain way of doing things here."

And wasn't she just enjoying the hell out of that certain way?

Laissez les bon temps rouler.

She rolled over onto her back. Grinned up at the ceiling as she thought about how many times she and Nick had let the good times roll last night. And how much she wanted to go rolling in them again.

She could hear him in the shower and was sorely tempted to join him, then decided that since neither of them had gotten much sleep last night, she'd surprise him with coffee, one of the few things she actually knew how to make.

As water began dripping through the coffeemaker, she decided to go outside and enjoy the morning.

With warm thoughts of last night's lovemaking spinning sensually in her mind, Kate was totally unprepared to be greeted by the horrific sight of fresh blood all over *The Hoo-yah*'s gleaming deck.

36

NICK HAD JUST PULLED UP HIS BRIEFS WHEN Kate's strangled scream jerked his mind from a hot replay of last night's sexathon.

Not bothering to grab his jeans, he dashed out of the stateroom and up the stairs, where he found her standing in the doorway leading out onto the teak deck.

"What the hell?" The door was draped in a fringe of black feathers. What appeared to be chicken bones were scattered around the deck, along with ashes and—what the fuck—blood?

"I'm sorry." She was standing there, dressed in a T-shirt and jeans he hadn't even realized she owned, her hair tousled from the wild night they'd shared, a riot of red curls falling over her shoulders, a hand over her mouth. "I didn't mean to scream, but . . .

"Oh, God." She dragged a shaky hand through her hair. "I was just surprised. We get some weird stuff in Chicago. But nothing like this."

"It's not exactly common here, either." He drew her into his arms and pressed his lips against her hair. She was putting up a good front but he could feel her tremble. "Let me get some shoes on and I'll scrub it down."

"You don't think it's human blood, do you?"

"Nah. From the looks of things, some unlucky chicken gave his all. As soon as I get it cleaned up, I'll call Téo, see what her best guess is about the meaning."

"Well, if it's that Jean-Renee Bertrand guy from Algiers and he's trying to scare me with dark Voodoo, it isn't going to work. Because I don't believe in that sort of stuff. But you know what really creeps me out? That someone was on the boat and we didn't know it."

Yeah. That was pissing him off, too. It was the second time in a week he'd been caught off guard.

"We were occupied with other things."

"Well, that's true enough." Color rose in her cheeks.

A man who'd always enjoyed contrasts, Nick loved not only that his tough-as-nails cop was sexy as sin, but that somehow, despite having had to grow up too fast, despite all her years working Chicago's mean streets, she'd managed to keep an innocence that allowed her to blush.

He was thinking about just letting the cleaning-up wait and taking her back to bed and making her blush all over when his phone rang.

"It's Remy," he said, glancing at the display. "Hey, *cher* . . . Okay. Sure, we'll be here." He flipped the phone closed.

"He's got the autopsy report," Kate guessed.

"That'd be my guess. He didn't say, but that's probably because by sharing it with us, he's breaking all sorts of departmental rules. He's comin' over in an hour or so."

"I'll go shower and change."

"Do me a favor?"

"What?"

Call him perverse, but he also liked that she didn't agree right away without finding out what the favor was first. She wouldn't be his Kate if she was that much of a pushover.

Life with Kate Delaney could be a challenge. But it would sure as hell never be boring.

"Go with the jeans instead of that official pantsuit thing. And if you've got another pair of those sexy-as-sin panties, it would give me a great deal of pleasure, while I'm cleaning up here and we're having to deal with the grown-up serious crime-fighting stuff, to anticipate stripping them back off you."

"You're terrible." She was fighting to keep her luscious lips, which were even fuller than normal from having been fully kissed all night long, from breaking into a smile.

"And you love it."

She went up on her toes and planted a quick, hard kiss against his mouth. "Abso-fucking-lutely."

"What could you have been thinking?" Téophine's red silk dressing gown swirled around her legs as she furiously paced the floor. "Taking such a risk?"

"No one caught me."

"They could have. Nick Broussard used to be a U.S. Navy SEAL. Trained in covert military combat."

"That may be," Toussaint said mildly. "But he was not playing soldier last night. And between the rain and his and Desiree's sister's lovemaking, an entire enemy army could've stormed onto the boat and he wouldn't have noticed."

"It was still foolhardy."

"The woman is in danger."

"And what business is that of yours? You don't know her."

"She is Desiree's twin. Desiree's blood. Desiree's other half." He pushed himself off the sofa with a heavy sigh. "The woman you were once friends with, the woman I loved with all my being, is a *lwa* now. Can you tell me that you don't believe she expects me to protect her sister?"

"Like you were able to protect Desiree?" Téo flared, batting away at his hands as he tried to take her into his arms. "Oh, God. I'm sorry."

She turned her back. Closed her eyes and pressed a hand tipped with bloodred nails against her breast. "That was unnecessarily cruel."

"Don't feel the need to apologize. Because it's all too true."

Her brother's turquoise eyes glistened as he stood behind her, shaping her shoulders with his hands. He wasn't sure which of them he was attempting to soothe. "I wasn't able to save Desiree. I won't allow this Kate person to suffer the same fate."

She turned and framed his face with her palms. Her own expression was tortured. "And if it gets you killed?"

"Broussard is a good man. He'd never kill an innocent person."

"I wasn't talking about Nick. I was referring to whoever it was who threw Desiree to her death. Did it occur to you that you may be murdered as well?"

"Of course."

"And?"

"Then my soul would be together with Desiree's in Ginen. I can't think of anything that would give me more pleasure. More peace."

"Peace," Téo scoffed bitterly. "That is not a word anyone would ever use in connection with Desiree Doucett."

"She was growing in the faith. She was finding peace within herself. And when we were together, honoring the Gédé with our bodies, well, I don't know how to describe it, but lying with her afterward was the most peaceful I have ever felt."

"Sex is like that."

"Sometimes," he agreed. "But it was different with her."

She pulled away again. Resumed pacing. "How many men do you think gave her money to feel exactly that way? She sold her body, Toussaint! She knew what men wanted. And she gave it to them."

"I never paid her anything. And she was leaving that life."

"So she said."

She stopped again. Took a deep breath.

"I wish you'd never met the whore."

"If I'd died without ever having known Desiree, I would have died without ever knowing true joy."

"Or pain."

"Life consists of two sides," he said, reminding her what she'd told Nick Broussard and Desiree's sister when they'd come into the shop seeking information about left-hand magic. "Light and dark. Joy and sorrow. Without a balance, one cannot fully experience a full and well-rounded life."

He took hold of her upper arms again, restraining her when she tried to twist away. "Don't worry."

"I'm your older sister. It's my fate to worry."

"I'll be fine. Now I must go."

"Where?"

"I had a dream last night. Of the woman, Kathleen, out in the bayou. In danger. I must watch out for her."

"That's Broussard's job."

"Yes, you'd think that, wouldn't you?" he agreed. "But in my dream, he was bound hand and foot by trumpet vines and hung over a deep, dark pit."

"But alive?"

"He was when I awoke." He touched his lips to her forehead, which was uncharacteristically marred with deep horizontal lines. "But just in case—"

"Be careful," she begged. "Stay safe."

"*Si Dieu vlé,*" he responded. God willing.

Truer words were never spoken. He'd done everything he could to save Desiree. But all his efforts and prayers and spells had failed.

For some reason, while he'd been serving gumbo and overly sweet Hurricanes to drunken tourists, she'd left his home and gone to her own apartment, only to plunge to her too-young death. Since then Toussaint had not been able to escape the feeling that the world, at least his little corner of it, had spun totally out of control.

37

"I HAVE SOME GOOD NEWS," NICK SAID AS KATE joined him in the galley.

"Tell me Remy called again and told you they've caught Tara's killer." She took the mug he held out to her, cupped it between her hands, and breathed in the fragrant steam.

"Sorry. But I described the woo-woo Voodoo stuff to Téo and she says the feathers were probably from a black rooster. The blood and bones as well. It's a protection charm."

"I suppose that's good news." Kate still wasn't so sure. The idea of any Voodoo person skulking around on the boat while she and Nick had been making love, or sleeping, was still more than creepy. "Does she have any idea who did it?"

"She thinks it might have been some guy who was sort of mentoring your sister in the religion."

"What?" Kate nearly choked on her coffee. "There was some guy in her life and Téo Jannise knew it and never said anything when we were at her shop?"

"Yeah, I asked her about that. She said she hadn't thought to mention it because she was so shocked to learn Tara was dead."

"So, what did she have to say now?"

"Only what I told you." He broke some eggs into a bowl.

"You asked her his name, right?"

Nick gave her a look.

"Okay. Sorry. Of course you did. What did she say?"

"Not much. In fact, she pretty much dodged the question."

"Which we're not going to let her get away with, right?"

"Right. I figured we'd drop by her shop after Remy leaves. Which is going to be a while, by the way. He called again and said something had come up."

"About Tara?"

"No. He caught a case. A carjacking went bad last night and two tourists are going back to Baltimore in pine boxes."

"That's tough."

"Yeah, even tougher because Remy doesn't think they were real tourists, given that they had rap sheets as long as your legs."

She smiled at the compliment and gave him a quick, light kiss. "Does he think they were in town on business?"

"Yeah. Like I said, things are pretty wide-open right now, what with all the gangbanger drug dealers fighting over turf. So I suppose it's not unexpected that out-of-towners would be trying to muscle in. But I don't envy Remy."

"Why not? It sounds fairly routine, as far as drug murders go."

"It would be. Were it not for the little fact that one of the victims just happens to be the son of a Maryland congresswoman."

"Ouch." Kate whistled. "I don't have my crystal ball with me, but I think I see a red ball case in Detective Remy Landreaux's immediate future."

"Yeah. He figures he's got about four hours, tops, before the media leaps onto the story."

"So what are we going to do for the next four hours?"

"I was thinking about mixin' up a little batter for *pain perdue*. But if you've got something else in mind . . ."

Kate did.

And it was the last thing either one of them was to say for a very long time.

It turned out to be closer to six hours. Since even they couldn't make love all that time, Kate found herself enjoying being forced to sit around and do nothing.

Well, not exactly nothing. They played several hands of gin rummy, finally tossing in the towel with them tied.

And they talked. She shared stories of cases she'd worked, he told her about missions his team had been on around the world. At least the ones he was free to talk about; she accepted that others would have to remain classified.

He also told her about returning home early from a mission and discovering his wife was having an affair with her hairdresser. She thought it said something about his character that he didn't seem to blame her, but only said that being the wife of a SEAL could be tough duty.

They discovered they both loved books, enjoyed many of the same authors, although he didn't share her fondness for romance novels, which she decided was fair because she really didn't "get" Westerns, either.

Neither were that wild about reality TV shows, although Kate admitted to being a sucker for any program about animal rescues on the Animal Planet, and Nick liked *Cops*, which made Kate laugh because, after all, how many drunks in how many trailer parks can any one program show?

They both had eclectic tastes in music, with a preference for country, although she liked jazz, which he believed sounded like "warm-up" music, and she was still trying to gain an appreciation of hip-hop.

And in a discussion she thought should have been uncomfortable, they learned they both someday wanted a family and children. But not now.

And when they weren't talking, they just sat out on the deck, enjoying the warm South Louisiana winter day, and the company.

At first Kate felt a little strange. Off center. As if she'd been at sea for a very long time and hadn't quite gotten her land legs back.

Then, finally, as the sun lowered on the horizon, she

realized that what she was feeling was relaxation. It had been such a long time since she'd let go of her anxiety and stress, she'd forgotten what it felt like not to be emotionally and mentally tied up in knots.

"Wait until we get you out in the Gulf," Nick said when she shared that revelation with him. "You'll never want to come back to the real world."

When he'd first suggested sailing away, Kate had scoffed, considering just lifting anchor and heading off for parts unknown the height of irresponsibility. Now there was something wonderfully appealing about the idea.

She was about to tell him that when an unmarked police car pulled into the lot. Without even thinking of what she was doing, Kate held a hand out toward Nick, who laced their fingers together.

"Whatever it is," he said, "we'll work on it together."

Like a team. And wasn't that another concept that had seemed unthinkable when she'd first arrived at *The Hoo-yah*? One that now seemed as natural as breathing.

Even knowing how Remy must've been under the gun, and working his tail off on his political red ball murder case, Kate had to marvel as he strolled toward them on a long, sexy stride that reminded her of a sleek panther.

"What the hell does he do?" she asked, taking in the navy blazer, the crisp white shirt topped off with a perfectly knotted navy-and-red-striped tie, gray slacks creased to a razor's edge, and loafers shined to a mirror gloss. "Take a Teflon shower every morning before going into the station?"

"He's always been that way," Nick said. "He was the only kid in our first communion class who ended the day with his shirt and shorts as snowy white as when he'd put them on. Hell, I've been on stakeouts with him, and not once did he ever spill hot sauce from his po' boy onto his shirt. And don't even think about tossing a burger bag on the floor. It was a lot like bein' stuck in a car with Felix Ungar."

"Well, I'm glad someone's having a good day," Remy drawled when Kate laughed at Nick's description.

"We're just sharin' a joke, *cher*," Nick said.

"Well, share it with me, because I could sure use a good laugh."

"Sorry." Nick exchanged a look with Kate, who was studiously biting her lip. "It's sorta private."

Remy flicked a quick, judicious look from Nick to Kate. Then back to Nick again. Although his eyes were hidden behind a pair of designer aviator shades, once again Kate had the feeling they weren't putting anything over on the special-crimes cop.

"Well, I can't stay long. I just wanted to bring you this file. Which, by the way, you've never seen."

"Roger that," Nick agreed as he took the manila envelope Remy handed over. He in turn passed it to Kate. "How's your murder going?"

"Don't ask."

"Want a beer before you get back to the salt mines?"

Remy glanced down at his gold-banded watch. "Yeah. Sure. Sounds great."

As Nick went below for the beer, he sprawled in one of the deck chairs.

"I appreciate you taking the time to do this for me," Kate said. "Especially when it involves going against policy."

"Hey, if you can't break the rules for friends, what's the point?" he asked. "Besides, in case Nick hasn't told you, this is—"

"The Big Easy," Kate said with a smile, trying not to blush about some of the things Nick had done to her using just that excuse. "Folks have a certain way of doing things down here."

"Fuckin' A," he said, returning her smile with a dazzling one of his own.

As good-looking as Nick was, Remy Landreaux seemed more like a TV or movie cop than a real one. He and Nick must've cut quite a swath through the girls of New Orleans, back in their high school years.

"Here you go, *cher*." Nick was back, carrying three brown bottles of Abita Bock. He handed one to Kate, another to Remy, and kept one for himself.

Kate held her breath as she pulled the papers from the envelope. As much as she wanted to know, *needed* to know the facts of her sister's death, there was another very strong part of her that just wished she could sail away.

She cast a quick glance up at the mizzenmast, then caught Nick watching her and realized he knew exactly what she was thinking. She also knew that although he wanted to solve his father's murder as much as she did Tara's, if she said the word, they'd be off.

Despite having always considered herself a strong, independent woman, knowing Nick Broussard was in her corner gave her the strength to begin reading.

Rather than start with all the dry details, height, and weight—which she noticed was within half a pound of her own—Kate skimmed down to the final page.

"Manner of death undetermined?"

"There wasn't enough evidence, *cher*," Remy said, speaking to her more as a grieving survivor than a cop. "The cause of death was clear enough—"

"A broken neck." She momentarily closed her eyes as the image of her sister hitting that stone fountain flashed through her mind. She imagined she could hear the crack of bone.

"Even Dubois called that one," the detective said. "But manner . . ." He gave her a palms-up shrug. "Bein' a homicide detective yourself, you know the coroner could've found for murder, accident, or suicide. Though I know it's tough to accept, my money's on suicide. But it's still just an educated guess."

Kate knew he had a point. But the determination had knocked so much wind out of her sails. Where to go next?

Rubbing her temple, she went back to the beginning and began to study the report, line by line.

"There's no mention of that tattoo you told me about," she said to Nick.

"What tattoo?" Remy asked.

"A gad," Nick answered. "It was of a coiled serpent. Supposedly to represent both some Voodoo goddess and the snake Marie Laveau used to dance with in Congo Square. It was on her breast."

As if worried he'd wandered into dangerous conversational waters, Nick immediately turned his attention from his former partner to Kate, who only shrugged. However Nick knew the location of her sister's tattoo was the very least of her concerns right now.

"Maybe it'll show up later in the report," he said.

"Maybe." Though unlikely, since that type of information was always the first to be written up. "Do you have the photos?"

"Sorry," the detective said. "Not yet. This was faxed over because the ME knew we were in a hurry for it."

It was difficult to separate cop from sister as she read about the semen that had glowed fluorescent beneath examination from the Woods light.

"Has anyone checked to find the man she'd last been with?" she asked Remy.

"We're working on that. Actually, *I'm* working on it, because, well, how do I put it politely, my current partner is pretty much a—"

"Dickhead," Kate and Nick said together.

Remy nodded. Shrugged. "That's it. Anyway, although it was one of the busiest party nights of the year, she didn't work the ship that night."

"You sure?"

"There wasn't any record, and none of the girls I spoke with remembered her being there."

"So whoever she was with was either off the books or a personal friend." Kate exchanged another glance with Nick and knew that once again they were on the same wavelength. They needed to find the Voodoo guy.

"That's pretty much what I was thinking," Remy agreed. "Problem is, we get a helluva lot of out-of-towners during Mardi Gras. A lot who probably are long gone."

"Back to their safe, boring worlds," Kate muttered. It would be like looking for a damn penis in a haystack.

They shared the same blood type. Her lungs were a dark and sooty gray, revealing her to be a heavy smoker, her enlarged liver evidence of alcohol abuse. Which wasn't surprising. Kate couldn't remember meeting a prostitute who didn't feel the need to self-medicate.

Her blood chilled as she read the next item.

"She was pregnant?"

"So it says," Remy said. "Not uncommon in the business. Even the best precautions aren't one hundred percent effective."

"That's not the point." Kate's head was reeling. There had to be a mistake. "It's impossible."

"Why?" Remy, who'd remained comfortably sprawled in a deck chair, enjoying his beer, abruptly sat up. He was now openly alert, giving Kate hope that Tara had just knocked the red ball gangbanger down to number two on his crime-solving priority list.

"She had an STD her sophomore year of high school. Life had been complicated, she'd been looking for comfort and love in all the wrong places—"

"No one's judging her, *chère*," Nick said gently.

"She wouldn't be the first fifteen-year-old to have sex with the wrong guy," Remy seconded.

"No." Kate sighed. "And unfortunately she probably wasn't the first fifteen-year-old to end up sterile because of it."

"Christ," Remy muttered, shoving a hand through his sun-gilded hair.

"If the coroner didn't make a major mistake," Nick said, "that means the girl in the courtyard wasn't Tara."

Kate had known her sister hadn't committed suicide. She also hadn't believed, when Remy Landreaux had first called her, that she could be dead.

But the idea that she was alive, perhaps still somewhere in this city, proved staggering.

38

THE IDEA OF TARA BEING ALIVE DIDN'T DETRACT from Kate's need to solve whatever crime had taken place. On the contrary, now that she knew her sister wasn't dead, there was even more reason to find her before the bad guys learned they'd killed the wrong person.

"Maybe they meant to kill this other woman, whoever she was, in the first place," she suggested.

"Then Tara wouldn't be hiding," Nick pointed out.

"Maybe she doesn't know. Maybe she took off on a vacation somewhere." Kate knew she was grasping at straws. "Damn. I guess the thing to do now is go back to the beginning. Try to track down her Voodoo lover. And talk to LeBlanc."

"Let's not tip our hand to LeBlanc. It makes sense for Remy to interview him one last time to close out the case. If Leon knows we're interested, he might start wondering what's changed since the other night. If he believes his goons have killed her, he won't be out looking for her again."

"But maybe the reason he isn't looking for her is because he already has her."

"Good point. But LeBlanc runs his operation on a take-no-prisoners basis. Though I hate to say it, *chère*, given that we're talking about your sister, if he or his kid or his goons found her before I could, he would've gotten the information from her real quick. Then . . ."

His voice dropped off. Kate realized he was searching for some words that wouldn't hurt her. But she'd been a cop too long not to know exactly what path his mind had gone down.

"Then he'd dispose of her body."

"Plenty of places to do that," he said. "The bayou's a big place. And after a few days, between the gators, the snapping turtles, the fish, and the tides, there wouldn't be much body left to pop to the surface."

She shivered. Closed her eyes. Drew in a deep breath, then recaptured her resolve.

"Well, then, we're just going to have to find her alive."

Kate knew their chances were slim. But she also knew that she'd never be able to live with herself if she didn't try.

The one thing that very few TV shows ever got right was that being a cop wasn't about guns and car chases. What it mostly entailed was wearing out shoe leather.

While Remy went off to interview the LeBlancs again, Nick and Kate returned to Téo Jannise's Voodoo shop, only to find it closed and shuttered.

"Coincidence, do you think?" Kate asked as they looked past all the alligator heads and displays of beads in the front window, trying to see into the darkened store.

"It could be. Then again, NOPD has always leaked like a sieve. Could be there are more copies of that autopsy floating around than the one Remy gave us."

"But the key was the pregnancy. Who else could know Tara couldn't get pregnant?"

"LeBlanc, for one. Since one reason his business does so well is that he's got a mandatory health-screening process for his girls. And, although I haven't tested it personally, I'm told that any girl who doesn't practice safe sex is out of there. No matter how popular she is."

"So any doctor who works for him—"

"Would've probably mentioned her not needing additional birth control with her condoms."

"So we're back to LeBlanc being at the top of the suspect list."

"Him and his kid, Stephen, yeah."

"And—"

"Her Voodoo lover," they both said together.

"Which makes your old friend Téo's shop being closed less of a coincidence."

"*Mais*, yeah," Nick agreed with a dark frown as he started punching buttons on his cell phone. "Let's see if we can find out where she lives."

The hurricane shutters on the single-story shotgun in the Faubourg Marigny Historic District were closed, which made it impossible to see inside, but when no one answered the bell, Nick and Kate had to assume the owner wasn't home.

"I could break in," Nick offered.

"If her house is even half as cluttered as her store, it'd take an eternity to find anything that might be helpful," Kate muttered. "Besides," she added as a black-and-white police car cruised by, slowing as it viewed them standing on the porch, "one thing neither of us needs is to get busted."

They were back in the much more visible Hummer, having dropped the Escalade back at the parking garage, then placing an anonymous call to the cops telling them where to pick it up.

"Good point."

They decided to try Antoinette again. When the butler informed them she was at the hospital visiting her husband, they tracked her down there, only to run into another dead end.

"I'm not that surprised," Kate said as they left the hospital. "I wouldn't share any of *my* secrets with *her*, either. And even if Tara had tried to tell her about the trouble she was in, she wouldn't have listened unless it immediately impacted her life."

"Which is screwed up enough," Nick said.

"Now, there's a surprise."

"We could go back to the left-hand guy," Kate suggested as he gave her a boost up into the passenger seat. "Push on him a bit more, see if he'll be more cooperative."

"I doubt that. The guy didn't seem all that intimidated the first time."

"You could threaten to shoot him," she said after he'd come around and gotten into the Hummer. Unlike when they'd been in the rental car, or even the Escalade, she felt as if he were sitting in a different zip code. "Or, hey, better yet, let him know that he's dealing with a trained assassin."

"It's nice to know you find me useful."

"Oh, I do." She leaned across the Grand Canyon of a gulf between them and pressed her lips against his. "For more than the fact that you know how to break a bad guy's neck."

"And you learned this where?" he asked as he splayed a hand against the back of her head and deepened the kiss.

"Hey, I read. Watch the History and Discovery Channels. You SEALs are hot these days." She trailed a fingernail up his thigh and felt an almost giddy sense of feminine power as the muscles clenched. "If only people knew how hot."

"You keep that up, sweetheart, and you're going to find out what it's like to have sex in a Hummer."

That had never been on her to-do list before. But because it was suddenly sounding more than a little appealing, she clasped her hands together in her lap to keep them out of trouble.

"So, what do you suggest we do about the guy in Algiers?"

"Let's send Remy out there," he decided, flipping

open his phone. "Jean-Renee Bertrand might be as co-operative as a stone, but unless he's independently wealthy, he's still got to make a living. I'd be real surprised if that place meets code. Maybe if Remy flashes his badge, suggests a possible visit from the fire marshal, he might be able to shake something loose."

39

TARA WAS UP TO HER ELBOWS IN BREAD dough when her cell phone began playing Rihanna's "Unfaithful."

She froze. Then assured herself it had to be a wrong number. Or someone trying to get her to change her phone service. Or buy vinyl siding.

The call couldn't be for her. Because everyone believed she was dead. Didn't they?

Some people were able to ignore a ringing phone. Tara had never been one of those people.

Wiping her sticky hands on a dish towel, she dug into a pocket and pulled it out.

And blew out a relieved breath when she recognized the familiar number on the caller ID.

She flipped it open.

"Hello," she said cautiously, because you could never be too careful.

"Hey, girl," the all-too-familiar voice said. "Welcome back to the living."

∙ ∙ ∙

Nick and Kate had just made it back to the marina when Nick's phone rang.

"Yeah, Remy?"

"Hey, *cher*. Look, you know that guy you asked me to check? Runs that restaurant where you were thinking of throwing your new girlfriend that party?"

Nick hadn't just fallen off the crawfish truck yesterday. "Sure," he said, playing along with whatever ruse his former partner had going. "What about it?"

"Well, he says he needs to talk to you. That he's not gonna agree to any deal unless he gets his down payment and your signature on the contract for the party room."

They both knew there was no party. Or restaurant. Which could only mean that Remy had reason to think his phone calls were being monitored. Which wasn't good news.

"Well, that could be a problem tonight," he said. "Because obviously I can't take the lady with me." He put a finger up to his lips, warning Kate to keep quiet. "And although you nailed her shooter, just in case that pissed-off Chicago boyfriend hired himself a backup, I don't feel real comfortable about leaving her alone right now."

He could tell Kate was less than pleased by that comment. Which was too damn bad. He was willing to meet Remy in Algiers, but no way was he leaving her alone just when things had taken a turn he hadn't yet figured out.

"No problem. Remember my little brother Johnny?"

"Sure. We used to sit on the top of your parents' couch and knock him down with throw pillows back when he was learning to walk."

Despite the seriousness of the subject, Nick grinned as Kate lifted her brows.

"That's him. He's a patrolman uptown. I thought I'd send him over to babysit Kate."

"That might work." Nick still didn't like the idea of leaving her, but Remy seemed determined, which meant something big was up. "So long as he isn't still holding a grudge from those toddler days."

"Hell, no. He's the easiest-goin' guy you'd ever want to meet. Kid reminds me of a cocker spaniel puppy, he's so eager to please."

"Okay, then. But if I were you, I'd advise him not to use that *b* word when describing his assignment."

Remy laughed. "Got it. So, we're on?"

"Yeah. I guess so." It would, Nick thought, be like the old days, when they were kids and Remy used to play cops and robbers. Thinking back, more often than not Johnny Landreaux would get cast as the robber and end up being locked into one of the kennels the Landreauxs kept for their hunting dogs.

"I'll meet you there after Johnny shows."

"Great." Remy hung up.

"So?" Kate said. "What were you trying so hard not to tell me?"

"Remy couldn't talk. Not sure why, but he wants me to meet him in Algiers."

"I'm coming with you."

"No, you're not."

"Excuse me?" She rose to her full height. Folded her arms. "There's no way you're leaving me here with a babysitter while you go out and play cop. Which, may I point out, you no longer are."

"Johnny Landreaux isn't a babysitter. Think of him as another member of the team."

"It's the same damn thing."

"Kate." Talk about your timing, Nick thought as he saw the black-and-white cruiser roll up to the dock. "Please. You hired me. Let me do my job."

"Dammit, Broussard—"

"Okay, here's the deal," he said. "I'll call you as soon as I get there. If there's not one helluva good reason for you not to be in on the conversation with Bertrand, I'll tell Johnny to bring you right over."

"Did I mention I don't like compromise?" she asked as the young man in the spiffy blue uniform and shiny badge came walking toward the boat.

"I seem to recall you saying something along those lines. But give me this one thing, and I promise as soon as I get back here, you can compromise me all you want."

"I'm pissed at you."

"I know."

"But I suppose I did hire you because it's *your* town."

"Right." He lowered his forehead to hers. "We're wasting time here, *chère*. I swear I'll call as soon as I get there."

He felt her beginning to cave in. She wasn't happy. But he could fix that later. Right now, although he knew it was chauvinistic as hell, he just wanted to keep her safe.

"All right." Her frustrated sigh feathered her fiery bangs. Then she gave him a long, level warning look. "I want to know exactly what you know. When you know it."

"Absolutely."

Nick turned to the cop, who didn't look much younger than the rogue cop who'd held a gun to his head only three nights ago. Damned if Johnny Landreaux hadn't grown up to be nearly as good-looking as his big brother. And didn't it just figure that his uniform would be starched, his black cop shoes spit-polished?

"Hey, Johnny."

"Hey, Nick." The face, smooth as a newborn baby's bottom, split into a big smile. "Great to see you again. I was thinking about you a while back. While I was watching this special on SEALs on the Discovery Channel."

"Is that so?" Nick glanced over at Kate, hoping to share a smile. No such luck. "Well, I shouldn't be long," he said after introductions were made. "Meanwhile, don't let anyone on the boat. And whatever you do, don't let Detective Delaney out of your sight."

"Don't worry." Johnny stopped just short of saluting. "The lady's safe with me."

"Give the kid a break," Nick murmured in Kate's ear as he gave her a quick hug. He hadn't missed the sparks that had shot out of her eyes when she'd been referred to as a lady. "He's young. Green."

"An idiot," she muttered, refusing to smile. Or hug him back.

But she did let him go.

Kate watched Nick walk down the dock. Climb into the Hummer. Then drive away. He didn't look back, but she knew he was watching her in the rearview mirror, so she crossed her arms again and shot the departing vehicle her darkest scowl.

"I'm sorry, Detective," the kid cop said, his downcast expression echoing his words.

Kate had two choices. She could take her frustration with Nick out on Remy Landreaux's baby brother. Which would be like kicking a puppy.

Or she could suck it up and try to make the best of her situation.

"You don't have to apologize," she said, turning back toward him. "After all, it's not your—"

Oh, damn, damn, damn! She'd been so busy glaring at Nick, she hadn't noticed Johnny Landreaux taking that syringe from his pocket. The needle flashed, and before she could knock it out of his hand, she felt the prick at the back of her neck.

"I'm sorry," he said again. The weird thing was, he actually seemed to mean it.

"What the hell did you shoot into me?"

"It's just a sedative. It won't kill you," he assured her. "We just need to get you out of the way for a while."

"Why?" Was it her imagination, responding to the suggestion of being drugged? Or did she already feel her tongue thickening? "And who's *we*?"

"You'll find out soon enough." He put his arm around her waist as she started to sway. "Now, we'd better get you into the patrol car before the stuff hits your bloodstream. Because if I have to call for backup . . ." He shook his head. "Let's just say you really don't want that, ma'am."

"It's Detective," Kate managed to correct him. "Not ma'am." Her head was floating and her legs were turning to rubber. "And you're going to be very, very sorry you did this."

She knew that if anything happened to her, Nick would go into scorched-earth mode and absolutely, positively destroy the bad guys' universe.

The problem was, Kate thought, as she concentrated putting one foot in front of the other, despite what the kid cop said about the drug not being fatal, she still might not be alive to witness the conflagration.

40

KATE HAD NO IDEA WHERE SHE WAS. HOW SHE'D gotten here. Or how long she'd been unconscious.

She lay in a room that was as dark as a tomb, trying to take inventory. Her arms, particularly her wrists, ached. When she tried to rub her temple, which was throbbing with the mother of all headaches, she belatedly realized that she'd been handcuffed.

She was lying on some sort of canvas cot; when she attempted to move her legs, she found her ankles shackled as well.

"So, Sleeping Beauty wakes," someone said in a rumbling laugh.

Kate would recognize that voice anywhere. Even in her sleep.

Remembering what Nick had said about bodies disappearing into the bayou, she forced her foggy, aching mind to concentrate on getting out of this situation alive.

"Well, if it isn't Detective Dubois. Fancy meeting you here." She looked around. If there were any windows, they were covered, making it impossible to tell if it was day or night. "Where, exactly, is here?"

"No need for you to know that, bitch." The wood floor creaked as he lumbered over to stand beside her. "Since you're not going to be leavin'."

"I'm a detective," she reminded him. *Stay calm. Focus.* "And a woman." Although she wanted to gag on the words, she forced herself to sound as much like a poor, weak female-as-victim as she could. "You know how curious we are."

"Yeah." A match flared as he lit a kerosene lamp, allowing Kate to see how flat and reptilian his eyes were. "I also know what whores you are." He bent down, closed his pudgy, fat fingers over her breast, and squeezed hard. "I had your sister once."

Kate didn't believe him. From what Nick had told her, Martin Dubois wouldn't have been able to afford Tara. And she knew that her sister never would have willingly had sex with this dickhead.

"You don't believe me." His fingers tightened like a vise.

"Why would you lie?"

He didn't answer that question. Instead, he apparently decided to share a bit of the nasty particulars with her.

"She threatened to tell LeBlanc. Get me kicked off the security detail. But hey, you can't rape a whore, right? Besides, a guy can tell when a bitch likes being hurt. And your sister liked it. A lot."

Before Kate had gotten appointed to homicide, she'd worked sex crimes. Knowing what some men were capable of, having seen what she'd seen, Kate didn't want to think of what he must have done to Tara.

Which she feared wasn't nearly as bad as what he planned to do to her. Before he killed her.

"How about you?" His hand moved to her other breast. "You look like her." He released her long enough to grasp the rounded neckline of the T-shirt with both hands and ripped. "Do you fuck like her?"

"I don't know how she fucked." Relying on acting skills she'd only ever had to use on those occasions Vice would send her out to play undercover hooker, Kate managed to keep her tone matter-of-fact. "But I was always better at everything growing up." It wasn't easy shrugging while lying on her back, but Kate managed. "So, I suppose I'm better."

His hands, which were groping at her lace-covered breasts, momentarily stilled. Well, she'd definitely gotten his attention with that assertion.

"But," she tacked on silkily, "I suppose there's only one way for you to find out."

He was tempted. She could feel it.

His fingers tightened again, digging into her bared flesh in a way Kate knew would leave bruises.

It's okay. Bruises fade.

Death, she reminded herself as one hand moved to the metal button on her low-cut jeans, *is permanent.*

41

"LET'S GO OVER THIS ONE MORE TIME SO I CAN get it straight." Nick was sitting in the office of the St. Jude homeless shelter. Desiree/Tara's face was white as cold ashes, her eyes red-rimmed. Father Mike Gannon sat behind his desk, his expression grim. "Remy called you?"

She nodded. "Th-th-that's right. He told me that they had Kate." She still couldn't believe her sister was in New Orleans. And Remy and Dubois had captured her? How could that have happened? "That they were going to kill her unless I brought them the tape."

"The tape showing the murder of a hooker."

"Jasmine was my friend."

Tara still remembered how shocked she'd been when the john had hit Jas so hard, he'd knocked her off her feet. She knew she'd remember the sound of her head slamming into the metal leg of the bed, like the thunk of a ripe melon hitting the pavement, for the rest of her life.

"Sorry," he said. "Bad choice of words."

She could tell Nick was about ready to explode and

knew only his incredible control was keeping him from shouting. From putting one of those fisted hands through the wall. If he'd been anyone else, she would have been afraid, from the icy rage in his eyes, that he'd kill her. Just like that bastard had done to Jas.

"She *was* a prostitute," Tara allowed. "I just wanted to point out that she was more."

"Point taken." He heaved out a deep breath. Stretched out his fisted fingers, then thrust them through his dark hair. "All the more reason you should've gone to the police."

"Which ones?" she challenged. "Besides, I went to you."

"You only told me you had something on LeBlanc." Tara found Nick's soft, rigidly controlled tone more dangerous than a shout. "You didn't tell me it involved murder."

"How could I be sure I could trust you? After all, you were kicked out of the cops for taking a bribe."

"Then there was also a chance you could make some money on the deal," Father Mike suggested mildly.

Tara thought he was damn casual about all this, for a priest. Then again, he'd probably heard a lot of bad stuff in the confessional over the years.

"Look, it sounds worse than it was," she said, not quite believing her words herself. Hearing them out loud, they sounded pretty bad. Made *her* sound bad. "I was into LeBlanc for a bundle. From the surgery, which, by the way, I never asked for, and the drugs, back when I was using.

"Since I couldn't bring Jas back, I figured I might as well see if I could get enough bucks from that big shot to pay off my debt."

"By stealing that tape from LeBlanc?" Nick said. "You didn't think that'd piss him off?"

"Well, yeah. I guess that was a major flaw in the plan. But I was also thinking that maybe me and Toussaint could just take off to somewhere. Like Haiti. Where LeBlanc wouldn't bother to look for us."

She watched the two men exchange a look over her head and knew they were thinking she was an idiot. Which maybe she was. Hadn't Toussaint tried to warn her she was playing with a very dangerous fire?

"And Toussaint is?"

"Téo's brother. She owns the—"

"Yeah. The Voodoo place. Hell, I never even knew she *had* a brother."

"Technically he's her half-brother. He only came to the States a few years ago. From Haiti."

"Okay. So, your other friend—"

"Kels," Tara said. "She was hiding out at my place. I guess the guys LeBlanc sent after me mistook her for me."

"LeBlanc didn't send them," Nick said.

"How do you know that?"

"Because he told me."

"And you believed that SOB?"

"Yeah. Because he sent me."

"He sent you? To kill me?"

"No. To find you, and, I suppose, bring the tape back. Because it's my guess he was already milking the guy."

"Who, being a Homeland Security big shot, was able to make sure LeBlanc's companies got the bulk of the federal hurricane cleanup and reconstruction contracts." Michael Gannon filled in that blank.

"Got it in one," Nick agreed.

It was taking every vestige of self-control Nick possessed not to shake Tara until her teeth rattled for what she'd done. But he reminded himself that losing his temper would only make him lose focus.

He'd gotten his first inkling that things were going bad when he'd arrived in Algiers only to discover that Remy had never shown up. Then Kate hadn't answered her phone, and her mother—no surprise here—had professed not to have heard from her.

He'd been speeding back across the CCC when Desiree's call had come in. And his world, for a fleeting moment, had stood horrifyingly still.

"Those feds undoubtedly didn't go on their information-gathering tours themselves in those early days after Katrina, did they?" he asked the priest.

"Of course not. It would have been too dangerous."

His voice was dry, as if to point out life had certainly turned out to be deadly dangerous for so many local citizens. "They were given police escorts. I suspect, if you do a little digging into the logbooks from those days, you'll find your former partner was one of those escorts."

That made perfect sense. During the weeks after the hurricane, a lot of the politicians had been scrambling to cover their collective asses, which meant appearing on television. As they walked through the streets of devastated neighborhoods, such as the Lower Ninth, they were accompanied by cops.

Considering how bad NOPD had looked in the early days of the flooding, it only stood to reason that they would've wanted to present themselves in the best possible light. And who better to do that than a guy who could've appeared on a police recruitment poster?

"And Remy told you to tell me to bring you out to LeBlanc's camp?" he asked Tara.

"Yeah. I wondered about that, but—"

"He's wrapping up loose ends," Mike Gannon said. "He's already got Detective Delaney. You've teamed up with her, which means you know as much as she does, so you've got to go, as well. And, of course, he wants that tape."

"I think you've nailed it, Padre," Nick said. "And there's something more."

He gave Tara, who already looked as if her nerves were hanging by their last thread, his sternest look.

"My dad worked on LeBlanc's casino ship, didn't he?"

"Sure. But you knew that. He was head of the security detail."

"Which meant he could've been watching the cameras on the gambling floor and in all the rooms."

"He liked to watch." Tara shrugged. "A lot of the girls knew that and played to the cameras even more whenever he was on duty."

Nick hadn't needed to know that about his old man. But then again, he'd never had any illusions about Big Antoine.

It had taken a while, but the final piece of the puzzle that was his father's murder clicked into place.

"He bucked when it came to letting that guy get off with murder, didn't he?"

Tara's smile was sad. "Big Antoine was really mad. He said taking graft was one thing. Murder was another. Yeah, *cher,* he tried to stand for Jasmine."

And had died for it.

Christ.

"Who killed him?"

Tara exchanged a look with the priest, who'd been the one to insist she call him.

"Remy Landreaux," Father Mike revealed.

Oddly, it wasn't a total surprise. Because it all fit.

"And now Remy's gone off LeBlanc's reservation. He switched sides because the Homeland guy pays better."

Nick realized that there'd never been any elderly blue-haired aunties leaving his former partner money in their wills. Remy had probably been crooked from the beginning. He was also one of the few of LeBlanc's men his father would've trusted. Having known the fellow since Remy was knee-high to a crawdad.

He'd have to deal with his anger about this later. Big Antoine was in his tomb. There wasn't anything he could do for him now.

What he needed to concentrate on doing was getting Kate the hell out of there. Before she ended up as dead as his father. As dead as she'd believed her sister to be.

THE DICKHEAD WASN'T GOING TO LET HER GO. Kate had already figured that out. Fortunately, his ego required him to boast about how important he was in the plot to capture her sister and retrieve the video Tara had absconded with from LeBlanc's stash of tapes. Great racket the guy had had going for him. Get high rollers to pay to screw his hookers, then make them pay again so the pictures didn't arrive back in their hometowns, where their reputations—and their lives—could be shot to hell if their behavior became public.

Dubois seemed even more pleased by the idea that the plan had required Nick to bring Tara out here to the camp.

"We're gonna have a threesome: me, you, and your slut of a sister," he told her. "While Broussard's forced to watch. Then, since I'm a bighearted guy, I'm gonna let him pick which of you dies first."

There was no way it was going to come to that. Kate had had her fill of crooked cops. She also realized that all the stories Landreaux had told them, about Joe putting out a hit on her, and the Hulk being arrested, had all been lies. Part of a ploy to get them off track.

Neither she nor Nick were naive; but Remy, with all his smooth charm, and his personal history with Nick, had drawn them both in.

"What if I don't want to share?" she asked.

His eyes narrowed as he stared down at her. "What the fuck does that mean?"

"I mean, if I'm going to die, at least I'd like to spend the last minutes of my life having a little fun."

"Yeah. Right. Like of all the guys in all the bayou camps, I'm your ideal fuckmeister," he said.

Kate decided that he'd never believe an out-and-out lie, that he really was her dream fuck. So she opted for a middle ground.

"Hell no, you're not. Given my druthers, I'd rather bang Johnny Depp, or Russell Crowe, so long as he showed up in that leather skirt he wore in *Gladiator*.

"But neither one of them is here right now," she said. "And I strongly doubt they're going to show up out in the middle of this godforsaken swamp anytime soon. So, while you're definitely not my first choice, and would never even make my top-ten list, you've just lucked out, Dubois, because you happen to possess the only available penis out here."

He wasn't as stupid as he looked. She could tell he wasn't buying the entire story. Then again, she could also tell he wanted to.

"If I fuck you now, Broussard won't get to watch."

And, having heard the history between them, Kate

knew exactly how important that one-upmanship was to this cretin.

"What?" she asked sarcastically. "Are you saying you can't get it up twice? What's the matter, Dubois? You got prostate trouble or something? Hell, Nick managed to do me three times in an hour. And that doesn't count the number of times he made me come. Or scream."

Okay. Maybe she'd gone too far.

"I'll make you fuckin' scream," he threatened as his meaty hands went to his belt buckle.

"You win." She dropped the edge in her voice as he unzipped his jeans. "I'll admit it. I'm afraid you're going to hurt me." The tremor, she thought, was a nice touch. "And even more afraid I'm going to enjoy it."

Oh, yes. From the way his peanut of a penis twitched at that, she'd gotten to him.

"There's just one problem," she said. "You've got me tied up."

"That's the idea."

Kate had to struggle not to throw up as he began to stroke himself.

"I can understand keeping the handcuffs on."

God, she wanted her hands free! But beggars couldn't be choosers, and she had to take one thing at a time.

"That's kind of kinky. But if you keep my ankles tied up like this"—she jangled the leather-and-chain manacles—"I don't see how you're going to manage to get very deep."

She paused while he thought about that.

"Here's the deal," he decided. "I'll undo your legs so

you can spread 'em real wide for me. But if you even try to get away, I'll fucking kill you. By cutting pieces off you and makin' you watch while I feed 'em to the gators."

Well, that was certainly a more graphic death threat than any the Chicago cops had come up with.

"Deal," she said. A bit too quickly, perhaps, given the way he'd straightened his back again just when he'd been bending down to release her.

"You're stalling," he decided. "Hoping that Broussard will come riding to your rescue."

Again, she decided this was a case where the truth would serve her well.

"Absolutely."

"Dream on, bitch." He unzipped her jeans. Unlocked the bindings and began dragging her jeans down her legs. "Because he's fucking outnumbered."

"What are you talking about?"

The door to the cabin opened.

"I believe he's talking about me, for one," Remy Landreaux drawled. "Along with the two other men waiting outside as a welcoming committee."

He crossed the scarred pine floor, looking ridiculously out of place in the same jacket and slacks he'd worn when he'd come by the boat earlier.

"Put your dick away, Dubois," he said calmly, as if there were nothing out of the ordinary about a woman tied up in a cabin with her jeans down around her ankles. "If you're a very good boy, perhaps I'll let you play with our guest later. After we get the tape that D.C. bureaucrat is willing to pay through the nose for."

He smiled down at Kate. "It was looking as if we weren't going to be able to deliver. What with your hooker sister dead and the tape nowhere to be found. Then today, damned if things didn't make a one-eighty turn when you let me know she was still alive.

"Fortunately, I'd already taken your dear *maman*'s cell phone from her bag while we were all at her house. I'd thought it might come in handy. But I had no idea it would prove so useful so quickly.

"Your sister never would have answered a call from me. But fortunately she gets along with your *maman* much better than you do."

He reached down and ran a hand over her hair. Impossibly, his touch made her skin crawl worse than did the Dickhead's.

"Go outside," he instructed his partner. "I want to have a private chat with the detective."

"Chat, hell," Dubois grumbled. "You're going to do her."

"If I were to decide to dip my wick in our lovely visitor, that's none of your business." His outwardly pleasant tone was edged with deadly steel. "In case you've forgotten our organizational chart, I outrank you. Which means you do what you're told. When you're told to do it."

His teeth flashed. His eyes were hard and cold. "Is that understood?"

The Dickhead mumbled what Kate took to be a very reluctant affirmative.

"Don't worry," Remy called after him. "I'm not a selfish man. You can have her sister all to yourself."

"It's not the same thing," the Dickhead muttered as he closed the door behind him.

"Exactly," Remy agreed. The smile he gave to Kate was several degrees warmer. But it still chilled her to the bone. "Now where were we?"

"If I were you, instead of raping me, I'd be saying my prayers. Because when Nick gets here, he's going to kill you."

Kate hoped she'd still be alive to watch.

43

NICK WAS SURPRISED REMY WOULD GO INTO the swamp. Not only had he always had a fear of gators, he'd established a lifelong pattern of keeping himself on the sidelines.

Besides, getting into the fray was messy. And the one thing Remy Landreaux had never liked was messes of any kind.

Then again, greed was a prime motivator.

The night was dark, lit only by a cool winter moon as Nick piloted the pirogue through the bayou. Bullfrogs croaked, nutria paddled alongside the boat, furry shadows in water as dark and murky as Cajun coffee.

The pirogue's headlight cut through the rain falling from low-hanging clouds. Nick didn't need the GPS he'd brought along; thanks to those goons dragging him out here, the way to LeBlanc's camp was emblazoned on the map in his mind.

He was going to find her. Save her. And then together they were going to take off on *The Hoo-yah* and sail to romantic ports where they'd drink mai tais and feed each other passion fruit. Where there were no cell phones, or computers, or good guys versus bad guys.

They'd kick back for a change. Enjoy life. Enjoy each other. They'd make love, and maybe, one of these years down the road, they'd settle down in some big old house with a wide front porch—with a swing for making love—and start making babies. He liked the idea of a harem of little girls with bright red hair and slanted cat's eyes like their mother's.

Nick had never thought of himself as an optimist. Nor a pessimist. He'd always been a pragmatic realist, something that had been necessary in his line of work.

But as he headed deep into the bayou, he kept assuring himself that everything would turn out okay, and his admittedly rosy-scenario fantasies regarding his sexy detective were going to come true.

Because the truth was, he couldn't allow himself to consider the alternative.

He was about a thousand yards from the camp when he cut the boat's motor. He knew they'd be expecting him to come by boat. He also knew that a civilian could watch those Discovery and History Channel shows about SEALs 24/7 and they still wouldn't get it.

No one made it through training unless he found water to be a refuge rather than an obstacle. And you never knew who was going to make it through that all-important Total Immersion training. Hell, he'd watched LA surfers ring out in the first week, and farmboys from Iowa—who'd never been near a goddamn ocean until they landed on Coronado Island—hit the water like tadpoles.

The key was to swim more like a fish and less like a human. It was like swimming downhill, making your body physically longer in the water, reducing drag.

As he went over the side of the boat, Nick wished he had his Draegar, the rig that allowed him to swim beneath the water without leaving bubbles on the surface. Still, being that the sun had set, he was counting on the dark, and the element of surprise, to work in his favor.

Rather than skimming the surface, he dove deep, increasing the partial pressure of oxygen in his lungs, which allowed him to breathe longer. And swim farther.

At least that was the theory, and it'd always worked in the past. Then again, it had been more than six months since he'd trained with his team.

Nick was assuring himself that this was like riding a bike, that a guy never forgot the technique, when he started to surface near the camp and found himself eyeball to eyeball with the granddaddy of all gators.

44

OKAY, HER CAPTOR MIGHT HAVE CHANGED, BUT there was no way Kate was going to let Landreaux rape her. Maybe, in the overall scheme of things, rape was preferable to dying. But just as that hadn't been an option in Chicago, it wasn't now.

"Can I ask a question?"

"Of course."

"Joe didn't pay to have anyone try to shoot me, did he?"

"Very good." He shook his head. "No. I lied about that."

"To keep Nick and me from digging around."

"It seemed like the best way to get you both off track. Of course, if the shooter hadn't failed in what he'd been well paid to do . . ."

His voice drifted off. He took a deep breath, obviously regaining his aura of suave composure. "Of course, in the long run, you've turned out quite useful. So, I guess it was all for the best."

"I'm thrilled I could be of help." His partner might be a dickhead, but Remy Landreaux was a card-carrying sociopath. Which made him, in his own way, even more dangerous.

He had the upper hand, as hers were tied, and while he was lean and trim, she could tell that his body was well muscled.

Then there were Dubois and those other two cohorts lurking out there in the dark.

Her chances of survival weren't exactly rosy.

But if she *was* going to die, and it damn well seemed that was what they intended for her, at least she'd go down fighting.

Thunder rumbled in the distance, signaling a storm approaching from out in the Gulf. Meanwhile, Nick could've done without the moon lighting up the boggy land around the cabin, making it more difficult to stay in the shadows. He'd brought along his night-vision goggles, but unless one big-ass cloud happened to come along, he wouldn't be needing them.

Dark water ran off him as he pulled himself silently out of the water, kicked off the fins that fit over his boots, and positioned himself behind a huge cypress. From what he could tell, there were three guys standing guard outside the camp.

One was—no surprise—Dubois. He and the other guy were stupidly smoking, the tips of their cigarettes glowing like flares.

The third guy was dressed in cammies like the others, but holding an M4, which was basically just the old M16 with a shorter barrel and collapsible stock. And a lot more cool accessories, like a grenade launcher, which thankfully, the guy didn't seem to have.

Unlike Dubois and his pal, who were lounging against the weathered side of the old cabin, puffing away, he was lying on his stomach in full sniper mode. Which gave Nick the impression that he knew what he was doing.

If he'd been a former SEAL, or even a Ranger or Delta Force, living anywhere in the area, Nick would've known of him. Which meant that while he might present more of a challenge than the other goobers, he wasn't invincible.

Still, obviously, the key was to start with him.

His Ka-Bar was strapped to his thigh, where he'd put it after that stare-down with the gator. A stare-down he'd won when it swam away, leaving him to continue on. Nick could only hope this next encounter would turn out to be as uneventful.

Unlike in the movies, SEALs weren't really into hand-to-hand combat. In fact, if you ended up going mano-a-mano with your enemy, it was just a sign your primary, secondary, and tertiary plans had gone south.

There was also the problem that what might work in a war zone wasn't exactly acceptable in civilian society. Even down here in South Louisiana. If he took these guys out for good, he'd undoubtedly have some explaining to do.

Utilizing the crawl and walk parts of the SEALs' crawl/walk/run raid technique, he made his way through the flag-and-needle grass, pausing behind another cypress trunk shaped like a gigantic elephant foot. Fortunately, the rain had soaked the piles of dead willow leaves, keeping them from crackling as he crawled through them.

He approached the guy from the back, on his feet now, bent low, every nerve ending in his body primed to attack.

On three . . .

One.

Two.

Three.

The guy holding the M4 went out like a light.

The arm-bar chokehold could silently, quickly kill a man from behind. But there was also another way; if done right, it could merely render an adversary unconscious, which was Nick's intention.

And hadn't it worked like an effin' charm?

He plucked the assault rifle from the soggy leaves.

One down. Two to go.

Piece of cake.

Dubois, again no surprise, folded, just like the illustration in the SEAL Combat Manual.

Just as Nick lifted his arm to dispatch bad guy number three, the night silence was shattered by a scream coming from inside the camp.

45

"YOU BROKE MY FUCKIN' NOSE, BITCH!"

Wow. And hadn't Mr. *GQ* just lost his suave?

Remy jumped up, tipped over the cot, and knocked the kerosene lantern onto the floor, shattering the glass chimney.

Blood was gushing like Old Faithful from the nose Kate had managed to score a bull's-eye on. It hadn't been easy, swinging both arms with his heavy weight sprawled on top of her.

But she'd managed, and luckily the metal cuffs had hit just right, cutting a deep slice into his left nostril, which was hanging off his handsome face like a bloody piece of snot.

So caught up was he in his pain and fury, he didn't notice the wick from the lantern igniting the spilled kerosene.

Despite the rain, the building's wood was aged and rotting. Kate didn't want to still be here if and when it went up in flames. Deciding her chances were better outside with three armed men than in a burning building with an enraged cop, she scrambled to her feet and started running.

Proving that old military maxim about the best war plan falling apart upon contact with the enemy, the third guy spun around toward the camp, saw Nick coming toward him, and lifted a police-issue Glock.

At the same time, the door to the cabin burst open and Kate came racing out.

Into the night.

Nick called out her name, but his voice was drowned out by another rumble of thunder—closer this time— and the roar of a voice thickened with fury and, he thought, pain.

He shot off a round from the M4, nailing the third guard before the idea to pull the trigger could get from his brain to his hand. He dropped like a stone, the front of his fancy camouflage hunting vest turning crimson.

Three down, and Nick had no idea how many left to go. But he did know that however many there were, if any of them dared touch a hair on Kate Delaney's head, they were all going to die.

The scents of salt and oil rode on the night air with the dank odor of rotting vegetation. Kate felt the electricity of distant lightning beneath her skin. Or maybe that was just fear.

She'd always imagined the bayou to be an empty, silent place, but as she ran through the sharp marsh grasses that were ripping at her bare legs, she was vaguely aware of the hoot of an owl, the croak of bull-frogs, and the incessant, nerve-wracking whirr of crickets.

And then, worse, the unmistakable rat-a-tat-tat of an assault rifle.

Lowering her head, hearing the pounding of boots hitting the soggy ground behind her, Kate ran faster. Farther.

Damn, the woman could run! Nick hadn't held the team record for the hundred-meter dash, but he'd always ended in the top two or three. But he was having trouble keeping up with Kate.

Of course, fear was a prime motivator. Adrenaline a speed enhancer. Shouting out her name again, Nick kicked into overdrive.

Another gunshot rang out. A single crack that sent a bullet whizzing by her head, the snap of the sonic wave ringing in her ears before it embedded itself in a fat cypress stump.

Kate would have screamed if she could. But the sound was blocked by the major lump in her throat.

The earlier drizzle picked up, turning into a drenching shower, like piss poured from a boot. The leaves and rotting grass grew slippery. Tripping over a root, Kate went sprawling, which turned out to be a lucky thing as yet another bullet went soaring inches from her head. If she'd still been running . . .

No. Don't think of that, she told herself as she scrambled to her feet. Just keep going.

Nick was coming for her. All she had to do was stay alive until he got here.

"Kate!"

She paused. Was it really him? Or Remy pretending to be him to get her to slow down?

"Kate, dammit, it's me. Nick."

It *was* him!

She spun around and nearly ran smack into his chest.

"Are you all right?" he demanded as relief made her scratched and battered legs go numb.

"I am now," she gasped, clinging to him.

He looked nothing like the sexy Cajun PI she'd first met only three days ago. With every muscle of his magnificent body revealed by the skintight black dive suit, his rugged face streaked in shades of green and black and gray, he looked terrifying.

And spectacular.

"Fuck," he ground out as another bullet went flying by. "Who knew a guy could run in Italian loafers?"

"How do you know it's Remy? There are other—"

"Yeah. Dickhead and the other two stooges. I took care of them." He put a hand on the top of her head and pushed her back down to the wet ground. "But I didn't want to take time to get rid of Remy until I got to you, because I didn't want you running off half-cocked into the water."

Which, although she hated to admit it, she just might have done.

He turned around.

"Stay down."

It was the second time he'd instructed her to keep low.

While her plans were admittedly and uncharacteristically sketchy, she'd already decided—sometime between arriving at *The Hoo-yah* for the first time and meeting Nick, and when she'd woken up in that cabin tonight—that there was no reason for her to ever return to Chicago.

And since she wasn't about to risk getting her head blown off before she could see those Mexican cliff divers with Nick, Kate set aside her independent streak and did exactly as told.

46

NICK TURNED AROUND. CALMLY. WITH A COLD sense of purpose.

Remy was running toward them. He seemed a bit winded, but nevertheless managed to lift the police-issue Glock and point it at Nick.

Who, as coolly as if he'd been shooting targets at the SEAL range, lifted the M4 and pulled the trigger, and—

Nothing?

The freaking gun jammed?

"Oops," Remy said. Despite the blood gushing down his face, he managed a smile. A killer grin, Kate thought. "Looks as if your luck's just run out, *cher.*"

"Someone ought to tell you that when you're fighting for your life, stopping to gloat can be fatal," Nick said.

Moving so fast that Kate wasn't quite sure she'd actually seen it happen, Nick swung the M4 by the stock, sending his former partner flying backward, landing in the water with a huge splash.

He was shouting curses, struggling to tread water while dressed in that wool navy blazer that was now billowing out around his body, when a huge alligator, its eyes gleaming like yellow agates in the dark, swam like a pebbled torpedo straight toward him.

Unable to watch, Kate squeezed her eyes closed; dots like white-winged moths began flying behind her lids.

But she didn't need to be able to see to know what had happened when Remy Landreaux's high-pitched scream sent a flurry of night birds nesting in a nearby tree into the sky.

The horrible sound of bones breaking was like another gunshot. She opened her eyes again just in time to see animal and man disappear beneath the black surface.

"Oh, my God." Trembling like a leaf in a hurricane, Kate managed to get up on her knees as Nick dropped to his and gathered her into his arms.

"It'll be okay," he assured her. "You'll be okay."

And because it was Nick telling her that, Kate believed it to be true. "Was that all of them?"

"Yeah. Christ, I'm sorry, Kate." He was running his hands over her hair, her wet face, which she knew must've been filthy, her shoulders. "I'm so freaking sorry."

"For what?" She stared up at his tortured expression. "You just saved my life."

"You wouldn't have needed saving, dammit, if I'd just figured out Remy was the worst of the bad guys."

"He was your friend." How strange that despite her body still jangling from residual fear, she'd be the one trying to soothe him. "You've known him forever. You have to trust people sometimes, Nick. He was your partner. You were a team."

"He killed my father."

"I'm sorry." But not surprised. Once she'd learned the truth about Tara, she'd begun to suspect the connection.

"Dad was killed because he was going to rat them out."

She almost smiled. It was the first time she'd heard him call his father Dad. She'd come to accept how much she and Nick were alike. What a surprise to discover that she also had something in common with his father.

"That's too bad. But he left you with a nice legacy. Knowing that he was going to do the right thing."

"Yeah." He kissed her then. A long, sweet kiss that strangely made her want to cry. It was that tender.

As she kissed him back, with all her heart, Kate tensed when she heard another sound.

"Is that a—"

Please don't let it be a boat bringing more of LeBlanc's thugs, she prayed.

"It's okay."

As he helped her to her feet, Kate recognized the *chop chop chop* sound of rotors and looked up to see the huge black helicopter flying toward them.

"Father Mike borrowed it from the Coast Guard," Nick told her. "It's our ride home."

They were bathed in a circle of yellow light as the

copter touched down. Bending low, Nick and Kate ran toward the open door.

"Well, this is one helluva reunion," Tara greeted Kate as she scrambled aboard. "Next time, what do you say we just settle for brunch at the Court of Two Sisters?"

Kate laughed and threw her arms around the twin she hadn't seen for too long. "You're on."

47

IT WAS A PERFECT DAY. THE SUN WAS WARM, THE water smooth as an endless blue mirror as Nick and Kate sailed *The Hoo-yah* out into the Gulf of Mexico.

"That was fun last night," she said.

"Absolutely." He put his arm around her waist and lifted her onto her toes for a kiss that had memories flooding back.

"I was talking about before that hot, chandelier-swinging sex," she said with a laugh.

"Ah, the Voodoo wedding." He nodded. "Your sister made a beautiful bride."

"She did." And less like a movie star, now that she'd had her face changed back to pre-LeBlanc days. "Toussaint never stopped beaming."

"They're an odd mix," he said. "But I got the feeling they're going to make it."

"I did, too."

Téo's brother obviously adored Tara, who was clearly basking in his love.

Surprisingly, at least to Kate, he lived a fairly normal

life as, of all things, a sixth-grade science teacher who'd been moonlighting as a waiter, trying to help raise money to pay off Tara's debt to LeBlanc. A debt that had been forgotten at Nick's pointed suggestion after the tape, which she'd hidden inside the barrel of the Civil War replica cannon at Washington Artillery Park, had mysteriously arrived at the Baton Rouge FBI offices.

The government agent, when arrested, had pleaded guilty to second-degree murder and was already living in his new digs in Angola prison.

After a honeymoon to Haiti, to meet the rest of her new husband's family, Tara would be returning to work at Chelsea Lamoreaux's popular French Quarter restaurant.

"The jumping over the broom was a nice touch. And I'm really glad they decided to forgo the live his-and-her chicken sacrifice."

"You and me both, *chère.*" He kissed her again. Lightly. Quickly. "So, did it give you any ideas?"

"Only that if I ever do get married, I don't think it's going to be beneath a black velvet painting of Isaac Hayes."

"Yeah. That was a little weird," he agreed. "How about on the beach? Or maybe a quaint Mexican wedding chapel?"

She looked up at him. "Was that a proposal?"

He rubbed his jaw. "You know, I think it was."

"I believe a marriage proposal is something a person should take a proper amount of time to think about," she said. "Be very sure about."

Nick thought about Kate wearing a floaty white Mexican lace dress on a sun-drenched Mazatlan beach, with the ocean breeze feathering her bright hair, and her smile wrapping his heart in a shiny bow as she promised to love and honor and—hell, she'd never obey, but he wouldn't have her any other way.

He thought about slipping the ring he'd been carrying around for days onto her finger, thought about carrying her over the threshold into the stateroom, taking that lacy dress back off her, discovering what treats the lady had in store for him underneath, and did he mention that he flat out loved the fact that what shoes were to other women, frothy bits of silk and lace lingerie were to his Kate? He doubted she'd ever have enough and hooyah, wasn't that A-okay with him?

He thought about spending the next several months just sailing the seven seas, since he couldn't think of a better way to spend all that money he'd been socking away for years. Neither one of them was sure what they wanted to do next, but he wasn't worried about that, because so long as they were together, whatever they eventually decided would be fine with him.

He thought again about babies. And a dog. Kids needed a dog. He thought about getting old with her, sitting on the deck of whatever boat they'd have in their nineties, watching the sun set, then going below and . . .

"I think I'm going to be a dirty old man," he said.

"My favorite kind." Her smile told him he didn't have to explain his thought process to her. Because she just got it. Got *him*. And how cool was that?

"Okay. I've thought about it," he said.

"And?"

"It's a real proposal."

"It's about time. I was beginning to worry that when I told the story of our wedding to our grandchildren, I'd have to admit that I was the one who finally ended up proposing."

"We've only been together for six weeks." Six weeks that seemed like forever. In a good way.

"Six weeks and three days," she corrected.

"You're right. I was remiss."

He turned the ketch westward. "So, next stop, Mexico. And that little chapel on the beach."

"And then the world." Kate laughed, lifting her face to the wind as, together, she and Nick sailed into their future.

Dear Reader,

On August 26, 2005, my husband and I drove to Wetumpka, Alabama, where I'd agreed to speak at a luncheon to raise funds for the library. As we left East Tennessee, Hurricane Katrina came ashore in Florida as a Category 1 hurricane and was quickly downgraded to a tropical storm.

During the long drive we talked about my book in progress, which was, at the time, titled *Impulse*. Those of you familiar with my books know that New Orleans is one of my favorite cities—to visit and to write about. But even loving it as I do, I was still planning to have it hit by a major hurricane.

When I arrived at the event on the morning of August 27, I discovered that while we'd been away from newscasts, Katrina had turned back into a hurricane and the National Hurricane Center had issued a hurricane watch from Morgan City, Louisiana, to the Louisiana/Mississippi border. By the time lunch was over, the watch had been extended eastward, across southern Mississippi to the Alabama/Florida border. Given that Wetumpka's 190 miles from the coast, I never felt in any personal danger, but concerned about people in the watch area, I decided to take the hurricane out of my story.

Later that night the watch was changed to a warning and while we were driving back home to our mountains on August 28, NHC was warning people of a "catastrophic Category 5 hurricane" with "devastating damage" expected. New Orleans declared a state of emergency and the mayor called for the first-ever evacuation.

Katrina made landfall in Louisiana on the morning of August 29 and hell broke loose. Like much of the country, I spent days glued to my television watching as 80 percent of New Orleans became flooded—the water in some places twenty feet deep—and decided there was no way I could finish writing that particular book at that time. Even without the fictional hurricane, there were other events in my story I felt would be perceived as "piling on" a city already reeling. (Making things worse, New Orleans was rocked again by Hurricane Rita on September 24.)

So, I put my story on the shelf and began an entirely different book set in Wyoming, which kept the title *Impulse*. After I finished that story, I decided enough time had passed to get back to work on the book you've just read. Coincidentally, I finished *No Safe Place* in the early morning of August 29, 2006, during the same hours Katrina had come barreling ashore a year earlier.

I'm writing this letter on September 29, thirteen months after Katrina. Although the situation remains fluid, and numbers are always changing, at least 1,740 Louisianans died, 135 are missing, there are 52 unidentified corpses in the Orleans Parish morgue, and bodies are still being found. One-third of the hospitals and libraries remain closed. The residential Lower Ninth Ward, once home to 14,000 people, remains a devastated and abandoned ghost town, the only neighborhood in the city still lacking drinkable water and other basic utilities.

Less than half of the pre-Katrina 460,000 population has come home; again, numbers are hard to pin down, but the Postal Service puts the figure at 171,000, which is equivalent to the population of 1880. Only 56 of the 128 schools have opened and more than 18,000 businesses have closed permanently since the storms.

Daily life in New Orleans can be a struggle. In a recent poll, only 16 percent of the citizens felt their lives had returned to normal.

But there's also good news. Tourists are returning; the city has celebrated Mardi Gras and Jazz Fest; the Port of New Orleans is nearly back to normal; the convention center has bookings; the Saints won their home opener in a newly refurbished Superdome, which had been the site of so much suffering and despair; and although, according to the Louisiana Restaurant Association, 1,562 of the city's 3,414 restaurants are still closed, Commander's Palace, a famed New Orleans landmark since 1880, finally reopened this weekend with a celebratory jazz brunch.

One of my favorite things about New Orleans has always been its fabulous food. It's the only city in the world where, as soon as I finish one meal, I begin planning where I'm going to eat my next. People in my Louisiana stories are always cooking and eating, and Cajun and Creole recipes from my novels and local restaurants can be found on my website.

Which is why I'm going to end this letter with a quote from Charles Bohn, a talented New Orleans potter and optimist who owns Shadyside Pottery on Magazine Street: "Hell, you can't let New Orleans die. The food's too good."

JoAnn Ross

$\mathcal{F}all$ in love

with bestselling romances from Pocket Books!

Impulse • JoAnn Ross
A haunted man...A hunted woman...
Together they must stop a madman before he kills again.

BAD Attitude • Sherrilyn Kenyon
Sometimes even the good guys need to have a BAD attitude...

The Seduction of His Wife • Janet Chapman
He set out to seduce her for all the wrong reasons—
but fell in love with her for all the right ones.

Thrill Me to Death • Roxanne St. Claire
When a Bullet Catcher is on the job, he'll always watch
your back. But you better watch your heart.

Dirty Little Lies • Julie Leto
She's a sultry Latino bounty hunter armed with
sex, lies, and other deadly weapons.

FINALLY
A WEBSITE
YOU CAN GET
PASSIONATE
ABOUT...

Visit
www.SimonSaysLove.com
for the latest information
about Romance from Pocket Books!

READING SUGGESTIONS

LATEST RELEASES

AUTHOR APPEARANCES

ONLINE CHATS WITH YOUR
FAVORITE WRITERS

SPECIAL OFFERS

ORDER BOOKS ONLINE

AND MUCH, MUCH MORE!